VULTURE

VULTURE

Fletcher Michael

Queer Space
New Orleans

Published in the United States of America and United Kingdom by
Queer Space
A Rebel Satori Imprint
www.rebelsatoripress.com

Paperback ISBN: 978-1-60864-188-8
Ebook ISBN: 978-1-60864-189-5
Library of Congress Control Number: 2022930850

CONTENTS

For my parents, Michael and Laureen Bonin,
for putting words into my world.

CHAPTER 1

*God help thee, old man, thy thoughts have created a creature
in thee; and he whose intense thinking thus makes him a Pro-
metheus; a vulture feeds upon that heart forever; the vulture the
very creature he creates.*

—Herman Melville, *Moby-Dick, or, The Whale*

Finch massaged baking soda into the gash sliced across his
left palm. The sting provided a welcome burn. The sooner
the healing began the sooner the wound would close and
join the constellation of bumps and welts adorning his hands
and climbing up his arms. The maze of raised purple scars tex-
turing his fingers and wrists made it look as though he juggled
cactuses for a hobby, though the truth was far less whimsical.
Each scar told of a different encounter in which he'd managed to
skirt death. Some of them even predated Finch's memory, growing and stretching with him like a tortoise's shell.

The most recent wound, which he now wrapped in a withered gray sock, would leave a crescent scar of several tooth-sized
bumps. The wrap wasn't perfect but it held. He secured the
makeshift bandage with a rusty paper clip. Sometimes those bas-
tards got so hungry or drunk or both that they forgot to cook
you before taking a bite.

Finch rewarded himself with a handful of salmon berries. He
glanced down at the dwindling harvest wilting at the bottom of
the tin pail. Wild greens challenged the shallow lip of a neighbor-

1

ing paint bucket. Next to the bucket, a foggy glass jar housed a few wrinkled mushrooms. A small heap of rosebuds mixed with a fistful of unappetizing cattail shoots nestled in a cracked ashtray.

Stopping himself from swallowing the ripe fruits all at once, he savored the bittersweet flavor as each red-pink cap burst on his tongue. Like most people here, he luxuriated in any and every modicum of pleasure he managed to eke out of life in Vulture.

"Horatio, you hungry?" he called, his tongue swollen with tart red juice. Horatio's dark ears perked up at the sound of Finch's voice, cocking his boxy head quizzically. *Self-Reliance*, he thought, as he unbolted the lock, touching two fingers to the nineteenth-century essay he'd surgically excised from the *Collected Works of Ralph Waldo Emerson* and affixed to his door with a thin nail. The phrase had become a mantra of sorts, or perhaps a prayer or a charm, invoking Emerson's central exhortation for protection and success each time he left the refuge of the station and crossed the craggy threshold into Vulture.

Taking minor comfort in the unflinching afternoon sun's ability to hold the gangs at bay until dusk, Finch paused outside the door, waiting for his eyes to adjust to the searing light. The Regals would be holed up in the security of the cinema, confident in their precarious safety as the top gang but ever alert for inevitable challengers. According to the fresh graffiti he'd seen bedecking a mutilated shipping container near the city limits, the Regals had recently obliterated a squadron of Veins in truly triumphant fashion—at least to the extent that such propaganda could be trusted. The ornate portraiture and purple shades cultivated by the Regals would lead one to believe that they had marched into the Veins encampment at the ruinous museum and run their gold-hilted scabbards through the conspiring militants from teeth to toes. More than likely they had simply poisoned their water supply. Regals rarely liked to get their hands dirty, but a sword fight made for better wall art.

Taking in the collapsed buildings, the cratered roads and ruptured parking lots, Finch pondered for the umpteenth time the origins of the city's monniker. A glance skyward provided the obvious answer. The omnipresent birds hovered like black kites affixed to the ochre sky. Their freakish naked heads swung from side to side, slow but intent, as they scanned for earth-bound death. Every so often a chilling squawk would emanate from their grizzled throats, the haunting flap of their ashen wings disturbing the silent landscape.

The people, too, were vultures. They lived and died by the human carrion that reliably appeared each morning after the ritualistic violence of the night. Each painted corpse provided a foreboding message for all and a meal for some.

Staring out at Vulture, Finch was struck by its likeness to the vibrant coral reefs pictured in the torn pages of a *National Geographic* magazine he'd once come across. He'd discovered the tattered image on one of his expeditions, picking his way on this occasion through a bombed-out dentist's office. At the time, he'd hardly believed that such a sight could exist on the same planet as Vulture, so peaceful and serene the underwater world seemed. As with all the other textual scraps he'd scavenged on these hunts, the worn pictures and articles now rested in neat piles on his desk back at the station. Each one was carefully read and reread, expanding his mental vision of the world before and perhaps—when he allowed himself such fancies—the world beyond Vulture, before being gently replaced back on the stack.

A shadow passed slowly over Finch and sent a shiver up his neck. Peering upward, shielding his eyes from the sun's glare with his bandaged hand, he watched the ragged bird coast silently over his head in the direction of Vulture. He lost sight of it as it disappeared into a canyon of derelict skyscrapers and mountains of multicolored rubble. Every deteriorating surface and mound of metal in sight had been painted over countless times, suffusing into a vibrant, riotous collage. His eyes found no place to rest as they jumped from one manic, rainbow-splashed edge to the next. In the thick heat of the afternoon, the technicolor structures appeared to sweat runnels of green, blue, purple, silver, red, and orange. Touching his hand to one such mound of colorful brick, Finch's fingers sunk into the thick layers of paint that become soft and putty-like in the unabating heat. Each layer told a different story, some moment in history when a gang had asserted their presence through a spritz of graffiti or a splash of oil paint.

Following the Water Wars, the abundance of crumbled surfaces and vacated walls, all bearing the dusty, muted hues of a former cityscape, had effectively established a blank canvas upon which the gang artists now chronicled the triumphs and sacrifices of their respective tribes in rich detail. No inch could be left unmarked lest another gang claim it for themselves. The raucous colors of these ruins gave the landscape a jarring vibrancy that belied the depths of desolation that had inspired such an eye-catching veneer. Pocketing his key and wiping away the sweat that had already accumulated on his brow, Finch issued a sharp whistle through his pursed lips. Horatio stretched his meter-long spine, gave his muscled torso a quick shake, and trotted up to his side.

It took a certain amount of ingenuity (not to mention an unfastidious stomach) to track down and consume Vulture's spartan edible flora. Looters had cleaned out the supermarkets even before the Water Wars and by now the gangs had seized and stockpiled nearly everything remaining of any remote value—food, water, or otherwise. Finch often worried about the inevitable day when the gangs would exhaust these reserves, hoping this disastrous reckoning wouldn't occur during his lifetime. Almost nothing comestible proved resilient enough to grow through the solidified ash that caked the ground or the heaps of rubble and calcified garbage that swelled like boils from the brutalized tarmac. But the trick, as Finch had found, was knowing where to look. And thanks to over two decades of experience, several food poisonings, and a few key passages in Thoreau's *Walden*, Finch knew by now where to look. It helped to have Horatio around, too, his hypersensitive nose leading them in the direction of food more often than not.

Together they trotted out to the gulch and began wending their way along the dusty bank—their usual path. Horatio kept pace beside Finch, stealing off now and again in pursuit of some enticing scent, but always returning to his side. They froze in unison as a rustling sound broke the desert silence. Whipping his head around, Finch watched as the burned-out shell of a car that had disturbed the soundless atmosphere, tumbling down from the top of a heap of molten ash where it had hung precariously for years before finally succumbing to gravity. The metallic clunks wrent the air before settling in a dusty heap at the foot of the corroded mound. His pulse returning to its baseline apprehensive throb, Finch continued along the gulch, Horatio padding faithfully an arm's length away.

The radio station faded in the distance to their rear as they walked on. The vultures felt nearer than usual, circling close to the ground. Horatio froze and pointed his snout toward the birds as they hovered over the gulch, his ears flattening against

5

his wide skull. Hesitating, Finch followed Horatio to where they landed. The smell of rot burned at his nostrils and he clasped a hand over his nose. When the limp body comes into view, lying prostrate on the bank of the musty gulch that might once have been a coursing river, he isn't surprised. The defunct riverbed triggers his thirst, though he fights the urge to take a precious sip of water from the steel bottle in his backpack, instead forcing a swallow down his dry throat.

Stepping closer, he nudged the figure's emaciated ribs with a sneakered toe. The head lolled to the side, revealing hideously sunken cheekbones and sickly yellow eyes. A fresh streak of purple eclipsed the electric blue face paint typical of Vein troopers. Crude dashes of purple paint interrupted the hundreds of small blue arrows intricately tattooed on the Vein's skin, like a factory-patterned shirt stained by spilt ink. If only the explanation were that innocent. The Regals had marked their kill. An arrow protruded from the body's lifeless chest at a sinister angle. Finch tore his gaze from the grisly sight.

His eyes shot to the ground, scanning for the mushrooms he knew to grow by the gulch. Horatio lingered another minute, sniffing at the body before joining him, nose to the ground. Together they tracked deeper into Vulture, the afternoon silence ratcheting Finch's anxiety with each step. All around him the painted crags rose up, their formless shapes and hectic color patterns bestowing a surrealness on his surroundings that unnerved him the further he got from the station.

An hour passed slowly as their hesitant steps continued along the gulch, until Horatio finally trotted off a short ways up the embankment. Catching up to him, Finch, by now drenched in sweat, saw that his partner had uncovered a small cluster of mushrooms hidden beneath a dank stone outcropping. He gath-

6

ered several handfuls of these mushrooms, which he recognized as Black Trumpets, and delighted in finding a few Chanterelles growing nearby. Popping a single Chanterelle in his mouth, the smallest he could find, he let the rich, earthy flavor dissolve on his tongue. He placed the rest gingerly in his weathered gray backpack, thankful that the gangs remained as yet unaware or dismissive of the mushrooms' presence. They tended to cache and ration their food, using it primarily as a tool with which to consolidate power. Food was one of Vulture's chief currencies, overridden only by violence and water. Finch succumbed finally and took a delicate sip from his canteen, letting the cool liquid pour slowly down his arid throat.

Hunger and thirst were as deadly weapons as the crossbows that hung from straps across the Regals' well-fed shoulders. The Cannies recused themselves from this Darwinian cycle by opting into cannibalism, a depth of depravity to which no other gang had yet sunk. Finch often wondered whether the Cannies drank the vile Leak in order to make eating human flesh palatable or else to suppress their shriveling consciences as they indulged in their unethical meal. Or perhaps the Leak was the only thing keeping them alive, as it was composed in meagre part by water. Finch's mantra would certainly have resonated with the self-sustaining Cannies were they ever to stay sober long enough to hear it in its two word entirety. After all, Emerson unequivocally dictates that "Whoso would be a man must be a nonconformist," and the Cannies were nothing if not that, albeit to far more corrupted ends than the New England philosopher could ever have imagined.

With the mushrooms now trundling with a promising weight in his backpack, Finch turned back in the direction of home. Permitting himself a rare daydream, he imagined sharing the mushrooms with Viro, having a mild conversation over a rustic dinner like Jake Barnes and Bill Gorton in his battered copy of *The Sun Also Rises*. When the rickety bridge above him abruptly blots out the sun, he is recalled to reality, a sudden blanket of shade thrown over his head. A dull mechanical drone emanated from somewhere in the distance, sending Horatio charging off at a speed Finch couldn't follow. It was a sound he'd heard many times before, though he'd never been able to place its origin. Perhaps sensing the possibility of prey, Horatio's shaggy body disappeared behind a rotund, melted mass that might once have been a cement mixer before vanishing into the distance. Mushrooms and berries were enough to sustain Finch, but they could never satisfy Horatio's animal hunger. Finch knew his companion would return with the same confidence he had that it would never rain in Vulture, that each dry, scorching day would persist through the night and into the next morning.

"How 'bout some Leak, indie?"

Finch cursed himself for his lack of focus. The Canny, naked and streaked in haphazard orange stripes, dangled his bandy legs from his perch on one of the bridge's warped rafters. Gnarled toes capped with dissolving black nails swung lazily above Finch's head, the Canny's bony knees creaking with each pump of his legs. He sipped a brown, villainous looking substance from a rusted watering pot. Though the Canny sat nearly five feet above him, Finch could smell the acrid stench of the Leak from where he stood on the ground. The putrid scent accosted the back of his throat and he felt his stomach climb up into his chest. Finch took a ginger step backward, casting furtive glances around the musty area under the dilapidated bridge for any other potential threats. Horatio was still nowhere to be found, no doubt pursuing some distant prey that Finch's human senses could not perceive. Still scolding himself, he unconsciously rubbed the sock binding on his hand, the wound still tender from his most recent encounter with a Canny.

"Relax, iss jus' me *indie*," garbled the Canny through a toothless mouth, hissing out the last word like a slur. "And what's that yer arm there?"

"It's nothing," he replied after a painful pause, never breaking eye contact with the restless cannibal as he yanked his sleeve down over the thin line of text tattooed on his forearm. The amphetamines in the Leak functioned to keep the Cannies in a near constant state of motion. Finch mustered his courage, knowing that his best hope was to buy himself time by keeping the Canny talking. After another long pull from the watering pot, the Canny croaked, "I don' give a fuck what ya call yaself. You got no colors, you an indie-pendent!"

That the strength of his commentary alone almost knocked him from his precarious perch revealed the Canny's significant inebriation. Brown flecks of spittle leapt from his ghastly mouth and drifted just shy of Finch's perspiring face. If Horatio were by his side the Canny would likely have left him alone. He'd probably been waiting for the dog-wolf to leave this whole time.

Finch tried to detach himself mentally from the certain danger glowering down at him, denying his humanistic instincts in an effort to push Emerson's definition of *self-reliance* to its logical conclusion: defending the sanctity of one's own humanity even to the death. Easier to conceive of the Canny as less than human, a fly that needed swatting. Still, behind the Canny's monstrously dilated pupils, Finch could envision a man that might once have been decent, or simply scared like himself. Did not Ahab behave tenderly to his beloved Pip, though compelled by the vengeful pursuit of the white whale? Was not Milton's Satan briefly moved by humanity's beauty, though "ever to do ill" was his "sole delight"? Tearing himself away from the Canny's shifting gaze, Finch's eyes landed on the bodies stained with blue and purple paint, slumped like broken puppets in the ashy embankment. The stench of the corpses mixed with that of the Leak and choked Finch's lungs. Even the Cannies had enough sense not to eat the poisoned bodies. A Regal would have killed the impish Canny by now, yielding themselves instantaneously to predatory instinct and trusting in the numbers sure to back them up. If only Horatio were here…

"Don' go wastin' ya leak on this indie-baby."

The most wretched Canny Finch had ever seen—and he'd seen his fair share—materialized on the rafter. Her skin looked two sizes too tight. Swollen yellow eyes bugged out of her narrow skull and as she leered down at Finch, her teeth seemed to be slowly disintegrating like anthills in rain. Conspicuous stripes of orange paint adorned her bony arms and her lank, greasy hair. She could have been fifteen or ninety-five but Vulture had ravaged her, indiscriminate of time. She snagged the watering pot out of the first Canny's crusty hands and brought the spout to her cracked lips for a long pull.

"Wha's in that bag there on your back *indie*?"

She spoke in rough staccato bursts not unlike a squawking vulture. Finch again wished he was flanked by a gang or Horatio. Though tall, his limited diet had made him lean to the point of thinness and nothing about his appearance made him especially intimidating. Though her own body looked brittle enough to snap under a strong wind, her drunken confidence rattled him.

"Nothing. Just some flowers."

Finch commanded his feet to hold their ground. He created a sort of barrier with his words until he could figure out an escape.

The voice hollered in his ear and he felt the sweat prickling his scalp and neck go cold. Fierce runnels of orange sweat coursed down the reptilian skin of the Cannies' bare chests. Like them the bridge was covered in messy, concentric rings of orange, painted there by quaking hands.

"Well is it flowers or is it nothin' then?" chimed the girl after another long pull of Leak, twin streams of brown liquid dribbling down her sharp chin. Years of studying the Cannies' scratchy orange graffiti and observing their habits from afar had informed Finch that no two batches of Leak were the same, each concoction brewed with a different admixture of intoxicants. Much like its infamous founders, it followed no set recipe or guidelines. Upon discovering an intact vessel—be it a bucket, can, dog bowl, or flowerpot—in the throes of their stupor, the rest became simply a matter of preference and convenience. Old liquors from immense, secret Canny stashes would be mixed with Xanax, acid tabs, peyote capsules, Vicodin, toasted marijuana leaves, bath salts, hallucinogenic mushrooms, black tar heroin, cocaine and whatever else had been scavenged or stolen. The gangs had little use for such items, focused as they were on remaining constantly alert. If it blurred the vision enough to delude the mind into imagining Vulture to be livable, it went into the Cannies' makeshift pot. Any laughter heard in Vulture more than likely came from the drunken belly of a Canny. Until the last droplets had been feverishly licked from the rim of the canister, the Cannies imbibed continuously. They paused only when thirst, hunger, sleep, or madness begged to intervene. Cannies regularly died after just one sip or overdosed several hours after partaking in a particularly potent batch.

"Just flowers," he finally replied, licking his perspiring upper lip with a bone-dry tongue. He watched a momentarily lucid

11

glance pass between the mangy duo. It was the hungry look that everyone here wore like a mask.

Finch turned suddenly and made to sprint back toward the station. Fight or flight might as well have been the official policy of Vulture, and fleeing had sustained him this long. Not wanting to lead them directly to his hideout, however, he hesitated. In that moment's hesitation the girl leapt catlike off the rafter and grabbed his ankle with her claw-like hand. He kicked out behind him but the other one appeared in front of him, his steamy breath smelling of bourbon and crushed aspirin. He landed a lazy but effective punch on Finch's jaw. Finch threw his arm out in defense and knocked the drunkard back a few paces, nowhere near the damage he'd hoped to incur. The Canny behind him snatched up a rusty kitchen knife, which had previously been dangling from a long strand of her greasy hair wound loosely about its handle. He'd failed to notice it when she'd stood above him on the bridge. Tearing the knife from its makeshift noose, she slashed one of his backpack's straps, throwing Finch off balance as the weight shifted on his narrow shoulders. As she wound up for another jab Finch danced clumsily out of the way, suffering a small gash to his shoulder in the process. Though he could smell the distinct metallic odor of his own blood he refused to look at the wound.

"Come on there indie we're hungry," said the girl, a jagged smile carved into her face revealing plum-black gums.

Finch swung the backpack from its only remaining strap and caught the man in the neck. He wasn't nearly as alert as his compatriot, as he'd probably been sipping that Leak by himself all morning. He fell to one knee, grabbing at his throat. He rasped horribly as he scrabbled at his Adam's apple with bony, twisted fingers.

Finch turned to the girl. She looked feral, hopping and fidgeting frantically as she swiped at the air with her rusty blade. For a surreal moment time slowed down, and Finch was struck by a strange curiosity of human evolution; had this viciousness been lurking in humankind all along, or had the Water Wars somehow changed them just as the warheads had destroyed the city, the climate, and the earth? Everyone he'd ever encountered in Vulture had seemed more like Horatio than himself, and yet the people he read about in his books seemed just the opposite, exchanging instinct for contemplation, ever plumbing the depths of their complex interiors. These writers and their characters had comforted him in ways that he could not articulate. And yet at moments like this, with a rabid creature—alleged to be his same species!—slashing at him from mere inches away, he resented the influence of his precious books and the part they had played in softening him, ill preparing him for this dismal realm that mandated dispassionate callousness. What was it that Ishmael had so sweepingly pronounced? "It's only his outside; a man can be honest in any sort of skin." Not so if that skin was riddled with orange stripes. Though he'd purportedly met cannibals himself, clearly Melville's fantastical maritime adventures had never landed him in a place so disenchanting as Vulture. Finch almost respected the Canny's ruthlessness, so attuned to the demands of her environs, before reminding himself that she wanted to make a meal of his limbs.

He caught another blunt jab in his forearm as he blocked the thrust away from his rib cage. Blood joined the stains of electric blue, royal purple, orange, green, and yellow on his faded shirt and pants, the bizarre camo of Vulture. With his undamaged arm, he slung his handicapped backpack from one strap across his shoulders. Suddenly finding his strength, Finch lunged forward and pushed the waifish, knife-wielding Canny to the ground. She collapsed to the gravel and yet still the crooked smile was stitched across her face, as though glad that he'd finally shown a sign of vitality. As soon as Finch straightened up he was knocked back to the ground by a sharp kick to his shin, and he felt the backpack leaving his shoulders. The man bounced out of reach, knapsack slapping against his sharp shoulder blades. The girl flashed up like a striking snake, following her partner's bounding direction. They left behind a mist of orange-stained dust and a plume of rancid stench that momentarily waylaid Finch, retching and rubbing his eyes.

He watched as they scurried off with ungainly strides, relieved at their departure but humiliated by his loss. They'd certainly drain his precious water and convert his canteen to a Leak vessel, but worse they could discover his food source. While Cannies didn't have much taste for mushrooms of the non-hallucinogenic variety, the backpack and its revelatory contents could still be lost to a more competent graffiti gang. Allow that and he risked starvation, his foraging scheme really the only thing keeping him alive. He knew he must follow them despite the two cuts in his arm begging him to return immediately to the safety of the station. *Self-reliance*, he reminded himself begrudgingly.

The Cannies gamboled off with surprising speed despite their drunken steps. He decided to hang back, let them think he'd given up. He gritted his teeth as he pushed himself up on his good arm. Hot air choked his throat, surely as dry as it had ever been. He licked the sweat from his hands and arms and sucked the moisture from his t-shirt until the salty flavor made him wince. While he waited, he tried to catch his breath and calm the throbbing pulse of his heart. The last thing he wanted was to rush into a Canny Saturnalia where he'd go from guest to entrée in mere seconds. He'd once watched in horror as several wild-eyed orange streaks tackled and devoured an adult Vein in less than twenty-minutes.

Being sure to stay out of range, Finch hid behind one the many boulders of solidified magma that had been churned up out of the rocky earth when the warheads had hailed down from the sky, launched from thousands of miles away. The hot paint coating the boulder left multicolored prints on his skin and clothes, stains he'd long since learned to live with. For miles in all directions the ground looked both fluid and dense, like water frozen at the zenith of a rolling boil. Great hillocks of painted cement jolted abruptly out of the ground only to descend just as dramatically down into stony pits. A colorful blanket of ash and melted garbage covered the surreal landscape like an un-kempt beard. This made for ideal spying conditions, with many igneous formations to poke one's head around while shielding their body, though the threat of a surprise attack or an ambush remained equally likely.

As the Cannies bounded giddily back to their rotting bridge, the backpack clasped to the man's chest, Horatio's lethal form shot out from behind an overturned dumpster twisted gro-tesquely around a scorched telephone pole. Likely the spawn of the hardiest domesticated dogs of the past and the always-wild wolves of the American Northwest, Horatio's lean legs rippled beneath his charging, muscled body. The mixed offspring of these pairings had proved to be one of the few species capable of surviving Vulture's harsh conditions. Finch would never cease to be enthralled by the sheer power of the dog-wolves on the hunt, perfectly evolved to their environment. Watching Horatio now, he was flooded with a renewed sense of gratitude in hav-ing befriended this beast so long ago, and wondered why others didn't try to do so themselves. Perhaps the gangs had no need given their human ranks, though to see a dog-wolf pursuing its prey was to know its potential as an asset in a world that revolved almost exclusively on instinct and ferocity.

From his distant vantage, Finch watched as Horatio snapped at the girl's bare legs. The long canine mouth opened briefly to reveal two sets of unmistakable, jagged yellow teeth before locking shut on the target. The Canny screeched as she hit the asphalt and Finch winced as he heard the gnash of her frail bones snapping in Horatio's powerful jaws. It struck Finch that nobody embodied his mantra better than the dog-wolves. In fact, they possessed seemingly no awareness of any lifestyle alternative to self-reliance. Eat when hungry, sleep when tired, kill when necessary. The girl's whimpering disappeared, replaced by the carnal noises of the animal slaking its primal hunger. Finch watched in awe as Horatio's snout quickly turned from black to dark maroon.

Careful not to startle Horatio and remaining out of the sight-line of the other Canny, Finch shuffled from behind the boulder to another heap of rubble. The ideal sneaking conditions of Vulture's lumpy earth were invaluable to an indie like himself. The thick ash cushioned each footstep with a soft crunch. The Canny still clutching his backpack ran on a hundred more yards or so before deciding he was safe enough to take another swig of Leak. Evidently Horatio, having momentarily satisfied himself with one Canny, provided enough of a buffer for the other to once again tilt the watering pot to his eager lips.

Finch's heart pounded as he slunk up behind the preoccupied Canny. The drunkard murmured and hummed to himself as he spilled the Leak down his naked front, where it mingled with the sweat and grime of his exertion. The Canny's bulbous Adams' apple bobbed with each gulp of Leak, reminding Finch of his own thirst. As he crept closer, he could smell the vile liquid as the rivulets descended through the Canny's grimy toes and began to rush down the grooves of hardened magma toward Finch's worn out black sneakers. One blow to that stringy neck and he'd be home free, backpack in hand. He readied himself, his calves tensing for the final pounce.

But he stopped, fist frozen in the air. Or rather, his body stopped. Try as he might, he could not bring himself to throw the punch that would strike the thief. Fighting off involuntary pity for the Canny, he again wished he had some small portion of Horatio's animalistic resolve.

The moral hesitation cost him valuable time. The Canny wiped his lips with a ragged arm and turned to walk away. Feeling adrenaline rise to the tips of his ears, Finch made his move. With a swift, hard kick he catapulted the watering pot twenty feet in the air. The surprised Canny let out a strangled yowl, his yellow eyes wide and darting frantically from Finch to the can careening through the air. Leak spigotted wildly from the rusty pot as it arced in a high parabola overhead.

Finch didn't wait for the cannibal to connect the dots. He snatched his backpack and sprung backward in a dead sprint for the station. He hopped with practiced ease over the swells of cement and metal, mimicking moves he'd watched Horatio perform for so long. Hot, dry air filled his lungs and he blinked sweat out of his eyes. He dared a quick glance over his shoulder as he bounded away. The Canny, on hands and knees, was trying in vain to coax the spilled liquid back into the can with fumbling swats of his filthy hands. If he'd noticed the dog-wolf tearing into his partner a few yards away his reaction to the traumatic sight was none too strong, for he was now licking his fingers, sticky with Leak, and whimpering softly. Securing his backpack under his one functional arm, Finch sped up. Vulture receded behind him as his feet carried him to the outskirts. The sun was beginning to melt into the hazy ball of deep orange that denoted sunset. At night, Vulture belonged to the gangs.

Staggering up to the door of the station, he fished the key out of his pocket, relieved to find he had not lost it in the tumult of the afternoon. As he turned the lock, Finch heard the heavy, padded steps of Horatio approaching behind him, and turned to see his blood-spattered friend. The effort of opening the heavy station door sent a bolt of pain up Finch's arm.

Gritting his teeth, he let Horatio in first before locking the door behind them. Before collapsing onto the floor in exhaustion, he made sure to secure all three deadbolts and slid the two iron beams into place across the doorframe. Thus protected, he turned his attention to his latest injuries. He thought briefly of what Viro might say when he saw the wounds, ashamed at his desire to be pitied. Anything resembling intimacy, or even just simple care, would be enough, though he knew by now to quell these hopes.

Double-checking the locks, Finch finished off the ritual by again touching two fingers to the essay staked to the door.

" 'The height, the deity of man is, to be self-sustained, to need no gift.' What do you think of that, Horatio? Think old Emerson might have been on to something?"

He poured the remains of his canteen into a bowl on the floor, which Horatio eagerly lapped up.

"You earned it buddy, drink up. You were my gift today, anyway. Not the first time, either, is it?"

He ran a hand down Horatio's sleek neck and munched on a wad cattail shoots. To Finch's estimation, no feeling existed so sublime as getting back behind the multi-locked door of the station after a particularly harrowing outing. He wondered if people had always felt this way, or whether it was a phenomenon unique to Vulture. He'd deal with the cuts in his arm in the morning, too exhausted to move just now. His stiff spine cracked as he reclined back on his springy mattress, selecting a book at random from one of the piles on his desk. His fingers closed around a dissolving copy of Edith Wharton's *The Age of Innocence*, reading jealously of Newland Archer's trivial—but nonetheless heart wrenching—quandaries until his eyelids shuttered.

CHAPTER 2

All the lonely people,
where do they all belong?

— The Beatles, *"Eleanor Rigby"*

The purple paint jumped from the canister with a satisfying hiss. Rigby thought briefly about how arbitrary these colors were despite the significance with which they'd gradually become invested. From what she'd heard, it had been a mad dash to collect as much of any one color of paint as could be found once the color gangs started forming up. That had been long before her time. Back at Regal headquarters, thousands of paint canisters were arranged into a great pyramid, like a sacred offering to the color purple. Oil paint, house paint, spray paint, car paint, and anything else remotely similar joined the pyramid, with colors ranging from lavender to deep violet. Rigby pictured them now, all resting in a seemingly inexhaustible pile next to the equally impressive Regal food stash, plus the gigantic water tankard hidden behind a quadruple-locked theater door. The sputtering canister recalled her attention to the fresh corpse at her feet.

The mission had been a success, the Vein squadron blindsided by the poisoned ink. The plan had been Rigby's idea, and she smiled to herself at the successful execution. Knowing the Veins' penchant for tattooing numerous small blue arrows all over their skin, she'd suggested that their ink could be laced with toxic battery acid harvested from the junkyard behind the cinema. By poisoning the ink, the Regals hadn't had to spoil any of the food or water that they'd then stolen from the depleted Vein troop. Once the purple paint coated the dead Vein's eyelids to her satisfaction, Rigby placed the significantly lighter canister back in her pack, bracing herself for the lecture Milo would surely give her once she returned it to the inventory. She'd gone through nearly half a canister that afternoon alone. But even he couldn't be too upset with her, given the success of the mission.

Jimi Hendrix's "Castles Made of Sand" poured softly from the old-fashioned record player's boxy dual speakers. It was one of the few electronic items to go relatively unscathed during the Water Wars. Rigby ran her purple-spattered hand along the smooth edges of the false wood, careful not to disrupt the delicate needle. Hendrix was her favorite, at least currently. Her tastes changed constantly, and her current accommodations made this whimsy possible.

As the final charges of Hendrix's guitar faded into silence, Rigby scanned the bookshelf in front of her. She meticulously catalogued and maintained every record she'd ever found. It had all started with the Beatles' record *Revolver*, which she'd discovered in an abandoned luxe condominium during a raid with her fellow Regals. She had never heard music before that moment, other than the senseless chanting and arhythmic chest-pounding of the Cannies' firelit carousing, if that could be called music. And so when Richard had shown her how to use the record player, fitting the needle gently to the vinyl, she'd been smitten. She must have listened to that album over a thousand times by now, start to finish. She knew every track by heart. It was why she had started calling herself Rigby. That song, "Eleanor Rigby," still mesmerized her today just as it had the first time she'd heard it, a song and story told so delicately, so beautifully otherworldly, it might have come from a different planet. And yet Eleanor, with its soft, round syllables, was no name for a girl trying to make it in Vulture, she had decided.

So Rigby it was. Presumably she'd had a name before that self-christening, though she could hardly remember that early time in her life now, and rarely gave it any thought. It didn't matter, finally. Today mattered. Surviving until tomorrow mattered. And to Rigby, music mattered.

When Richard had shown her the peeling façade and smashed windows of the old record shop, Rigby had cried for the first and only time in her life. Of course, she'd refused to let Richard see her tears. She'd rushed inside and immediately begun rifling through the stacks of records, pressing each one to her chest as though to consume its sounds via osmosis. On that very day she had made a cramped home for herself in the attic above the shop. Gradually, painstakingly, she had curated her personal music library. The record player—a gift from Richard—looked retro and blockish, with faded turquoise paneling edged with imitation balsa. When she wasn't with the gang at the cinema or off on a mission, she was here, creating playlists for herself to drown out Vulture's oppressive silence. Each album sang of an unimaginable, paradisiacal time before the Water Wars, before her memory. She longed to relate even to the sad songs in some small way, though she was equally quick to quash these frivolous feelings. With great care she monitored her musical escapism, knowing that she was better off without the diversion.

The space that housed her modest collection of records remained fairly secure. All four walls still stood, which was more than could be said of most buildings in Vulture. And the tiptoeing other gangs posed little threat to her sanctuary this deep in Regal territory. The purple graffiti sprayed violently across her door left little doubt as to the occupant's affiliation. Wherever the architecture failed, the colors would protect her.

Still, she stood periodically and shuffled to the window, scanning the charred street below for any lurking threats. She kept the music volume as low as she could bear, avoiding attention at all costs but one. The batteries powering the record player were as vital to her enjoyment as they would have been useful to any savvy Vulture resident. Everything had a price.

A fresh purple X adorned her bedside window, standing out against the dozens of faded purple X's she'd since scrubbed away or had flaked off on their own.

Rigby swore to herself, instinctively removing the needle from the spinning record. Silence filled the room like an exhaled lung. The messenger must have come while she'd been sleeping, though she was surprised that she hadn't heard anything. Even the slightest rustle of street gravel was usually enough to snap her eyes wide open. She slept in her boots.

The record slid gently into its sleeve with a satisfying whisper. With the exception of her pristine record collection, neatly arranged on a shelf, the room was filthy. Purple spray paint canisters and paint-caked laundry were strewn across the floor in piles that grew with each passing day. Torn candy wrappers—Snickers, M&M's, Twix, and Skittles—poked out from laundry creases, shining gaudily in the pale morning light. She regularly secreted these treats from the Regal stash, succumbing to her sweet tooth rather than enduring the bland, meagre gang rations. She didn't have much time for cleaning, though even if she did have the time, she probably wouldn't have done so. Being a Regal required almost all of her time and, more often than not, all of her energy as well. But this was the price of being in Vulture's top gang, she often reminded herself. With status came safety, and she'd do anything to maintain her relatively comfortable life secluded in the record shop. Even if that life did happen to take place in the grim shadows of Vulture.

She looked at the sundial affixed to her windowsill. Not quite noon yet, but she'd be cutting it close all the same. Already a pulsating line of heat stretched across the horizon. Richard had taken a liking to her when she was young, but his moods were as fickle then as they were now. Like everyone else in Vulture, Regal or not, she feared winding up on the receiving end of his temper. She'd once seen him cut the tongue out of a ranking Regal for speaking out of turn.

Rigby swore to herself again, louder this time, as she finished retying her boots and applying a fresh swipe of purple paint across her brow. The paint dribbled down her cheeks, forming a jagged purple mask over her face. Thus adorned, she set out for Regal headquarters. To save time she took her shortcut. A wall of overturned and melted city buses blocked the gritty avenue that passed beneath her blissful attic. They were fused almost beyond recognition but for the large, wrenched wheels and axles poking out of the wreckage at violent angles. Portraits, shapes, X's, spray-painted words and graffiti covered every inch of the wall, clustering into a distorted frenzy of color. On several wide hunks of metal the words 'Spokane Bus Lines' were visible through the paint, printed in corroded metal letters. Rigby pieced the words together once, reading from several of the twisted steel and plastic slats that composed the blockade.

Rigby's compact, wiry frame allowed her to wriggle head-first through a small opening that might once have been a panel window. Dodging the broken glass and rusting metal as best she could, Rigby wormed her way to the other side. The smell of melted rubber clung to her throat. The cinema loomed three hundred meters in front of her, the northernmost point in Vulture. Beyond the theater miles of steaming junk dared even the toughest weeds to grow.

Out of those outskirts rose Vulture, its tortuous skyline grotesquely twisted like immense concrete and metallic cacti. Buildings crumbled around steel beams and tilted against the cloudless sky. Immense, multi-leveled mounds of striated iron fused to cruelly bent car axles and ancient lead plumbing systems burst through the ground to meet them, creating fragile bridges and catwalks of refuse and charred machinery. It looked like a giant rusting fungus lurching heavily toward the sun, a grisly, paradoxical lifeform seeping out of the scorched earth in the aftermath of the bombings that ended the Water Wars. Massive mushrooms of solidified magma that might once have been roads and highways stretched up from the earth's core and froze to give Vulture its swollen, bumpy skin. Colors vibrated off of every twisting angle and shard. Even the landscape of the city seemed afraid to stay in one position too long.

According to the lyrics on her records, girls her age ought to daydream, dance, drink, tell secrets, and have conflicted emotions about boys. They never sang about killing cannibals or poisoning rival gangs. She savored the image of the world these songs presented, so drastically different from her own life. Tossing her record player into one of the heaps in the junkyard should certainly have been her instinct as a Vulture survivalist, but she dreaded the thought of returning to a silent apartment after a long day of reconnaissance for the Regals.

At last, she reached the cinema. It's wide brick façade

stretched up imposingly before her, the glass oculus window facing Vulture, scanning the city like an unblinking eye. Compared to the rest of Vulture, the cinema looked palatial, its thick walls covered in intricate, stunning artwork. To avert one's eyes from the junkyard and the arching crags of Vulture, focusing only on the cinema, it might be guessed that the Water Wars had never happened.

Rigby noticed a new graphic had been added to the mural. The gang must be feeling confident, as the Triumph Mural grew in size with each passing week that they remained on top. The baroque black and white artwork of the Bleaks, the original (and now extinct) paint gang, had long since been painted over with endless shades of purple. This week's installation displayed a preposterously muscular Richard surrounded by his loyal Regals, nondescript purple men and women standing at hip height next to their fearless leader, their eyes staring stonily toward Vulture. Rigby rolled her eyes and walked up to the revolving door. A tall woman guarded the entrance. At six and a half feet, she stood more than a foot above Rigby's petite stature. The giantess arched a purple eyebrow at Rigby expectantly.

"Mohawk," Rigby mumbled.

"See you in their kiddo," said the guard, stepping heavily to the side.

Rigby nodded and trudged into the lobby, quickening her pace as she turned down the hall and into the main theater. The sea of turning heads and hushed voices cast a visible ripple through the dimly lit auditorium.

"Ms. Rigby, in the flesh. Not just urban legend after all."

Clearly word of her recent success had already spread.

"Hello Richard."

Best to speak as minimally as possible with Richard. She had learned early. He had slapped her for talking back once, before any hair had even grown on her legs. Once was enough for Rigby. Her jaw smarted at the memory.

He stared at her intently for a full half-minute that felt like hours. He sat upon the stage on a sturdy Captain's chair, purportedly nabbed from a rotting harbor deeper into the outskirts than anyone had ever gone. Most people considered this to be a concocted rumor typical of Richard's hyperbole, though none had undertaken the dangerous journey to confirm its merit. Still, Rigby had a hard time picturing water in a place so bone-dry as Vulture. The thought reminded her of her thirst, and she made a mental note to fill her canteen at the tankard before heading home after the meeting.

Looking at him now, or rather being trapped in his searchlight gaze, Rigby began to wonder if the depiction on the building's mural was as preposterous as it first appeared. Even beneath his thick, purple-spattered corduroy jumpsuit she could see his massive chest rising and falling. He was certainly taller than the guard outside, and perhaps twice as dense. His thick, simian arms hung heavily at his sides. His massive fingers, each one the length and width of a dagger, tapped absently against the legs of his throne.

An eternity passed before he spoke again. The Regals seated in the creaky theater chairs stared silently from Richard to Rigby and back to Richard. Even the junkers standing limply at the back of the theater roused themselves from their usual aloof exhaustion in order to watch this silent destruction. Rigby felt circles of sweat beginning to form under her arms and behind her knees, though she refused to break the gaze. Richard took a long, deliberate pull from a massive canteen handed to him by a trembling Regal attendant. A collective, audible swallow rose from the thirsty audience, tortured by Richard's gluttonous swig. It was a subtle move on Richard's part, but an effective reminder of his absolute authority.

"Take a seat Rigs, please. We have much to discuss today." His words were too kind, dripping in syrup. He knew he had punished her sufficiently for her tardiness with the painful, public silence.

The room let out a collective exhale and Rigby shrank into a chair before he had even finished his sentence. She folded her small frame as tight as it could go into the sticky purple theater chair, though she couldn't manage to make herself disappear. Out of the corner of her eye she saw Milo, Richard's second in command, shaking his head conspicuously. Rigby knew that he, and many others, resented her for the favoritism that Richard often forgot—or refused—to hide.

"The Veins are dead. The poisoning was successful, as I knew it would be. It seems not even the Cannies will touch their bodies." A nervous laughter filled the pregnant pause that Richard provided for this very purpose.

"So we keep food out of their mouths as well, an added bonus," he continued, his voice thick with gravitas. "But we must remain vigilant for retaliation. While we have reduced their numbers, they are far from extinct."

Nobody spoke. Richard stared icily into each set of eyes, as though daring someone to open their mouth. It was well known that Richard harbored an especial hatred for the Veins, as many of them had once been Regals. At some point they'd grown tired of Richard's dictatorial style of government, his success as a general in the Water Wars paving the way for his increasingly violent rise to power in the postbellum wreckage. Wanting a more democratic system in Vulture, the Veins had emerged as an alternative faction, taking a couple dozen Regals with them and positioning themselves just below the Regals in the Vulture food chain. Of course, the vicious realities of Vulture had eventually undermined the Veins' democratic ideals, and they'd been forced to become just as heartless as the Regals simply to stay alive. Rigby had been young at the time, though she remembered Richard's fury upon discovering the betrayal. The blue V's had emerged throughout Vulture overnight, the painted letters splashed hastily over every convenient surface. Richard had taken their defection personally, which was likely their intent. A junker wheezed at the back of the theater, stifling a cough.

"Our numbers are strong. But we can always add to our ranks. Though I know they are rare and have mostly been eaten by Cannies at this point, keep alert for independent's that might want to join us here at the cinema. If they are still alive it is a testament to their constitution. And we can't let the Vein's gain any more members, not now that we have them on the precipice of extermination."

At this point in the oration Richard could barely conceal a wan, prideful smile. He continued, "an invitation to join the Regals would be a gift to the common indie, I would think."

Rigby saw Milo squirming in his seat. As Master of Inventory, each additional member meant another mouth he'd have to feed, another water ration deleted from the tankard, another body to cloak in the increasingly rare purple paint.

"A problem, Milo?"

Richard's voice resonated in the cool silence of the theater.

"No, sir."

"Worried about our stockpile, yes?"

"Always, sir."

"Well good, that's your job, isn't it?"

"Yes Richard."

"I'm in a good mood this morning Milo, let me help you. Would you like that?"

"Of course, Richard."

Richard's serpentine eyes scanned the crowd. The junker's wheezing started up again, this time more violent.

"A volunteer, wonderful."

Richard reached his immense arm out in the direction of the junker, beckoning him onto the stage with one flick of his plate-sized hand. With difficulty, the junker relieved himself with a short coughing fit before his compatriots gently nudged him toward the stage. His steps were timid, every Regal watching silently as the pigeon-toed feet made their hesitant journey up the aisle. At last he reached the stage and clambered up pitifully on his hands and knees before rising to stoop in front of Richard.

Without ever leaving his seat, Richard's muscled hand shot out at the junker's neck. The frail figure's eyes bulged briefly before rolling back, Richard snapping his neck with a slight twist of his heavy wrist. The limp body slumped off the stage with a sickening crunch. Two purple-masked attendants quickly scurried to the body, dragging it out of sight.

"One less mouth to feed, yes Milo?"

"Yes, thank you Richard."

Milo was beaming, his fidgeting replaced with a relaxed slouch.

"And for the rest of you lucky Regals, a lesson. We do not have the resources to support deadweight. Every Regal must contribute every day, yes?"

Emphatic nods rippled throughout the crowd.

Rigby settled into her seat, never comfortable at these meetings but thankful to be out of the spotlight for now. She yearned to be back in the record shop attic on her thick mattress, Jimi Hendrix's powerful chords transporting her far, far away. She imagined herself laughing with Jimi and singing along to his songs in a place called California. It sounded surreal and far from Vulture.

Rigby thought sometimes about running off and joining the Veins, escaping Richard's wrath once and for all. But each time she considered leaving the Regals, she realized the futility of such an endeavor. Not only did the Regals provide the best security and stockpiles in all of Vulture, but Richard had also found her as a child, giving her food and water and patiently training her to survive in the ruinous new world. He'd just about raised her. Plus, she hadn't become the Regals' Master of Reconnaissance without making a few enemies along the way. Why would the Veins welcome a high-ranking Regal after the years of espionage and violence she'd committed against them? And if she were rejected, Richard would never take her back. She'd be killed on the spot or left to die as an indie, eaten by a Cannie or a dog-wolf in the outskirts. Likely the many other loyal Regals had come to a similar conclusion, though they'd never discuss it out loud. Furthermore, the impregnability of the cinema and the guarantee of food and water was nearly impossible to walk away from. So long as Richard's iron-fisted rule kept them alive and their stomach's somewhat full, they had no convincing reason to defect. Richard's booming voice startled her out of her reverie.

"Now. Your turn to talk," he said, flicking away a Regal attendant proffering his canteen as he stood up to survey his wards. The room was beginning to take on that cloying dermic smell of too many people packed into a tight space. Two hundred seats plus standing room would soon be inadequate. From all over the rotting city these people, each one covered in varying amounts of purple paint, had scuttled here to await Richard's instructions. Rigby often wondered where they all lived. Some probably slept in a different haunt every night, still searching for a place secure enough to stay for more than a few nights at a time. Others probably holed themselves up in the ruptured and tilting buildings of Vulture, making homes out of cave-like dwellings that still had a few walls intact. Had any building large enough to accommodate the whole gang still stood, they would probably all sleep together in a massive purple herd. Rigby was glad that most of the buildings that had once held such a capacity were by now reduced to rubble. She would have missed the privacy of her record shop. Maybe others would miss their own small pleasures, too.

"Milo, start us off," commanded Richard, his tone conveying boredom at the thought of listening to someone else speak.

"Yes Richard. The food cache inventory has been updated and, with proper rationing, should last us comfortably through the next seventy-three moons."

"Should?" Richard cocked an eyebrow at Milo.

"Uhm… That is, it *will* last us seventy-three moons. My apologies, Richard."

"Let us be precise with our words, please. We are the Regals, not the 'uhm' Regals. Continuing, then. Painter?"

"Yes Richard. The Mural of Triumph is nearing completion and –"

"When?"

"Sorry Richard. In three sunsets the Mural of Triumph will be complete and we will celebrate with a feast in your honor." Milo winced at the mention of the feast. Regal feasts were never factored into his intricate rationing system.

"Again. Precision with our words now Regals, remember Milo's mistake." The agitation was building in Richard's voice. For someone who hated repeating himself, he never seemed to tire of hearing "yes Richard." Rigby forced herself to focus. Her turn was coming up.

"Miriam, what do you have for us today?"

"Yes Richard. No independents to report this week," responded Miriam's faltering, high-pitched voice. She sat a few seats in front of Rigby, and she watched a thick, purple bead of sweat course down Miriam's temple as she spoke. Her slender shoulders trembled like her voice.

A silence followed Miriam's report as Richard attempted to stare through her. His swollen forearms pulsed and his jaw worked back and forth in tense gyrations. Rigby had become fluent in Richard's body language, a knowledge born of fear and time. Few Regals had been with the gang as long as she. Finally he spoke in a measured, low tone.

"Well. You were precise with your words, Miriam. But, Miriam, I am upset with your answer. Come up here please, Miriam." His voice was ice. A barely audible whimper escaped Miriam's lips as she stood to walk to the stage.

Rigby has always thought 'Miriam' to be a name ill befitting Vulture, its syllables too soft or weak to withstand the harshness of its environs. The victim made her way cautiously to the stage where Richard, enthroned, glowered down at her.

Before Miriam had reached the steps Richard's massive hand shot out like a striking python and froze inches from her cheek. Miriam fell to the ground, too stunned to scream. The omnipresent hush that hung over the audience intensified. The theater became a constellation of wide eyes and pursed lips.

"Darling," cooed Richard. "Would you prefer I send your brother into Vulture in your place?"

"No! Please Richard, I can do it," Miriam whimpered, still

prone on the ground, her limp palms tilted upward in supplication.

The tense moment doesn't surprise Rigby. Richard's patience had been wearing thin ever since Milo's simple error, and Miriam should have lied rather than reporting nothing. Recruiting numbers had plateaued, indies becoming more scarce than ever. When Richard spoke again, it was to the entire audience.

"Never. Never report nothing. Miriam's job is locating independents. If one week is not enough time for you to find one person who is not affiliated with a gang, then perhaps you are not quite talented enough to be a Regal! Not worthy to eat our food, drink our water, or celebrate our victories!"

Miriam all but crawled back to her seat, fighting back the tears no doubt begging to spring forth. Richard's threat would mark her far longer than any slap could. Her coltish legs carried her back to her seat where she crumpled into a silent ball.

"Rigby!"

Richard shouted her name but she was ready, speaking with almost robotic clarity.

"Yes Richard. General gang surveillance: the Veins are severely diminished, twenty-six dead and less than eighty remaining. They lick their wounds at the museum."

"Good. And what of the others?"

Perhaps he was testing her, making sure she has done more than lounge about in the auditory bliss of Hendrix, Tom Petty, Nina Simone, and The Beatles. As Master of Reconnaissance, her responsibilities included keeping tabs on all the gangs, a demanding task despite the flexibility allowed by its ambiguity. After inventory, Milo's responsibility, reconnaissance was the most important job in the gang. Nonetheless she was prepared. It would have been unlike Richard not to include a follow-up.

"Yes Richard. The Scorps' numbers remain low, not totaling more than sixty members by my latest estimate. They've been hard to get a read on ever since they went subterranean, though the reappearance of green tags in the southeast is disconcerting enough to warrant vigilant observation. The Veins have added members this week after last week's losses, and graffiti commemorating the additions has been painted on the water tower in Vulture-west. The Cannies remain drunk."

This last bit she included as a joke, intended to chip away at the oppressive tension that had engulfed the theater. It was certainly a risk, especially given the verbal lashing Miriam had just received. But Rigby usually got away with these liberties.

After a brief and horrifying pause, Richard let out a deep chortle. The room collectively exhaled for a second time and a few Regals even ventured a staccato laugh. Rigby smiled and shifted in her seat.

"Very well. Thank you, Rigby. Painters, be sure to add our mark to the Veins' new art. They must be reminded of Vulture's hierarchy."

"Yes Richard," responded the gang's guild of artists in unison. Their job was riskier than might be expected. They consistently had to work behind enemy lines, and Richard had been known to cut off fingers for depictions of himself that he found unflattering.

The meeting ended and the Regals began filing out of the old cinema. They met during the day because the large holes in the roof created natural skylights, though the brutal heat that seeped into the theater in the late afternoons hardly felt worth the meagre light. Otherwise, the venue would be blindingly dark, and Richard liked to be seen as well as heard. He took another long slug of water as they filed out.

The purple-clad herd diverted like a river as the Regals crept back to whatever homes they had carved out for themselves in the various caverns of Vulture, one of the city's few naturally occurring resources. Some scurried quickly through the fossilized debris while others trudged steadily, scraping their boots along the gritty earth.

It would be six sunsets before they saw each other again *en masse*, unless Richard called an impromptu meeting as he had today. Regals with some form of status like Rigby had their own departments to take care of until that time, but the rest of the rank and file would be responsible for spying, supplementing the stockpiles through thievery or ingenuity, and leaving the gang's markings on the endlessly available surfaces of Vulture. Each tuna can added to the stockpile or rival graffiti vandalized would be an opportunity for promotion up the Regal ladder toward the safety of relevance. Water, food, and paint: the strange currencies of Vulture. Power and plentitude for the gang meant safety for its members.

Rigby began her walk home, humming an Amy Winehouse track to herself in anticipation. She accidently makes eye contact with Miriam and quickly looks away, though not before she notices Miriam's face, contorted against the tears welling at her eyelids. Rigby wondered when she'd finally let them go, yielding herself to her perilous vulnerability. Probably not until she was safely back behind some kind of wall that physically separated her from the rest of the city, even if her mental barrier had been rendered porous. Rigby looked away and returned to her humming.

"Rigby – hi."

Rigby's head whipped around, her hand instinctively forming a fist before she saw the slender figure shuffling up behind her.

"Don't sneak up on me like that."

"Oh, sorry… It's Miriam."

Miriam stretched out her tiny hand, sniffling and adjusting her face into a warm smile. It was a motherly smile, Rigby thought, though she had no way of knowing that for sure. After another moment she stiffly shook Miriam's hand, a skeptical eyebrow arched beneath the paint on her forehead. Such greetings were rare in Vulture.

"People say you know Richard better than anyone."

"They're not wrong. I've known Richard a long time. You'll get used to him. It'll all feel easier once you figure him out a bit."

"Well, thanks," shrugged Miriam, making an effort to compose herself.

Ashamed that Richard's favoritism was so ubiquitously known, Rigby felt a sudden compulsion to comfort her less fortunate fellow Regal. Despite the fact that they all wore a second skin of purple paint, the Regals rarely felt like a team. Really everyone was out for themselves. The gang just made it easier to stay alive. Other gangs weren't as cynical about their mutual affiliation, but the Regals had discovered success in shirking even platonic relationships, instead rallying around a common animal desire to survive.

Rigby turned to leave, assuming by Miriam's silence that the conversation was over.

"Wait! Sorry. People say you know Vulture better than anyone, too."

Rigby stared at her for a moment, taking in Miriam's shuffling feet and earnest face, hands clasped and writhing behind her back. Regals rarely asked for help, and it was painful for Rigby to watch. She tried to make her mouth say 'no', but it refused, withering under Miriam's pitiful gaze.

"Miriam, listen. If you want some help finding an indie before next week's meeting, I can help you."

"Oh my gosh! Really? Rigby, you wouldn't mind?" Her eyes stretched impossibly wide with genuine gratitude. It made Rigby uncomfortable.

"Sure. I can do my field checks at the same time. Two birds, one stone, ya know?"

Rigby blamed the sappy Amy Winehouse song in her head—"Wake Up Alone"—for her submission to Miriam's plea. Her preference had always been to work alone.

"Oh my gosh," she gushed again. "That's so nice. Thank you so much Rigby. This really is so nice."

Miriam bounced on her toes before shrugging giddily and hugging Rigby, though she retracts the hug quickly when Rigby's stunned arms remain stiff at her sides.

Miriam's sincerity flummoxed Rigby. Though strange, she had to admit the hug felt nice, the pleasant embrace sharply contrasting the body-blows she spent most of her time dodging. Who had been the last person to hug her? A father? A mother? Had it ever happened?

"Don't mention it," she called over her shoulder, picking her way over the refuse back toward the record shop.

CHAPTER 3

Until I feared I would lose it, I never loved to read.
One does not love breathing.

— Harper Lee, *To Kill a Mockingbird*

The sunrise woke Finch as it always did, filtering in through the grime-coated window by the door. Yawning, he stretched his sore limbs up from the mattress and stepped softly to the window, careful not to wake Horatio, who snoozed peacefully by the door. From the station's locus on the threshold of the outskirts, he watched as the rising sun cast Vulture in brilliant polychromatic hues that belied the city's rotted core. The paint-stained, ruinous remains of the city might once have been named for something other than birds with a taste for deceased life. Like his own name, the city's original moniker had been forgotten and replaced in the days and years since the last electrical bulb fizzled to defunction. Turning from the window, he looked down at the various newspaper shreds and magazine fragments that rested like fallen leaves on his desk. Next to these stood short towers of books and paperbacks, some more intact than others.

The sturdiest stack was composed of the leather-bound law books he'd found in the crumbled remains of a law practice not far from the station. These tomes were in the best condition of the modest library collected atop the desk. They'd been the first books Finch had ever found, and before he'd even been able to read them he'd sat for hours wondering at their inscrutable symbols, breathing in the sweet must of the pages. Though he'd read them cover to cover by now, he rarely returned to them, finding that Vulture's sole law—survive—had rendered the dense verbiage of these legal texts essentially moot. Still, it had been the weighty quality of these books and their mysterious symbols that had piqued his interest in reading in the first place, nearly two decades ago.

He'd eagerly combed through the magazines and newspapers so many times that he'd nearly memorized them, scanning for any clues about Vulture's history, his own origins, or useful information that might increase his chances of survival. But all he'd come up with (besides irrelevant items like pie crust recipes, home decorating tips, profiles of Hollywood actors, cologne advertisements and the like) were a few mentions of the impending Water Wars, lengthy Jeremiads about climate change, and a longer piece on the antebellum economy that he couldn't follow but seemed somehow important. None of the articles he'd pieced together were complete and most had dissolved beyond readability anyway, but he could never bring himself to throw them away.

Alone on one corner of the desk rested the three thin books that Finch had procured from the heartbreaking ruins of a hospital maternity ward. He'd noticed the books trapped beneath a pile of shattered transparent bassinets, and had rescued them from the jagged mess. The first was a children's book called *Goodnight Moon*, which he'd eventually learned to read with the help of the second book, an alphabet guide complete with simple pictures. From 'A is for Apple' to 'Z is for Zebra', Finch had taught himself to read with dogged slowness, matching the pictures to words he already knew, always eying the imperial stack of law books and the untold secrets hidden behind their rich mahogany covers. Though simplistic to look upon now, Finch would never forget the world that the alphabet book had opened up for him, a master key to a universe beyond Vulture. The third book listed names for newborn infants, and Finch often entertained himself by reading through select alphabetical lists of names, wondering if one of these names had once belonged to him.

The final pile on the wide desk was Finch's personal favorite. These spine-broken paperbacks he'd discovered years ago on an expedition with Horatio, picking their way through a collapsing wing of a high school that had at some point sunk several feet into the earth. In one classroom (which he'd determined to be devoted to an English literature course, given the half-erased sonnet scrawled on the chalkboard) he'd found the novels tucked haphazardly in the mouth of an overturned desk. Rushing home with these treasures weighing down his backpack, he'd read each book, one after another, straining his eyes by candlelight when the bright sky gave way to darkness. *The Age of Innocence, Hamlet, Moby-Dick, Paradise Lost, Walden, To Kill A Mockingbird, The Great Gatsby, The Collected Essays of Ralph Waldo Emerson, Heart of Darkness, The Sun Also Rises*, and a poetry anthology called *Transatlantic Romanticism* continued to be his surest portals of escape from Vulture's grim reality. Over and over again he had read Thoreau's line, "Books are the treasured wealth of the world and the fit inheritance of generations and nations," as though it had been written for his eyes alone. After so many rereadings the novels were held together by little more than bits of floss, and the pages were so worn and yellow that Finch feared they would disintegrate in even the mildest of breezes. While he knew them to be works of fiction, he couldn't help but to hope that they were anchored by some former reality. *To Kill A Mockingbird* had inspired him to call himself Finch, awed by the imaginary family's compassion, honesty, and rigid belief in justice. Often while reading he'd pretend to be a part of their family, the fourth Finch.

He gazed lovingly at the neat stacks on his desk. The thought of further undiscovered books haunted him, inspiring his risky jaunts into Vulture in eternal pursuit of printed words. In whatever form they might appear, Finch wanted all the words he could get his hands on.

He would've liked very much to fill his home with books, lining the walls with overstuffed shelves. For now, the piles on the station desk would have to do. It no longer felt strange to call the abandoned radio station his home and hadn't for a long time. For the first several years banked in his memory, he'd lived on the run, hiding where possible and eating only what insufficient rations he could scavenge. Then, a year or two before he'd met Horatio, when a Canny had chased him deeper into the outskirts than he'd ever dared to venture, he'd discovered the radio station. For the first few months he'd thought of it as a temporary residence, a haunt good enough to last until forced to run again. But he'd soon realized the security offered by the cramped space. The door had several working locks, the walls were insulated with soundproofing, and the building had somehow dodged the major destruction of the Water Wars. All four walls remained sturdily intact, and rain had yet to test the roof for leaks. And most gangs clung to the familiar terrain of Vulture, rarely risking forays into the unknowable outskirts. Still, the Cannies occasionally came hollering and pounding on nights when they'd drunk themselves senseless on Leak and wandered beyond city limits.

The station must once have occupied a somewhat remote part of town, given its desolate location outside of Vulture proper. It had been part of a squat strip mall, abutted by a barber shop with its roof caved in, a tattoo parlor with its inner construction now jutting through the wide front window, and a methadone clinic reduced almost entirely to ash but for the limp, corroding sign that sheepishly displayed the clinic's name and hours. While the shattered satellite dish and crushed radio tower affixed to the station's roof squandered the space's radio capability, Finch had found it to be a more than adequate bunker.

Above the door were printed the words 'The Spokane Independent Voice' in faded black lettering. Finch had no idea what that first part of the name meant, though he'd seen the word repeatedly in various iterations throughout Vulture's ruins. A few of the newspaper clippings in his pile had once been plastered to the walls with peeling lengths of duct tape when he'd first overtaken the radio station. From these scraps of news—mostly small-time local media shout-outs and a few gushing fan letters—Finch had deduced that 'The Spokane Independent Voice' had positioned itself as the unfiltered rebel on the front lines of journalism, warning of a "coming reckoning not hyperbolically defined as an apocalypse." Finch marveled at these accounts now, wondering how the intrepid broadcasters had felt about being so dreadfully correct.

Finch massaged his throbbing shoulder, aching where the Canny's blade had punctured his skin. He stooped to pick up *The Age of Innocence* from the floor, where it had landed like a broken-winged bird when he'd fallen asleep reading.

Horatio, rousing himself, watched silently as Finch disinfected and dressed the slashes on his arm and shoulder. After a moment, Horatio lifted his snout to gently lick at the wounds with his rough tongue. The tenderness of Horatio's concerned lapping reminds Finch of the day he'd met Horatio, and he smiled at the recollection.

Barely a teenager at the time and nearly starved to death, he had tripped down by the gulch and sliced his knee on the sharp fragments of a shattered car windshield. As he'd tended to the scrape, picking the incisive pieces of glass from his skin, a dog-wolf pup had appeared on the crest of the gulch. It watched him furtively with its already large head cocked to one side. He had been too far from the station to make a run for it, not that he could have outrun the adolescent dog-wolf—even if both of his knees had been unscathed. And at that point, Finch had been thin enough to make a perfect snack for the growing pup.

Though still the size of a wheelbarrow, the pup had seemed more curious than vicious. Perhaps it had been lost, or abandoned, or maybe it had never seen a human before. It looked far too young to be hunting on its own just yet, and their mothers usually kept them close by their flanks for the first couple of years. But this one, like Finch, had been alone. Its overlarge ears flopped comically to one side of its head, its moist brown nose twitching ceaselessly. On tentative, oversized paws, it had stepped closer to Finch, leaving large prints in the ash-caked mud that foretold of the immense dog-wolf to come. Finch felt his breath catch in his throat as he froze in the dog's emotionless stare, smelling the wild musk of the animal's fur. Taking several ginger steps toward him before stopping again, the young pup never broke eye contact. Its red tongue lolled, panting in the heat as it sized him up.

Finch had been terribly thirsty, scouring the gulch for any budding succulent he could crack open for liquid relief. This was long before he'd devised the water-catching system atop the station's roof. The pup had looked thirsty too, and where its hot breath reached Finch's perspiring face it felt as dry as the desert air. Even as a pup the panting mouth had displayed menacing rows of two-inch long teeth, sharp as the broken glass that had punctured Finch's knee. Nobody drank enough water in Vulture, probably not even the dog-wolves, thought Finch. Slowly, and with deliberate, surgical movements, he had extricated his emergency water bottle from his backpack. Careful not to make any sudden movements, he'd poured some water into one of the natural clefts that freckled the igneous ground. As the water collected in the shallow rock pool, Finch prepared to make his slow escape from the dog-wolf's dispassionate black eyes.

The pup's spine bristled slightly as he poured the water. Finch forced himself to remain composed, though he felt his heart beating in his eardrums. The young beast sniffed cautiously at the water. Still avoiding any frantic movements, Finch rose to his feet, preparing to back slowly out of the gulch without turning his back on the predator. His legs wobbled involuntarily beneath him as he stood up.

Thirst proving one of Vulture's great equalizers, the dog-wolf lapped up the water in several flashes of its wide tongue. Once the last droplets of moisture had been licked from the smooth crater, the pup lifted its head expectantly back up toward Finch, still panting heavily.

Canteen at the ready, Finch poured more water into the natural bowl. He refused to consider the cost of such wastefulness when those powerful jaws hinged open and shut mere inches away from his face. However, just then, the pup began licking at the scrape on Finch's knee. He'd had to clamp a hand over his mouth to keep from crying out as soon as the warm tongue surprised his tender, bleeding skin. At first he'd been paralyzed with fear, his feet rooted to the ground. However, after several seconds of the strange, rough sensation, he'd found himself relaxing. There was something deeply considerate—even protective—about the dog's attention to his wound. After looking out for himself for so long, the sympathy had felt foreign to Finch.

He gambled several more slow, backward steps in the direction of the station. The sun had nearly set, its orange rays casting long, jagged shadows from Vulture's ruinous skyline. The pup watched him go.

At about twenty paces, however, its ears pricked skyward. Again, Finch froze where he stood. He'd never forget that first look, an expression akin to recognition forming in the dog-wolf's dark eyes. Finch shook the empty canteen as though to summon a few more drops, but it was empty. He took one more cautious step, testing the pup's intentions. The dog loped straight toward him, appearing almost playful in its explosive bounds. Finch was awed by the adeptness of the animal's movements, skirting the larger chunks of metal and cement and carving its way athletically through the shallow canyons on its wide paws, its fluid movements sharply contrasting his own gawky, pubescent limbs. It swished quickly about his legs before halting and looking up at him again. Finch took another couple of steps and the pup did the same. The coarse fur that formed a ridge on its spine came up to Finch's waist, and the ears atop its wide head came nearly to his chest. Finch exhaled the breath he hadn't realized he'd been holding.

The dog-wolf had been by his side ever since, dubbed Horatio for his stalwart companionship (not that Finch thought of himself as in any way resembling the moody Prince Hamlet). Basking in the pleasant reverie, Finch bent down to give Horatio a rub behind the ears. The oil that gave Horatio's black coat its metallic sheen coated Finch's fingers, and he rubbed the shiny essense off on his pant leg. That moment when they'd met felt so long ago now, and yet the years had gone by in a blur of day-in, day-out survival. Unlatching the door, he watched Horatio amble into a cool spot under the barbershop's tattered awning and laid down.

Finch filled a bowl from one of his water jugs and brought it back outside. Feeling nostalgic for those days when they'd both just been young pups, and still buoyed by gratitude for Horatio's last-second intervention with the Cannies yesterday, he added a few of his walnuts to the offering he set a few feet from the dog-wolf. Horatio cleaved the walnuts in halves with efficient brutality, reminding Finch of the effortless bone crunching he'd witnessed the day before.

CHAPTER 4

There's people runnin' 'round loose in the world
Ain't got nothin' better to do
Make a meal of some bright-eyed kid
You need someone lookin' after you.

— Stevie Nicks, *"Stop Draggin' My Heart Around"*

Rigby met Miriam at the cracked fountain in Vulture's center plaza. A distended steel pipe cleaved the fountain in half at its center, rising vigorously from the ground like a great, writhing earthworm. They weren't too far from the cinema, making the fountain a relatively safe place for two Regals to meet. Daylight beamed down onto Vulture, carrying with it a thick heat. Most of the gangs would be sleeping or conspiring in their respective quarters, waiting for the cover of night to scuttle about the city executing their plots. The Cannies would be getting drunk on the rotting bridge, and the Veins would be planning out their next move at the crumbling site of the old museum. The Scorps could be anywhere, though they rarely ventured above ground, preferring the safety of their tunnel network. The area around the fountain was wide and circular, making surprise attacks unlikely. Besides, it would take a particularly confident—or perhaps just stupid—gang trooper to attack the Regals in broad daylight, given the city's current hierarchy.

Rigby and Miriam wore faded grey corduroy jumpsuits with

large splotches of purple paint bedecking their arms, legs and torsos. It looked like the patchy skin of some exotic desert lizard. Both wore their hair long and dreadlocked into dry stalactites of solidified purple paint. Beauty had been forgone ages ago; the purple markings were not decorative but protective. Richard's wrath was widely known and, more importantly, feared in Vulture. Anyone that encountered Richard was now either his sworn enemy, a Regal, dead, or else a junker in the expansive landfill behind the cinema.

"We should check the city limits. I'll scope out the Cannies and see if any more Veins need to be tagged. I've heard lots of independents have retreated into the outskirts."

"Ok! Thank you so, so, so much Rigby. You know I've been having trouble with this new position. And Richard can be so..."

"I know. Really, it's fine Miriam, don't mention it." Miriam's unending gratitude was beginning to make Rigby feel uncomfortable. They each took a judicious sip of water before setting out in the direction of the outskirts. A vulture sailed between the cavernous buildings, coasting on a few languid flaps at a time.

As they stole through Vulture's winding alleyways, formed by the skeletal remains of skyscrapers and collapsed buildings, the sun stretched closer to its daily zenith. Rigby had grown accustomed to sweat trickling down from her scalp and soaking her collar—one of several reasons why life in Vulture was generally nocturnal. Typically, she wouldn't conduct her reconnaissance work until close to sunset, as that was when the gangs roused to visibility. But for Miriam's sake, today they worked during the day. Most indies felt safe enough to leave their hovels during the daylight hours for the same reason that Rigby operated at night; orchestrating their lives around the movements and habits of the gangs.

The bomb-rent buildings gave way to flattened strips of former shops and restaurants. A burst apartment building looked like the exposed innards of a wasp's nest, its walls collapsed to reveal a messy hive of concrete foundations and piping. The rocky, metallic substance of the ground rose and fell in bulbous hills and shallow canyons. As the outskirts entered their sightline, their steps trod more easily on the flattening ground, no longer impeded by the massive hunks of metal and ore that crowded the paths of Vulture proper. Wide, cracked asphalt lots soon dominated the scenery. Muted tones of black and gray replaced the riotous jumble of colors that characterized the city.

A Canny sang a garbled tune to himself from the depths of a badly dented yellow dumpster. A Scorp had hung himself from a third-floor window in a lonely burnt out house, his body rotating rhythmically from one side to the other at the end of the taut rope. The neon green paint on his body glinted in the bright afternoon sun, catching the light with each turn.

Miriam looked away but Rigby paused to watch the gentle undulations of the swinging corpse. She wondered how many dead bodies she'd seen in her life, and how many a person her age ought to have seen. Had Stevie Nicks ever seen a dead body?

"Cannies still drunk, check," said Rigby, more to herself than Miriam.

"What is that, over there?" Miriam's slender finger pointed towards a low building in the distance, about a quarter mile into the cement wasteland. It looked like the remains of an old strip mall. Rigby followed her outstretched finger. She noticed that Miriam had painted her fingernails a pale lavender color, some private vestige of femininity. Rigby glanced down at her own nails. They were stubby and lined with grime. Dried paint peeled and melted in webs across her digits.

"How the hell do you keep your hands so clean?"

Miriam blushed. "I found an old toothbrush, and I scrub them every night."

Rigby nodded but said nothing more.

"I like your…" Miriam seemed to feel pressured to return a compliment, though she struggled to summon anything worthy of remark from her interlocutor's grimy exterior. "Oh, your tattoo!" she finally declared, relieved to notice something that might have been an aesthetic choice rather than a functional necessity.

Rigby tugged up her sleeve to reveal the tattoo in its entirety, printed in neat lettering on her forearm. Half the time she forgot it was even there, it had been with her for so long.

"Oh, thanks," said Rigby, sheepishly.

"What does it say?"

"You can't read it?"

"No, I never learned how," blushed Miriam.

Rigby often forgot that most people in Vulture were illiterate, as there was nothing to read anyway. Still, Richard had taught her to sound out the letters when she was young. It had been a thrill when she could finally read the words tattooed on her slender arm. With uncharacteristic patience, Richard had taught her to ride his motorcycle, too—the only operant engine in Vulture — which he pridefully puttered about the city, now and again revving the engine for effect. After such days, tutor and tutee would sit side by side in an empty theater, and Rigby would ask Richard to tell her about the past, about the time he'd found her. He'd get a thoughtful look on his face before telling her about the shipwreck, the young boy who'd been crying nearby before tearing off on his own into the outskirts, and about the tattoo.

"It says, 'To thine own self be true, Ophelia.'"

"What does that mean?" asked Miriam, staring down at the

faded ink lettering.

Rigby did not answer right away. "I don't know," she finally said. That was the truth, anyway. But she stopped herself from telling Miriam about the song she'd heard that mentioned that strange word, 'Ophelia'. It was a Bob Dylan track called "Desolation Row," and he'd sung, "Now Ophelia, she's 'neath the window / For her I feel so afraid." So it was a name. Had it been her name, before she'd been taken in by Richard? Another weak name, she'd decided. Even Dylan was afraid for her. She didn't tell Miriam how thrilled she'd been the first time she'd heard the lyrics, hoping desperately that they might offer some clue about her past. But no matter how many times she'd listened to the song—hundreds of times by now—she couldn't determine with any certainty its significance to her tattoo. Not even Richard had known what to make of the thin, tattooed line of text, other than registering shock that her chubby young forearm bore the permanent ink when he'd discovered her.

"Hey is that... a dog-wolf?" ventured Miriam. Her gaze had returned to the distant building when Rigby's reverie had stretched into silence, ending the conversation. Rigby rolled her sleeve back down over her wrist.

"Yeah, looks like it, and a big one, too." Rigby continued to stare. She pulled an ancient pair of binoculars to her eyes. An enormous black dog-wolf paced back and forth in the shade of the building's awning.

She passed the binoculars to Miriam. "They're rare, but you hear about these dog-wolves out here. I've seen their paw prints in the junkyard a few times. I've never seen one this close to Vulture, though. He's huge, isn't he?"

"Wait, now look!" Miriam thrust the binoculars back to Rigby, who immediately put them to her eyes. The faded lettering of

'The Spokane Independent Voice' came into view. Some kind of wide tarp hung across the top of the squat building, secured on one end by a busted satellite dish and tied to a cruelly bent radio tower on the other. Through the magnified lenses she watched as a tall, thin man emerged from a door nearest the dog-wolf and set down a bowl on the shaded concrete. The man paused on the door's threshold, watching the shaggy dog lap up the water before returning indoors. Even from this distance she could see the animal's long yellow teeth. The man placed something else beside the bowl and the dog-wolf immediately snapped it up, a bone-chilling crunching noise echoing into the outskirts.

"Is it his...pet?" Miriam asked, incredulous. Without answering, Rigby continued to stare at the spot where the man had stood. Though she couldn't see his face, she could tell that he had long dark hair, which he wore in a short braid.

"He's not wearing colors. Looks like an indie to me," said Rigby, breaking the silence. She picked up her canteen but set it back down without taking a sip, deciding to wait out her thirst a little longer.

"Should we...go over there?" Miriam inquired. Rigby weighed her fear of the dog-wolf against her fear of Miriam returning to Richard empty handed again. Something about Miriam's delicate, neatly painted fingernails triggered a protective feeling in Rigby. Miriam didn't belong in Vulture, had done nothing to deserve its continual punishment.

"Yeah, let's go."

They began to trudge toward the dilapidated radio station, hugging the boulders until they could no longer avoid exposure in the flat, textureless land of the outskirts. The indie disappeared back behind the door he'd emerged from. The station appeared to have remained relatively undamaged in the war, at least from the outside. Maybe the man had fixed it up. Most indies looked hungry both in their withered bodies and their furtive movements. But the man, though thin, had not looked starved. Perhaps he was surviving better than most.

Rigby blinked the sweat out of her eyes. Nodding to Miriam, they descended the final crest into the outskirts, leaving Vulture behind. Within a hundred yards of the station, the dog-wolf sprung to its feet, its back bristling and its black eyes staring impassively in their direction. They slowed to a stop.

"I don't like this," said Miriam, her voice betraying a quiver.

"Me neither. But would you rather Richard chew you out or take your chances with the dog-wolf?" Miriam considered this for a while before shaking her head in despair. Rigby saddened at the prospect of killing Miriam's innocent ebullience, though she knew it would have to happen eventually.

Slowly, they resumed their journey. Within fifty yards, however, the dog began barking territorially, making hopping bounds in their direction. Rigby placed a ready hand on the triggered crossbow strapped to her back, grasping Miriam's shuddering elbow with the other.

"Maybe we'll have better luck somewhere else," suggested Miriam. Rigby doubted it. The fact that they'd seen an indie was rare enough. But as the dog-wolf charged toward them, its round shoulders lowered and pointing straight at them, she relented.

"Yeah, let's get out of here."

Visibly relieved, Miriam exhaled a breath she'd been holding. Rigby all but dragged Miriam back up over the crest, sprinting back into Vulture. Even once they were out of sight of the dog-wolf they could still hear it barking, loud and wild, in the distance. Finally they came to a stop, huddling behind a school bus that had been melted into a lumpy yellow mass. Holding their breath, they waited for the wretched barking to cease.

"Let's check the old mall, I bet there's some indies holed up in there."

"Should we just try tomorrow?" Miriam asked pitifully. Rigby fixed her in a hard stare. Miriam nodded without further argument.

"But I thought the Cannies had the mall?" They walked slowly toward the large shell-like structure in the distance. The afternoon heat thickened the air, requiring labored effort of each step.

"Cannies are everywhere, honestly. They're all too messed up on Leak to stay anywhere for very long."

Almost immediately upon reaching the mall's dank garage structure, they saw a slender silhouette dart behind one of the few sturdy cement beams remaining intact. Their feet crunched on a thick bed of broken glass that layered the ground. Buildings that once featured immense glass walls had fared poorly during the war,and skeletal metal rods were all that remained of the mall's frontal facade. The majority of the structure had slid beneath the ground, while bulbous plateaus of rock and steel awkwardly propped up the architecture that remained above the surface.

"Bingo," whispered Rigby, nodding in the direction of the cement beam.

She motioned for Miriam to hang back. Miriam seemed perfectly happy with this suggestion, crouching against the nearest pillar of corroded metal. Rigby stepped cautiously toward the cement beam behind which the silhouette had disappeared. Creeping up behind it, she kicked a cluster of loose glass littering the ground just before the pillar. A young boy shot across the parking lot, aiming for the smashed double doors that led into the mall's intricate alleyways.Rigby was faster, better nourished and more experienced than the fleeing boy. He probably hadn't had a sip of water in days. Overtaking him, she snagged his baggy white shirt, stained with soot and paint, and brought him to the ground as ceremoniously as she could manage despite his flailing, skinny limbs. He thrashed out with his arms and legs, his eyes jumping frantically in his skull. Glass shards made small cuts on his back and arms. He couldn't be older than sixteen.

Though coltish and skinny now, he might be handsome one day, strengthened by a Regal diet and training regimen. Of course, Rigby was aware of the possibility that she'd be handing the kid over directly into the junkyard. He was exactly the type that Richard liked to add to his junker crews. Young and lithe, he could work his way into the tightest crannies of the junkyard in search of any item Richard deemed valuable – half empty paint cans, crossbow arrows, blades – anything that could be used or bartered. Most people gave the junkyard a wide berth, its toxicity levels nearly palpable in the cloying steam that overhung the landfill. Junkers never lived long, though some were eventually welcomed into the ranks of the Regals. She pushed away the thought, holding onto hope that the boy could be developed into a useful trooper. It had worked for that kid Ledo she'd picked up a couple years ago, now thriving in the gang's upper echelons. Maybe things would work out for this kid, too.

"Sorry about that. You thirsty, kid?"

CHAPTER 5

There are more things in Heaven and Earth, Horatio,
Than are dreamt of in your philosophy.

— William Shakespeare, *Hamlet*

Finch dropped his battered copy of *Hamlet* when Horatio started barking. His thunderous howls echoed off of the cavernous ruins of Vulture and reverberated throughout the crusted wasteland. He'd seemed content with the water and walnuts Finch had just brought out to him, what could be agitating him now? Sweating now not just from the heat, Finch leapt to the window and peered out through the foggy double pane.

His mind jumped to the possibility that Viro might be trying to pay him a visit. Finch stood sentinel at the window a few dozen times per day, both in hopes of seeing Viro approaching and to check for approaching threats, though Horatio had become a reliable alarm in that regard. Many years ago, he'd found a pair of binoculars with one of its lenses cracked, but even in its half-functional state he'd cherished its utility in such situations as this. But he'd recently dropped them in the gulch, pursued by Cannies, and when he'd gone back to find them, the other lens had been shattered. The loss had forced him to undertake more rudimentary means of long-distance vision. Slowly, he opened the door a crack and took a tentative peek outside. The great hound's back bristled and his ears pointed low over his skull, long yellow fangs bared. Following Horatio's pointed snout,

Finch looked out towards Vulture. It was rare that he had visitors this deep in the outskirts, besides Viro of course, though it had been known to happen. Usually it was just Cannies bumbling madly in the throes of their sinister beverage or else other indies scurrying across the horizon.

But today two figures stood about a quarter mile from his makeshift home. The heatwave painted across the horizon line blurred them into shimmery vertical blobs. From the looks of their slight, wiry figures and longish hair they appeared to be girls. But he couldn't tell for certain, as they both wore shapeless grey jumpsuits. Being clothed alone disqualified them as Cannies. The thought of gangs this close to the station disquieted him.

As his eyes adjusted to the light, he could vaguely make out their colors. What would gangs troopers be doing this deep into the outskirts? And why hadn't they waited for nightfall? They almost never ventured beyond the city limits, as their painted affiliations didn't mean much beyond those settled lines. Dog-wolves cared little about arbitrary color demarcations when hunger struck, and drunken Cannies were always liable to attack at random. Many gang members had never even left the Vulture proper, fearing that the dangers of their home might pale in comparison to the world beyond. Purple splotches streaked the two figures' bodies, as though a car driving through a puddle of purple paint had caught them in its wake. Twisted purple dread-locks sprouted from their heads like tarantula legs. Long cross-bows poked out from over their shoulders. They were Regals, no doubt about it. Finch's pulse quickened.

The decaying Veins by the gulch were proof enough of the Regals' current confidence. But what were they doing out here? Had he been discovered? Finch's thoughts ran wild. He should move, change locations. He paced the small station room, walking back and forth from the window to his mattress and back again. A few well-placed arrows from their crossbows would neutralize Horatio, his only line of defense. And even if the multiple locks on his door foiled their entrance, they could easily stake him out, waiting for him to exhaust his paltry food and water supply.

Back at the window, Finch picked at the scab on his shoulder. His mind began whirring away at the debate that persisted eternally and irreconcilably within his skull. As a member of a gang he might enjoy stability, regular meals, and the protective support of all who bore his colors. But he'd be expected to submit his identity—his mind as well as his body—to a violent hierarchy and destructive system of beliefs he did not and could not hold. His eyes landed on the essay pinned to his door. *Self-reliance.* But at what cost? Could not joining a gang be rationalized as a drastic gesture toward self-reliance, compelled by dire circumstances to submit some fraction of his independence for the betterment of his whole? No, Emerson had been right: "I appeal from your customs. I must be myself." As an indie he answered only to himself, a trait he hesitated to yield after so many years of reading and contemplation. This, he prided himself, was what set him apart from the gangs and their unthinking violence and their blind thirst for domination. His books had made him *Finch*, had made him feel human where before he'd felt himself to be little different than the rodents that fled under rocks at the slightest noise, had awakened in him an interiority long latent. He refused to play the conspiring Guildenstern or Rosencrantz simply to appease some Vulture Claudius. *To thine own self be true, Laertes.* Was this not the line inscribed in permanent ink on his forearm? Were these words not the only vestige of his immemorial past by which to navigate his present circumstances?

And any gang willing to take him would certainly hesitate to take in Horatio as well, if the dog-wolf even gave them such a chance before sinking his teeth into their well-fed legs. Furthermore, an indie was safe from the gangs so long as he remained a prospect for their recruiters. However, after turning down an offer the indie became toxic, a potential threat liable to join a rival gang. For years he'd gone unnoticed here in the outskirts. The two Regals advanced and Horatio's barks grew louder. Finch tugged at his braid as he paced. He doubted that the purple duo now lingering on his horizon had ventured out to the station for anything benefiting his self-interest.

In moments like this, Finch held out hope that Viro would make good on his promise to vouch for him and let him join the Scorps one day, and he didn't want to ruin his chances with them by joining the Regals or the Veins in the meantime. At first he'd resisted the notion of joining the Scorps, thinking them to be just as villainous as the other gangs, an evil entity of a different color (in this case, green). According to Viro, however, the Scorps operated differently than the Regals or the Veins, promoting peace and democracy, recusing themselves from the violence of the surface by establishing themselves underground. The promise of safety under these circumstances appealed to Finch's most closely held virtues, especially if it meant more time with Viro. Still, the idea of fleeing pained him now as it always did when the thought of abandoning his roost in the radio station crossed his mind. Prior to the station, he had been a creature of the outskirts for nearly five years, and as a child no less. He had slept in snatches behind boulders and in torched cars until inevitably ousted from these hovels by the threat of gangs or Cannies or dog-wolves much like the snarling adult male that now growled aggressively outside his front door.

And then he'd discovered the radio station, and the law books, and then, himself. He had recreated himself—literally and figuratively—within these walls. Surviving and outsmarting Vulture with the help of Horatio and his precious books had been his life's work. There was still so much to unearth about the past, Vulture's and his own. He hesitated at the thought of abandoning the place where it had all happened, where it continued to happen. Like the mushrooms that sprung forth in the shade of ash-covered boulders, he had grown, lived, and survived through inhospitable circumstances.

He stared out at the two Regals for several seconds before backing away from the reinforced window, careful to hide his face. Staying away from the window, Finch opened the door a sliver to check for any new green thumbprints—the Scorps' system for recruiting, leaving a singular ivy thumbprint on a conspicuous wall or door for the indie to find. Sometimes Viro left a fresh print as a signal that he'd be coming by for a visit, though more often than not he simply appeared out of the blue. The first green thumbprint that Viro had left on the station door last year was still there, faded by sunlight and time. Finch had caught him in the act and pinned him to the wall, considering him a threat like everyone else who wore gang colors. But then their grappling had suddenly taken on a more intimate zeal, the tearing of limbs giving way to the tearing of clothes, and they'd gotten together that first night. Since then, countless green thumbprints had appeared, not on his door but on the yellowing pages of his scant library. The books fascinated Viro. Finch had taught him how to read beginning that first night, delighted to at last be able to speak to someone about the stories he loved so much. It had been arduous work, and Viro was as impatient as he was stubborn. When he'd made it through "Ozymandias" entirely on his own, Finch had nearly cried. Even Viro had blushed a little with secret pride, pinkish splotches appearing where the green paint did not cover his cheeks. But no fresh thumbprint adorned the door tonight. Finch closed and locked the door. He wished that Viro were here, that they could experience this fear together. Perhaps it was time to discuss again his admission to the Scorps. *Self-reliance* or not, the two Regals were standing not two-hundred feet from the station. If he'd been seen, he wouldn't be safe on his own for much longer. He was no longer too young or too inexperienced, as Viro had argued at first. Now Finch knew it was because of Viro's wife, Gajjea, the Scorp leader, that Viro had resisted. However idealistic and enlightened the Scorps might be, Finch and Viro's liaison placed them both at fatal risk.

Horatio's barking subsided to a low growl. Peering out of the corner of the window, Finch watched as the two figures receded back toward Vulture, picking their way westward over the lumpy, painted earth. Judging from their direction, they were heading for the mall. Perhaps the Regals were expanding territory or hunting down more junk-slaves for the notorious Richard. Whatever their purpose, Finch didn't like it.

Had Horatio's barking had deterred them, or was it something else? Either way, they probably hadn't felt especially inclined to tango with a roaring adult male dog-wolf. There weren't many weapons in Vulture suitable for slaying an animal of Horatio's size, at least not easily. Several well-aimed arrows might do the trick, but then one risked losing the arrows that might be needed once something with thumbs came charging their way. And if one arrow missed, a charging dog-wolf wouldn't offer the assailant much time to reload. The Bleaks had successfully removed and destroyed all the guns from Vulture, their first decree after the violent wreckage of the Water Wars. The historic moment was memorialized in one of Vulture's most faded frescoes, depicting a man bedecked with black and white paint stripes breaking a rifle over his knee. Two extra arms emerged from his sides, each clutching a flower. It was one of Finch's favorite images in Vulture, and the various gang artists had yet to vandalize it with their own declarative symbols.

Surging with gratitude for his companion, Finch grabbed a handful of walnuts and stepped back outside, whistling to Horatio. As Horatio jogged up amiably to his side, Finch tossed a walnut in the air. At the apex of its arc the hound snapped it out of the air in one quick click of his twelve-inch jaws. He looked back to Finch expectantly, a string of oily drool escaping from his jowls. Finch repeated the process, tossing the walnuts higher and higher until Horatio's powerful limbs were launching him five feet into the air to snag the flying morsels. Finch ran his hands through Horatio's thick coat, his long tail swishing back and forth.

Even in the shade the heat drew beads of sweat that trickled down Finch's back. Horatio rolled onto his back, revealing his taut stomach. Finch squatted to scratch Horatio's waiting belly, and his friend's tail beat contentedly against the dusty turf, staring up at him with his fathomless dark eyes. Finch can't help but wish that Viro might look at him that way, a look of mutual need, vulnerability, and companionship. With Viro, such elation seemed to remain only as long as they occupied the same room, whereas this moment felt like it could stretch on indefinitely. Finch didn't need much convincing. For the next hour he sat outside with Horatio, smoothing his friend's large velvet ears and peering up intermittently to check the horizon for movement.

With Regals showing up so close to the station, Horatio was certainly a blessing, though it pained Finch to admit his helplessness had his snarling friend not warded them off. In Vulture, becoming dependent on something —or someone—simply meant adding to the list of vulnerabilities to be exploited. The less he relied on others the more time he could spend ruminating on his own survival. Horatio—and Viro too—crippled his self-reliance, and yet to cut himself off from them would be to reduce the humanity he had so studiously and so strenuously cultivated for himself. What worth had a life strictly interested in the self, if it meant none could share in the scanty pleasures of life in Vulture? No, his self-reliance would be pliant enough for friendship and love, so long as the threat they posed to his safety remained worthwhile to the bolstering of his humanity.

A low, satisfied rumble emanated from Horatio's cavernous chest as Finch worked his hands up and down his long belly. He hadn't realized how lonely he'd been until Horatio came along. Unlike Viro, the dog-wolf still rested happily just outside his door each morning. It was the longest, deepest relationship he'd ever known—just as Shakespeare's Horatio had been Hamlet's sole trusting confidante. It was a perfect name for the stalwart and trustworthy dog now panting happily at his side. A creature of this magnificent incorruptibility was worthy of a name as magnanimous and unfailing as Shakespeare's principled character.

Up close Finch could see several long scars tracing rivets under Horatio's dense fur. They'd been there when they'd first met and had since faded and stretched but had not disappeared. Finch refilled the water bowl with his canteen. Horatio slurped loudly and gratefully, blissfully unaware of the pains Finch took to procure this most vital of liquids. He took a long pull from his canteen before guiltily spitting half the sip back into the bottle. The flatness of the outskirts made for long, lugubrious sunsets that bathed the landscape in saturated ochre hues. The chemical stains left imprinted on the sky by both the Water Wars and decades of pollution had at least made for some gorgeous sunsets. Pinks and reds combined for bursts of color that stretched simultaneously violent and sublime across the hazy skyline.

Finch follows Horatio's stare out to the wasteland scrub. The crisp, toasted smell of the outskirts seems to intensify at night. He wondered how far Horatio had ventured into the outskirts. He'd seen him eat Cannies a few times, but he wondered if that could that really have been his main food source. The thought reminded him of his own hunger. His mushroom supply was already running low and he'd thought of a new spot to check for Nettles. As the sun set over Vulture's jagged skyline, he noticed a band of Cannies far in the distance, dancing around a flaming pyre and hooting wildly at the sky. Three vultures circled impatiently overhead. He watched them until one by one they passed out on the ground, the bonfire dying down to a faint glow of embers.

"Horatio finally ditch you?"

Finch jumped at the sound of Viro's voice. He still wasn't sure he liked that Viro picked his locks to surprise him like this. But the joy brought by his infrequent visits made it difficult to stay angry. Still, it could just as easily have been a foe sneaking in to ambush him unawares. The Regals that had paid the station a visit yesterday still fresh in his mind, he determined to add another cross beam to the door. Placing the wild Nettles he'd just harvested in the tin pail on the floor, Finch locked the door and set his backpack on the desk before joining Viro on the mattress.

"He's just hunting," says Finch, trying to disguise his pleasure at the surprise visit. "How'd you get past the cross beams?"

Viro's electric blue eyes peered out at him through the band of green paint that masked the top half of his face. He lay on the mattress, one large hand clasped behind his head. A coverless copy of *Paradise Lost* lay propped open in his other hand. His long hair was already leaving traces of green spray paint on the faded grey sheets. Green streaks from past visits gave the sheets a leafy pattern.

"Window. Are you hurt?" he asked, gesturing to the bandaged knife wounds on Finch's arm. Viro's sinewy form sprung upward as he leapt balletically to his feet, dropping the book and grabbing fresh bandages from where he knew Finch kept them on a shelf over the mattress. He redressed Finch's wounds quickly and effectively with dexterous, practiced movements. Viro's slim green fingers played lightly over the bandaged wounds as he worked, and Finch basked in the intimacy of the brief moment, distracting him from the mental note he'd been making to secure the window.

"Just some Cannies. And there better not be green fingerprints all over those pages." Finch shrugged off the harrowing experience with the Cannies as though the cuts left in his arm had been nothing more than bee stings. Sometimes he felt the need to act Viro's age rather than his own.

"Oh that's right," Viro said, clasping his hand over Finch's, "I forget how tough you are."

"What's that supposed to mean?" Finch pulled his hand away.

"Nothing. I'm just joking around, Finch."

"You don't think I'm tough enough." Finch looked away, regretting the accusation as soon as it left his lips and ashamed of the pathetic timbre in his voice. He picked at a scab on his knee, not meeting Viro's gaze.

"I do, Finch. You know that."

A green hand wormed its way back into his palm.

"Not enough to let me join the Scorps," Finch mumbled, turning away.

Viro sighed and removed his hand, leaving green traces on Finch's fingers. A heavy silence settled between them.

"It's not time yet, Finch. We've talked about this. The day will come."

"When?" asked Finch, struggling to keep the exasperation out of his voice.

Again Viro reached out for his hand, pulling him back to the bed.

"I don't have much time," he said.

The line didn't surprise Finch though he bit his tongue, deciding against pressing the fight tonight. Viro probably did have places to be. Perhaps he had a recruiting mission to complete, petitioning an indie that wasn't Finch. Or maybe Gajjea was expecting him back at their underground home.

"Two Regals were out here yesterday."

Viro jumped to his feet.

"Yesterday? What did you do?"

Finch couldn't help but to feel pleased at Viro's response, the alarm and concern that he so rarely showed now written all over his green-smeared face.

"Nothing. Horatio started barking and they just walked off."

"Did they see you?"

"I'm not sure."

Still noticeably disturbed, Viro sat back down on the mattress.

"You have to be careful. Horatio isn't always going to be around to protect you."

"I know Viro that's why -"

67

"Stop." He silenced Finch with a wave of his large hand. Viro sighed. "I want you to join the Scorps too. Remember that. But trust me when I say that the time isn't right. The democracy is stabilizing but it has been difficult to unlearn the savagery we're all so used to. Once Gajjea's term as leader is up, she'll have less power to retaliate against you—against us."

"But that's not for another three years!" Finch whined.

Viro stooped to pick Milton's masterpiece back up off the floor but did not respond. Finch changed the subject, knowing that further argument would be useless. He didn't want to spoil their evening together, either, rare as they were.

"Good part?"

Viro shrugged. "Pandaemonium kind of sounds like Vulture, doesn't it? That's how I picture it, anyway."

As usual Viro took off all too soon, offering a flimsy excuse as he pulled a shirt over his green-painted brow and wrestling it over his broad shoulders. Stepping to the window without bothering to get dressed, Finch watched as Viro's lithe figure disappeared into one of the many burrows that the Scorps had created as a secretive network beneath Vulture's bulbous surface. Finch looked to Horatio, who hadn't stirred when Viro skipped past him on his noiseless green feet. The dog-wolf snoozed comfortably beneath the awning, blissfully unaware of Finch's human pains.

Collapsing back onto the mattress, Finch rooted out *Paradise Lost* from where it had become buried under the thin sheets. He'd never thought of Vulture as Pandaemonium, the capital of Satan's underworld empire. The only part he'd ever been able to picture with images derived from his own world had been Adam and Eve's banishment to the outskirts under the watchful gaze of St. Michael and his fiery sword.

CHAPTER 6

I hit the city and I lost my band
I watched the needle take another man
Gone, gone, the damage done

—Neil Young, *"The Needle and the Damage Done"*

The boy went by Pip and he didn't talk much. Rigby had to snatch her canteen away before he could gulp the whole thing down. He walked beside Rigby and Miriam, shuffling his feet, resting chin on his chest. Despite Rigby's assurances that he was not in danger, his flickering blue eyes spelled pure fear. Rigby knew that his was a trepidation born of a life on the run. Trust was foolish, especially in Vulture.

Though he walked beside them, he said very little. He greedily accepted the handfuls of salted almonds that Miriam rationed into his filthy palms. Rigby noticed that he ate the almonds from a hand that had only three fingers. His ribs stuck out, visible through his tattered shirt, and his short, dark hair was matted into dramatic angles with grit and sweat. A couple hundred calories a day would certainly do him some good, add some strength to his skinny limbs. Hopefully Richard would agree, not just for Pip's sake, but for Miriam's.

Pip began using the almonds as a bargaining piece, exchanging words for nuts. He was the picture of survival and Rigby half admired his resolve. Watching him subtly work to elevate his own status by way of the nut bargaining, Rigby felt half depressed at the cynicism Pip, this young boy several years shy of childhood, had had to accumulate. Not that she'd had much of a childhood herself. Apparently, he'd been cast out by the Cannies as a child after having a bad reaction to the Leak. His nightmarish screams had so disquieted their addled minds that they'd excommunicated him. He had grown up definitively homeless, on the run from the very people that had birthed him. Splashes of green, yellow, purple, red and blue covered his clothes, the typical indie garb.

They trudged back into Vulture's rugged city limits, adjusting their steps to the bumpy terrain so unlike the flatness of the outskirts. Twisting, multicolored columns rose up around them. They didn't necessarily lead Pip. He knew where the Regal headquarters was located. He had probably avoided it his whole life. His pace slowed as they got closer to the imposing cinema. The massive graffiti portrait glistened on the building's hot brick siding.

"Pip, we promise you're not in danger. Not today, anyway," said Rigby. She knew it was a lie as the words left her mouth. The chances of Richard forcing him to become a junker were plenty high. But her concern as always had to be her own survival, and right now that meant pleasing Richard with a freshly caught indie. She kept her eyes forward, refusing to look at Pip directly.

"Sure, you just pluck me up out of the trash and I'm suddenly a Regal, is that it?"

Rigby considered this, again admiring his skepticism.

"You won't be a Regal today. There is a long initiation process that you will have to complete."

"Yeah? And what does that entail?"

"I can't tell you that now. But if you've survived this long on your own, I'd say you're pretty decently prepared."

Pip stared at her with round, questioning eyes before returning his gaze to the portrait.

"Is he really that big?" He struggled to make the question sound casual.

"Yeah, pretty much," said Miriam. She too avoided making eye contact with Pip, and Rigby could see the struggle causing creases on her furrowed brow. Pip looked to be about the age of Miriam's brother.

After issuing the password, they marched through the revolving doors. However, they doubled back to snag Pip again when he made another attempted break for it as they passed under the sign that had once read 'Regal Cinemas Spokane Valley'. Now only the 'Regal' bit remained, fortified and brightened with purple paint, though some of the other, original letters could still be made out. The tall guard nodded at them as they passed through the entrance. Her eyebrows rose almost imperceptibly as she looked Pip up and down with appraising eyes. Again resigned to his fate, he walked between Miriam and Rigby up the staircase at the rear of the theater. His bony knees knocked together as he traversed the stairs. He suppressed a sniffle, his eyes now puffy and red.

At the black oak door, Rigby knocked a few notes to the beat of "Dissident" by Pearl Jam, a personal favorite. This wasn't the password, but she took what joy she could. Almost instantaneously the door was cracked ajar. Two thick, muscled men streaked in purple paint stared back at her with emotionless eyes. Their jumpsuits strained against their bulging chests. Veins throbbed in their necks and pulsated along their clenched jaws. They cradled heavy, menacing crossbows in their massive arms.

"Password?" Grunted one.

"Violet Violence is Verifiably Vicious." Rigby hated Richard's insistence upon using long, contrived, alliterative passwords. He probably thought he was some kind of poet. After ensconcing herself in the sonic poetry of her records, the trite passwords wormed at her ears and caused her to grit her teeth. The door swung wide and the trio entered Richard's opulent quarters. Opulent was a word rarely used in Vulture, perhaps reserved exclusively for Richard's not so humble abode. Several large crossbows were mounted like trophies on one wall. What before had been simply a theater storage area now boasted marble floors, plush leather couches, a four-poster king-sized bed and a massive boudoir brimming with purple garments.

A handcrafted tapestry hung on the wall facing the bed. It depicted Richard's victorious battle with—and ultimate extinction of—the Bleaks back in Vulture's earliest days. This would have been soon after the Water Wars had begotten this scab of a city. The extermination of the Bleaks was Richard's most prideful accomplishment, the battle that had fused his name inextricably to the fear it inspired. Pip's trembling figure clearly registered the reputation that Richard had cultivated. Miriam too shuffled her feet, clasping her hands behind her back so hard her knuckles went white.

Beside the bed was the only other image in the room. This too depicted Richard, a faded photograph sealed into an old bronze frame. While hunger and fear had shrunken most people since the Water Wars, Richard had somehow grown larger. In the photo he looked younger, not yet bald and wearing a crisp military uniform. For the people old enough to have been drafted into the catastrophic Water Wars and who had survived its destruction, the gangs of the reordered world that followed must have seemed a natural progression. Rigby had seen the photo before but never asked about it. In her experience, veterans of the Water Wars generally became uncomfortable when discussing the world before Vulture, if they discussed it at all. Richard could launch into his spiel about ridding Vulture of the cancerous Bleaks at any given moment, though he never told stories about the Water Wars.

"Rigs! A house call? This must be important." Richard's voice boomed from the center of the room, where he sat on a luxurious couch eating peanut butter out of a massive jar with his proportionally large index finger. Rigby was glad to hear the gleeful tone in his voice. Many had paid the ultimate price simply for catching Richard in an ill temper.

"Actually Richard, we're here on business of mine," said Miriam, piping up and straightening her spine. She had significant ground to make up after yesterday's fiasco.

"Is that so? Have you brought me a new warrior?" As he spoke he rose up to his full height, towering above the trio standing in the entryway. Rigby felt Pip take a step backwards, cowering behind her.

"Yes Richard, this is Pip. We found him by the mall earlier today."

"We?"

"Yes Richard, Rigby and I went together to scout the area-"

"Rigby has her own job. Acquisition is your job alone, Miriam. Or have you forgotten already?" His eyes flickered to Rigby before turning back on Miriam with a piercing gaze.

"I'm sorry Richard, I just thought that maybe – ," stammered Miriam, lowering her eyes and forming a shell with her shoulders.

"I do the thinking for you, you must remember that. I have given you a job and now you have seen fit to improvise, is that it?" Richard's tone took on a menacing quality and the words left his mouth in articulate rasps, escaping like steam from his vice-like jaw. The peanut butter jar shattered in his clenched fist, causing Pip to jump backward. One of the guards lurched forward to gather the plastic shards from the floor, doing a poor job of scooping up the sticky mess in his hands. Rigby grimaced on Milo's behalf, thinking of the wasted food now smearing the clean marble floor tiles. The guard stepped back against the wall, holding the destroyed jar and a brownish yellow blob of peanut butter awkwardly in his plump fists.

"Richard, I was scouting the outskirts checking on the Cannies anyway. We walked together but we worked separately." Rigby risked the interjection. Richard regarded her with intense eyes that popped out of his bald head. Blood rushed to his face and the purple paint coating his bare scalp took on a maroonish hue. Miriam's mouth formed inaudible words.

"Let's see the warrior then," he said finally.

Rigby had to pitch Pip forward to remove his thin frame from her shadow. He stood pathetically in front of Richard, his eyes at his feet and his thin arms hanging limply at his sides. Richard's eyes played over the slender figure before him.

"What happened to your hand?" He asked, hoisting Pip's three-fingered hand up to regard it more closely. It looked like a just-hatched bird in Richard's immense hand.

"Dog-wolf." Pip managed to squeak out through his chattering teeth.

"Pip, is it? Welcome aboard."

Rigby nudged Pip in the back, prompting him to speak.

"Thank you," he whispered.

Richard nodded and released Pip's arm. The red fury disappeared from his face, returning to his giant head a healthy, pink pigment. He turned his attention back to Miriam.

"Well done Miriam. I am pleased. But next time bring me a

warrior. Junkers are useful, but we need fighters. Preferably with ten fingers." Richard gestured casually over his back in the direction of the landfill as he spoke. The miles of heaped refuse were visible through a wide picture window on the wall adjoining the tapestry. Dozens of thin, bare-chested figures shuffled like ants over the hills of molten garbage. Pip hid his hands behind his back.

Rigby refused to meet Pip's pleading gaze. His wide eyes threatened tears and his Adam's apple bobbed noiselessly in his throat.

"Richard, are you sure? He is rather quick and with work could be a great Regal, I think," petitioned Miriam, frantically. Rigby winced at her outburst.

"Didn't I tell you to leave the thinking to me?" His voice was severe. Miriam's eyes shot back down to the floor.

"Is there anything else?" Richard asked. He barely looked at them as he spoke, simply addressing his periphery.

Miriam and Rigby exchanged quick glances. Rigby thought of the man they'd seen on the outskirts, though she didn't think it a good idea to mention it just now. Apparently Miriam misinterpreted her eyes. Rigby cringed as Miriam opened her mouth again.

"Richard, there is a young man living in the outskirts. We saw him today but he appears to be guarded by one of those dog-wolves that eat Cannies. We couldn't get to him but he looked tall and able."

Richard paused and looked from Miriam to Rigby. Then back to Miriam.

"Your job is acquisition. It's a simple job. You see a potential Regal and you bring them to me. Any independent that declines our offer is a potential enemy. Alone they consume resources that could be ours or, worse, they become affiliated with a rival gang. There is no in between."

Miriam gulped for air before she could get out her words.

"I'm sorry Richard, the dog looked very dangerous and we –"

"Enough!" Richard shouted as the back of his hand clipped Miriam's chin. Her head snapped back and lolled to the side as her limp body collapsed in a heap to the floor. A small yelp escaped Pip's lips and his three-fingered hand shot up to cover his mouth. Richard turned to Rigby.

"Looks like you're in charge of acquisition now, congratulations. Bring him to me." With that Richard turned away, dismissing Rigby with a flick of his massive hand.

Rigby knelt down beside Miriam, hoisting her light body back onto its feet. Miriam's eyes were glazed, a purple bruise already forming on her chin. She was lucky the slap didn't kill her.

As they left the resplendent room, Miriam leaning heavily on Rigby's shoulder, Rigby glimpsed Pip staring after her in a silent, helpless plea. The hefty guards slammed the door shut behind them. Guilt settled over her like the afternoon heat and she pushed it away, reminding herself that she was still alive. She all but dragged Miriam's silent form back down the stairs, her short, ragged breaths and occasional blinks the only indication that she was still alive. Why couldn't Miriam have just kept her mouth shut? Why couldn't Pip have had ten fingers? Rigby sighed as they exited the cinema, the intense sun momentarily blinding her.

Miriam roused after a few minutes in the sun, collapsing off Rigby's shoulder to dry heave, prone on the ground. Gathering herself, she wiped sweat from her forehead and paced silently next to Rigby.

"I'm sorry," she mumbled.

"Do you like music?" asked Rigby, ignoring the apology.

"I'm not sure," Miriam responded, refusing to meet Rigby's eyes.

"There's only one way to find out," said Rigby brightly, surprised by the chipper tone in her voice. Miriam nodded weakly, her hand touched tenderly to her swollen chin. They fell into step walking toward the record shop.

"Is it...battery powered?"

"Yes," said Rigby. Miriam's mouth gaped as Rigby placed the needle and flicked the machine to life.

"But...where did you get it?"

"Richard," she said. Upon seeing Miriam's reaction to the name, she added "a really long time ago." Miriam nodded and ran a finger unconsciously over her jaw.

"You won't tell anyone, right?"

"Of course not." Miriam gazed in wonder at the rotating disk as music began to spill out from the boxy speakers.

"Not even your brother. I'm serious Miriam."

Miriam nodded and Rigby adjusted the volume.

"So who is this one?" asked Miriam.

An unfamiliar pleasure washed over Rigby as she watched Miriam's irrepressible excitement grow with each song she played for her. A thin smile crept across Miriam's face as she listened, her eyes closed. Rigby picked carefully from her music library, having never played music for someone else before. Each track that she had enjoyed alone for years took on a new thrill when played for an audience. In peaceful silence they listened to Sly and the Family Stone, Tom Petty and the Heartbreakers, Stevie Nicks, and The Who. Rigby wasn't ready to share Hendrix or The

Beatles with someone else just yet.

"That's Carly Simon. Isn't she great?"

"She sounds so happy!" Miriam squealed with delight, the misery of the afternoon briefly displaced by rhythm and lyrics. Their purple heads bobbed along to the beat, Miriam's manicured fingers tapping gently against the floor.

"Miriam, how do you…never mind." Miriam's round blue eyes wondered back at her. Carly Simon's high tenor was replaced by Neil Young's croon as Rigby shuffled discs. Miriam shot a warm smile in Rigby's direction. The dark bruise on her chin was the only remaining indication that she'd been hurt.

"What is it? Ask me."

This sudden feeling of trust unsettled Rigby, the presence of another person in her home setting off alarm bells in her brain. And yet she couldn't bring herself to end the exchange, wanting to exist in this moment for as long as possible.

"You seem really…happy. How are you like that?"

Miriam opened her mouth to answer before stopping to consider Rigby's question.

"Never mind, sorry Miriam. You barely know me, I shouldn't have asked."

"No! No it's ok, really. Nobody's really asked me that before so I just had to think. I think I just feel lucky is all."

"Lucky? Here?"

"Yeah! Well, I guess that sounds kind of crazy, right? But things could be worse."

Rigby didn't answer. She ran her finger over the smooth edge of the record player before shrugging and looking back at Miriam's round, earnest face.

"I guess so."

"Well, we're in the top gang right now, so that's good. We

have enough to eat and drink. Richard's a horror but he keeps us safe, right? I had five siblings and four of them are still alive. So yeah, lucky I guess. And you're number three so that makes you really lucky, right?"

Rigby stared back at Miriam, unsure whether she was insanely positive or just plain insane. She scratched at a patch of dry paint on her scalp, sending a cascade of purple flakes to the floor.

"Jeez, you make me feel... I don't know. Cynical I guess. I never think about that good stuff."

"Well, do you have any family still alive? I lost my parents during the war like most people but all my siblings are Regals and it really helps to have them around, you know?"

Rigby thought before answering. She decided to change the subject.

"You know, you're the first person I've brought here. Nobody knows about this," she ran her hand lovingly over the record player, "besides Richard."

Miriam nodded and placed a tender hand over Rigby's. Unsure what to do, Rigby held her breath but didn't move her hand, even when a thick sheen of sweat accumulated on her skin. Cross-legged on the ground, they sat silently listening to music for what felt to Rigby like hours, Miriam's hand blanketing her own on the floor.

"What's this one?" Miriam held up *Synchronicity* by The Police. Happy to shift into a familiar action, Rigby carefully fit the record to the turntable. In her head, she wagered she'd outlive her new friend, who now swayed with closed eyes to "Roxanne." Rigby stood up to make her periodic window check. The sky had taken on the indigo hue of night. She hoped Miriam wouldn't die anytime soon. There were too few Miriams in Vulture.

Thoughts of the meeting with Richard gnawed at her psyche.

She'd have to return to the outskirts for that indie. Why, just to add one more digit to the Regals' ranks? To sacrifice another free individual to the slavery of the junkyard? Richard's temperament had begun to wear on her. He'd have her risk her life for a number, one number more than the Veins or the Scorps, at the risk of getting chewed up by a dog-wolf. Richard had proved today that he would just as soon kill an existing member than add a new one.

The day sickened her. Vulture sickened her. But she had decided long ago that her only course of action was to become sick alongside it all, becoming the disease so as not to be destroyed by it. Music was crucial. The records helped her like no medicine ever could on days like this. It disgusted her sometimes how quickly and effectively she could tune out her awful thoughts with the gentle rotation of a black disc.

CHAPTER 7

You shall no longer take things at second or third hand, nor look through the eyes of the dead, nor feed on the spectres in books, / You shall not look through my eyes either, nor take things from me, / You shall listen to all sides and filter them from your self.

— Walt Whitman, *"Song of Myself"*

The pale tangerine sunlight of dawn streamed through the window into the station, casting its interior in a faint amber hue. Though awake, Finch clamped his eyes shut, not moving a muscle as he tried to recover the images that had played behind his eyelids while he'd slept. He'd had the dream about the sailboat again. Wind thrashed against the top sail and walls of steely gray water thundered down on the deck. Who were those other people aboard with him? A man and a child, both drenched in sea water. Their faces were blurs of pinkish color. A throbbing pain thrummed on Finch's forearm, but he could never look down at its source. As always he'd awoken just when a final crash of water tore through the ship's hull, sinking the vessel beneath the surface into a black silence.

How could he have such a dream, when he'd never seen so much as a creek let alone the ocean? And though it bore eerie resemblance to the Pequod's doomed end in the final pages of *Moby-Dick*, he'd had the recurring dream long before he'd even been able to read. Could it have something to do with his past? All of his early memories were a hazy blur of life on the run. Each time he strained his memory, hoping to come up with some forgotten detail of those earliest days, his recollection disappointed. Waking from the dream, he'd snatch out at the images fluttering just out of reach behind his eyelids, fading into intangibility as once he'd awakened. For all he knew, he'd been born here, in Vulture. Maybe he had been one of the wailing infants he sometimes saw in the stony gulch below the bridge or on the cool cement of the crumbling parking garage.

Whenever he scoured Vulture for texts, he secretly hoped to find some clues pertaining to his past. If only for the pacification that he hadn't always been alone like this. It was bad enough to have grown up here; he wanted to have at least come from somewhere else. Finch savored the day's first sip of water before tightly capping the canteen. The tattoo was his only clue, and for years he'd been unable to read it, let alone understand its significance. He hadn't known its meaning until, in a moment he would never forget, he came across the line in *Hamlet*. But whoever had inscribed it on his arm had misquoted the Bard, adding Laertes's name to the end of Polonius' advice: "To thine own self be true." In the scene Laertes's name was implied, but on his arm it had been made explicit. If only Finch's own father would return as a ghost to provide some explanation as King Hamlet had done for his son. At first Finch had thought to call himself Laertes, but ultimately he'd decided against it. He'd chosen to christen himself with a name that felt right, a name of his own choosing, rather than submitting himself to a word on his arm that had been placed there by a dubious originator. He'd elected to follow Emerson's suggestion to "Trust thyself: every heart vibrates to that iron string," rather than adhering to Polonius' not dissimilar advice simply because it was printed in faded black ink on his forearm. Of course, Finch's unremitting preoccupation with the tattoo's origin defied Emerson's other dictate, which held that a man "cannot be happy and strong until he too lives with nature in the present, above time." But Finch could not help himself in this regard, the recurring dream triggering his interest in the past afresh each time he awoke with still unanswered questions.

That *Hamlet* had proved to bear some minute relation to his past had redoubled his interest in the fragmentary pages of his collection. But this, too, had become a distraction from the present, generating questions about the past more often than answers. Indeed, Finch often had difficulty tearing himself from the pages of his books. Though he rationalized that they sharpened his mind, which might have been true, he knew that he fundamentally enjoyed the act of reading, and that it was this joy that returned him to their pages on a daily basis. But pleasure was dangerous in his current circumstances. It bred optimism, lethargy and in turn, vulnerability. The books transported him momentarily from the wretched, painted expanse of Vulture and the constant threat of the graffiti gangs. The moments of sublime freedom that reading the books engendered were quickly deflated by his knowledge that, ultimately, they only made his reality more painful by comparison.

Stretching up from the mattress, Finch looked out the foggy station window to check on Horatio. He bit into the last mushroom in his stash, chewing it slowly. Horatio was absent from his favored place beneath the awning, likely off on a hunt deep in the outskirts. The smooth patch cleared of pebbles where he liked to sleep was the only indication of Horatio's presence. It troubled Finch sometimes to think that Horatio might be just as well without him, that their relationship was not as special or mutually significant as he perceived. Perhaps all his reading had ruined him in this way, made a romantic of a man that ought to be a realist and better yet a nihilist. His introspective mind was poorly suited to a world that operated almost exclusively on action and impulse. He ran a loving hand over the flimsy cover of *To Kill A Mockingbird*. He couldn't give up his books anymore than he could give up Horatio, Viro, or the station itself. He'd seen more genuine humanity in those stories and characters than he'd ever witnessed in Vulture. Surely these books had been written based in a world concerned with values beyond survival.

Finch sighed when he tilted his canteen back and a single droplet of water slithered across his tongue. Stepping outside and walking back through the gaping edifice of the barbershop next door, Finch climbed atop a sagging barber's chair and heaved himself onto the roof of the radio station. The effort sent soft throbs pumping through his bandaged shoulder. The radio station was not tall but from his vantage on the roof he watched a distant figure sprint across a brief scrubby lawn of gravel before its green head disappeared entirely, no doubt descending into the Scorps' secretive tunnel network. He thought of Viro, picturing him somewhere underground, on a recruiting mission, or with his wife.

A thin gray sheet hung limply in the windless air. He'd draped it over a long, coiled wire he'd ripped from headphones in the radio station below his feet, winding each end tightly around the defunct satellite dish and the twisted radio tower until the cord had been taut enough to bear the weight of the large, rectangular sheet. The mesh sheet felt damp and cool in the dry heat of early morning. Careful not to lose a single drop, he twisted the sheet in his hands, sending a weak trickle of absorbed condensation from the night before into a bucket at his feet. He'd gotten the idea years ago from the dew-covered wild greens he sometimes harvested early in the morning. The wide sheet spanned nearly the entire width of the radio station roof, and yet the arduous process of wringing out its folds yielded only a few inches of water. He flipped the mesh to the other side, readying it for tonight's accumulation of dew before heading back down, his canteen now half full.

Horatio's spot remained empty in the lot below. Sighing, Finch left to gather food alone, forcing himself out of the station on his own. He felt naked without Horatio by his side, but he had barely enough food to last him through the week, and his cached mushrooms and greens were already beginning to rot. Crumbles of plant and nut material dusted the bottom of the empty jars shelved over his bed.

Dodging behind melted cars and scorched scrap heaps, he made his way to the gulch. Within twenty minutes his shirt was soaked with sweat. The effort made him hungry and thirsty but he knew he could not return home empty handed. Today none of his usual spots yielded anything more than dry earth and gravel. He decided to risk venturing deeper into Vulture despite Horatio's absence. The city's signature smell of tar hit his nose as soon as his feet crunched onto the crusted city limits. He headed in the direction of the mall.

Trudging up to the wide patch of shade behind the mall, he paused to wipe sweat from his brow. He took a long sip from his canteen. Then he began digging into the rocky dirt in the shady ditch behind the mall, but his efforts were rewarded with little more than inedible roots. His vision began to go fuzzy as the heat sent rivers of sweat into his eyes and hunger gnawed at his stomach. He noticed a patch of newly sprouted mushrooms nearby but, upon closer inspection, decided to leave them. Several Cannies lolled in the cool dirt close by, but they don't worry Finch. The very mushrooms he'd just avoided were now wending their poisons through the Cannies' brains, sending them on a psychedelic trip far away from Vulture. They laughed and wrestled in the rough soil, their movements clumsy and happy. If they weren't likely to die as a result of their dietary indiscretion, Finch might have envied their carefree lifestyle. While the Leak generally made them crazed and prone to violence, the hallucinogenic mushrooms eaten on their own seemed to occasion a bumbling, childlike quality in the Cannies.

The frequency of their procreation was the only thing sustaining the gang. Pregnancy swelled the bellies of several females, and naked children painted in rust-orange stripes ran about in gleeful packs on the shady earth. A shifty-eyed Canny lurked on one of the mall's cement beams, eying the family below hungrily. He sipped Leak from a cracked coffee pot, waiting for the painted figures to drift into a drug-induced sleep. Finch hung close to the shadows, wary of the preying Canny.

Inching deeper into the shade, Finch again began to dig at the sight of small green fronds sprouting from the earth. Two Cannies frolicced and giggled nearby, paying him no mind. At last, Finch felt his fingers close around a supple cluster of radishes. They were hardly ripe but he gratefully zipped them into his backpack. Digging further he unearthed several edible roots and a few bulbous wild onions. He yanked a handful of chickweed that he found springing from the cracks where the mall's cement foundation met the earth. Breathing a sigh of relief, he trudged back home through the sweltering city limits.

Nearly back at the door of the station, Finch stopped. Horatio's ears perked up and the great dog-wolf stood up, looking eagerly toward him. Scarlet blood adorned the animal's maw and at his paws there lay the ravaged remains of some small animal. Finch stepped closer, carefully patting Horatio on the head. He was rewarded with a lick on his hand that leaves a bloody stain on his fingers. Up close Finch could see flecks of blue paint peppered throughout Horatio's coat and a few new scrapes along his back.

Pleasantries thus exchanged, Horatio stepped forward out of the awning's shade and nudged the bloody mass toward Finch's feet. As it rolled into the light, Finch jumped backward in shock. It was a human head, filthy with the grime of the outskirts. Finch could tell neither the head's gender nor the age beneath the layers of dust and tar that had accumulated while Horatio no doubt dragged it through Vulture. He could only discern that it was a Vein by the telltale blue arrows distributed liberally over its mutilated face. Horatio presented it expectantly, like some kind of offering, his tongue lolling as he panted and staring directly up into Finch's face.

Feeling simultaneously appreciative and disgusted, Finch stroked Horatio's new scars tenderly, hoping to translate some portion of the gratitude and sympathy he now felt. But then Horatio stiffened, his snout shooting in the direction of Vulture with his ears pricked to attention. Whipping his head around, Finch too looked in the direction of the city. There in the distance stood three Vein troopers, staring back at him, at Horatio, and at the head of their fellow Vein. For a long moment nobody moved. Then their blonde heads whipped back and forth, their hands pointing and gesturing in the direction of the station. Finch held his breath, frozen. Finally one of the Veins raised a set of binoculars to his eyes and scanned the area briefly before settling definitively on Finch. Still Finch did not move, rooted to the spot next to Horatio. After another long pause, the Veins turned and walked unhurriedly away, presumably back toward their crumbled museum headquarters.

As soon as they disappeared into the ruins of Vulture, Finch sprinted into the station, flinging the door shut behind him and frantically setting all the locks. Ragged breaths escaped through his gritted teeth. The grisly clicks and smacks of Horatio eating the remains of the Vein's head troubled Finch, aware that the gang would surely seek revenge for their loss. For the next hour he stared out at Vulture, picking absently at a scab on his forearm. He wasn't sure what he was waiting for, but between the Regals and the Veins taking notice of his whereabouts, he sensed severe danger lurking on the horizon. Like the soft winds that signalled the beginnings of the dust storms that occasionally kicked up out of the outskirts, Finch knew he must prepare for the trouble sure to come.

CHAPTER 8

Fighting on arrival, fighting for survival

— Bob Marley, *Buffalo Soldier*

Rigby stared at the dilapidated radio station from the same distance that she had viewed it the day prior. A vulture squawked somewhere overhead. Her binoculars kept slipping in her sweaty palms. She had commanded her feet back to the outskirts, willing herself not to think that she could be potentially sentencing another person to Richard's wrath. Thoughts of Pip tugged at her conscience but she suffocated these inklings, reminding herself that survival came at a cost. The dog-wolf was nowhere in sight, though she knew that didn't mean she was safe. She had seen dog-wolves in action. As a child she had watched wide-eyed as an adolescent dog-wolf cleaved a Canny's femur in two with one sharp snap of its jaws. Some people believed that they ate Cannies because they, too, had developed an affinity for Leak. The drug-alcohol concoctions flowing through the veins of their intoxicated prey made for easy respite. Drunk, high, or neither, there were plenty of reasons to avoid the dog-wolves.

She walked carefully yet purposefully up to the front door of the station. The door was iron and looked to be made of a heavy, industrial quality. She peered through the thick-paned window that abutted the door. The glass was cloudy with age and grime. Cleanliness was probably not the occupant's first priority. Not too many people to impress out here in the outskirts.

A green thumbprint on his door frame caught her eye. So the Scorps had tried to recruit him too. If he'd accepted, he'd be underground by now with the rest of them. Clearly he'd chosen to remain independent. The thumbprint looked faded. Hopefully the man had had a change of heart about joining gangs, though Rigby was doubtful. Anyone that had entrenched themselves this deep in the outskirts clearly didn't want to be found. But Miriam's outburst had essentially contracted Rigby to bring the indie in, dead or alive.

From her limited vantage at the window, she saw little more than a tired looking mattress resting on the floor in a corner below a shelf of empty jars. Her eyes roved across the small space. Her eyes lingered on the sight of several piles of books on a long, low desk in one corner, squinting to be sure that her vision hadn't been deceived. It was rare to see a book at all anymore, let alone several at a time. Books had been irrelevant since even before the war, according to Milo. He'd made the pronouncement after her first raid, an ambush of the Veins, which had yielded several almanacs and a rudimentary map of Vulture. She rolled her eyes at the thought of Milo. His zealotry for Richard and the Regals had always discomfited her, as though he were perpetually sniffing out the veracity of her allegiance. Of course, it was exactly that wariness that had earned him the number two rank in the gang. They had burned those books along with the rest of the useless cache. Other than herself, Rigby didn't know of anyone in the Regals who could even read. Surely Richard would be interested in another trooper capable of deciphering the older graffiti glyphs around Vulture. Perhaps the indie's literacy would even be enough to keep Richard from relegating him to the junkyard.

Overall, the place looked livable, comfortable even. The sun sustained its violent heat even in the shade of the awning. Tucked away in the outskirts, whoever resided in the station probably avoided most of Vulture's danger. Nobody appeared to be home, but Rigby's vision was limited, the foggier patches of the window obstructing her from seeing the whole room despite its compact square-footage. Looking to the rear, she saw a few small, rectangular windows up near the ceiling. They looked thin and probably used only for purposes of ventilation.

Rigby gave the front door another heave but it didn't budge. She circled around to the back. The windows were more than ten feet off the ground, eliminating the possibility of jumping. Plus she didn't want to surprise the indie with any abrupt noises. Silence was always safer. The station was connected to the remains of some other toppled strip mall unit, a fragile huddle of partially crumbled brick walls and a collapsed roof. This edifice, along with the other distorted brick buildings, was vacant save for a few rats and piles of cinder. Almost all of them were gutted, the exposed and melted steel beams of their foundations collapsing and bending at distorted angles.

In the ruins adjacent to the station, Rigby found a crusty, rusted metallic chair bolted to the ground. At one time it had been a barber's chair, with its sturdy iron base and black leather cushions, the latter of which now hung in tatters off the frame. She wondered how often people had gotten haircuts back before the Water Wars. She hadn't so much as run a comb through her hair in nearly two decades, a fact which accounted for the hellish tangle of dreadlocks that spilled off her scalp. She'd never really cared about her looks, and most people in Vulture wore their hair similarly. Long, unkempt, twisting, and paint-stiffened locks had essentially become part of the gangs' uniforms—a style not unlike that adorning Bob Marley's head on the cover of one of Rigby's favorite albums. Some gave themselves short, choppy cuts with rusty pairs of scavenged scissors or knives, though most allowed nature, time, and paint to work their hair into heavy ropes. The Veins stood out by keeping their hair close cropped and bleached blonde, perhaps to further differentiate themselves from the Regals. Climbing up onto the chair, the cushion's once soft filling now exploded out of cracks in the seams. Rigby leapt to a rafter above, hanging monkey-like before swinging herself up onto the rusty beam.

She dusted off her hands and surveyed the ceiling. What was left of the ceiling, at least. It looked as though an enormous fist had swung down on the roof of the building, caving the structure into a gaping hole. She hoisted herself up onto the stubby lip of concrete that served as the barbershop's remaining rooftop. From here, she shimmied along the crumbling stretches of cement and ironwork that crisscrossed the walls that remained of the building until she reached the rooftop of the radio station. On silent steps she crept up to the limits of the front ledge. Peering over the side, she still saw no signs of the dog-wolf or the man.

A wide sheet stretched nearly the width of the roof like some kind of massive flag. She ran a finger over the wrinkled mesh cloth that hung in front of her. Its dry fibers were interrupted by small patches of dampness. Noticing the steel bucket beside the tethered sheet, she wondered if this was not a flag at all but some ingenious water collection system. This, too, would certainly impress Richard.

Moving aside the sheet, Rigby glanced out at Vulture's scabby limits to her left and the expansive wasteland of the outskirts to her right. Even through the magnification of her binoculars, the outskirts stretched seemingly into infinity. Sweat drenched her back and chest and she paused for a small swig from her canteen. Nothing but dog-wolves and lost, raving Cannies for miles probably. She'd never ventured much further than where she now stood. Richard had told her once that he had found her deep in the outskirts, a sobbing toddler. When she'd pressed him for more details he'd become angry, advising her to forget the past and focus on her future, the future of the Regals.

She worked her way back to the other side of the roof. Slithering on her stomach, she approached the high windows from above. Careful not to lose her balance, her chest and arms hanging over the side of the building, she peered into the station through the thin window panes. Droplets of sweat dripped down off her nose and hurtled to the ground.

These windows, being both thinner and higher up, offered much more clarity than the thick, grimy window by the door. The man was nowhere to be seen. She tried to pry open the window but it was painted shut. Instead, she set about taking stock of the shabby residence from her birds-eye vantage.

The number of books amazed her, even more piled on the desk than she had seen before. The man must have secured them not long after the Water Wars, before anything remotely flammable had been used for kindling. All those obsolete books had been made relevant again by the need for warmth, safety, and cooked food. Pressing her face to the glass, she could see bits of plants, mushrooms, and nuts housed in various containers on the shelf above his bed. She'd always wondered how indie's managed to survive without gang rations in Vulture. Between the shelved jars and the hanging sheet on the roof, this indie had found a way. The space reminded her of her record shop home. Knowing that some other person in Vulture might settle down on an old mattress at the end of the day and enjoy something other than food, water, sleep, or vengeance filled her with empathy.

A new image of the indie began to form in her mind. He was not just another cockroach surviving on crumbs like Pip or the myriad other waifs flitting around the parking structure of the mall. By Vulture's standards, the man was thriving. Add in the tamed dog-wolf and she may be in over her head.

But Richard had been explicit, and the sky was burning its way toward the violet hues of sunset. The next meeting would be in a couple days. Rigby considered how Milo would handle a clever indie like this; certainly he'd opt for the most drastic or violent option. Shifting the crossbow strapped to her back, she knew that violence was always an effective option. But fear was often more persuasive. She would have to plan accordingly. Show up to the meeting empty handed and she risked ending up like Miriam, crumpled and bruised on Richard's marble floor. Even Richard's favoritism had its limits.

Rigby clambered back down to the ground the same way she'd come up. A white sliver of moon was etched in the lavender sky. While her colors rendered her relatively safe within Vulture's city limits, the outskirts provided no such comforts. Plus, the man could return home at any moment—or worse, the dog-wolf.

Hastily, she grabbed her canister of purple spray paint out of her backpack. She would have to leave her mark somewhere he would see it, letting him know that he had garnered the attention of the Regals. If it spooked him so be it. He would be easier to engage that way, his fear making him skittish and irrational. With practiced control, Rigby sprayed a large purple R on the station door, the only letter she'd ever written. Without ever removing her index finger from the nozzle, she encircled the letter in a clean arc, finishing the design with a professional flourish. The chemical smell of spray paint lingered at the back of her throat. Skinny dribbles of purple paint traversed the length of the door, giving the symbol an especially sinister look. Replacing the canister in her backpack, Rigby surveyed her work briefly before turning on her heel and trudging back towards Vulture.

Barely within city limits, she heard the soft crunch of feet on the pebbled ash behind her. Probably just a drunken Canny, but in this miserable dumpster of a city, safe was always better than sorry. Carefully and without any sudden movements, she removed a meter long length of black electrical cord from her backpack. The thick, rubberized wire felt smooth and familiar in her calloused hands. The end that finished in three mangled prongs was crusted with dry, brown stains of blood from its last usage. With guns made extinct by the idealistic Bleaks in those early days, and Regal crossbow arrows reserved only for emergencies, killers were forced to become more creative and, ultimately, more brutal. Her heartbeat hammered in her ears.

A shadow darted across the road and up ahead, disappearing behind boulders of twisted iron and truck-sized piles of refuse. The movements were too coordinated and fast to be a Canny. Rigby grew wary, her instincts humming on autopilot as she proceeded up the street. Sweat coated her palms and her throat felt dry but she doesn't risk diverting her attention to her water bottle. At least two miles stretched between her and the relative safety of Regal territory. The fact passed through her consciousness only long enough for her mind to register and plan accordingly. The purple paint on her denim jumpsuit might as well be a bull's-eye out here. Most of Vulture would delight in the death of a Regal.

The shadow jumped out suddenly, nearly catching Rigby by surprise. Had her reactions not been slingshot quick, she might have lost her head to the length of steel pipe now cutting through

95

the air. A thrumming noise she felt deep in her chest accompanied the swift chop, missing her ear by centimeters. Ducking at the last moment, Rigby rolled to her right and stood up, already plotting her counterattack. A quick glance registered the various shades of indigo paint splattered across the girl's jacket, a neat skull topped with short-cropped blonde hair, and the telltale blue arrow tattoos patterned on her skin.

"How do you live with yourself, working for that monster?" the girl snarled through clenched teeth.

Rigby knew immediately that the Vein referred to Richard. While many people of monstrous proportions populated Vulture, Richard surely provided the archetype to which they all aspired. The girl's short blonde hair lent her a ghostly appearance in the rapidly darkening light.

"He's worse than an animal," the Vein continued, Rigby remaining silent. "He kills for pleasure. Vulture doesn't have to be like this."

The words briefly disrupt Rigby's emotionless calculations. The Vein wasn't wrong, though Rigby had never thought of it this way. She had always considered Vulture to be simply evil, giving little thought to the gradations of evil that took place within its boundaries. But what was the point of telling her something she already knew? If this was some kind of recruiting tactic it was certainly pretty radical, thought Rigby, in the split second before frantically dodging another swipe of the metal bar.

Vulture's gangs had plenty of reason to hate the Regals, but none more than the Veins. Like the Regals, they too had sought to rebuild some semblance of humanity after the deposition of the idealistic Bleaks. But the Veins had believed, for a while at least, that this change was possible only through the formation of a republic. They'd split from the Regals, focusing their attention on navigation and outreach to other cities that might have survived in the wake of the Water Wars. Hence the arrow tattoos. As far as Rigby knew, their efforts had so far been fruitless. And in the meantime, the Veins had had to remain significantly violent simply to maintain hope of advancing their mission without succumbing to extinction at the hands of the Regals. Ideologically, Rigby often felt more aligned with the diplomatic goals of the Veins than the totalitarianism of Richard's vision for the Regals, though she considered the latter to be far more realistic compared to the naivety of the former. Richard, too, wanted to reach out to other survivors, but only for purposes of expanding his empire. But so long as her best chances of survival relied on being associated with Vulture's strongest gang, Rigby remained a Regal. With the recent demolition of the Veins' numbers by the poisoning orchestrated by Richard, tensions between the two gangs were running especially high. Rigby hadn't been a part of the poisoning mission, but in Vulture, you were synonymous with the colors that you wore.

And this Vein was no exception. She was probably on the hunt for food or indies and saw an opportunity in Rigby's solitude. Any opportunity to diminish another gang's numbers should and would be taken, almost without exception. The Vein's blond hair frizzed out wildly, clashing sharply against the thick blue paint covering her eyelids. Her knuckles choked the length of pipe and her forearms bulged through her tight jacket. She was taller and certainly stronger than Rigby, and against any other opponent the Vein would probably already be spraying down a corpse with blue paint.

But Rigby was alive at this moment for the same reasons she had survived for years here in Vulture. Faster and more agile than most, Richard had noticed the fight in her early on, and had cultivated it with intensive lessons in combat. Rigby sidestepped another swat from the pipe. Real loathing burned in those blue-rimmed eyes, her white lips pulled back over sharp yellow teeth. Gangs were family (a poor yet necessary substitute, at least) and this girl had been left relatively orphaned by the devastation of the poisoning. Rigby forced all thoughts of pity away, tensing her muscles and focusing on her opponent. She reminded herself that had she sided with her morals rather than the Regals, she too could have easily wound up poisoned at the bottom of the gulch.

As the Vein whiffed on another swing of the pipe, Rigby brought the cord down across the girl's neck in a vicious and practiced snap. The girl gasped, dropping her weapon and reaching for her throat, fighting for the air that had been there just moments ago. Rigby wasn't interested in games of cat and mouse like Richard. He might linger on a moment like this for twenty minutes, an hour even, before finally ending it. Rigby snapped the cord again, this time drawing blood at the girl's temple. The Vein dropped in a heavy heap to the ground. Rigby reached for her canister and quickly sprayed purple paint over the Vein's glazed eyes, the color mixing with the girl's bluish mask to create a dark violet color. Taking a breath and surveying the area for other potential threats, Rigby moved on without giving the body a second look. She dragged the cord behind her to dry off some of the fresh blood before replacing it in her bag. As she walked, the Vein's final words rang in her ears: *Vulture doesn't have to be like this.*

CHAPTER 9

Ugly. Yes, it was ugly enough; but if you were man enough you would admit to yourself that there was in you just the faintest trace of a response to the terrible frankness of that noise, a dim suspicion of there being a meaning in it which you—you so remote from the night of first ages—could comprehend. And why not?

— Joseph Conrad, *Heart of Darkness*

Finch smiled at Horatio's easy four-legged stride. He was panting harder than the dog-wolf. Though the sun was nearly set, heat reverberated off of the concrete landscape, scorching the soles of his feet even through his sneakers. Though their trek had yielded no books, they had come across a small patch of maple blossoms and peppercress. Sweat drenched Finch's shirt and glistened off Horatio's fur as the station came into view several yards away.

Finch froze. Though his heart pumped hot blood the sweat on his shirt went instantly cold. Horatio trotted on a few steps before halting too, staring innocently at his human companion with his parched tongue lolling. Taking a few cautious steps forward, Finch could make out a large R spray painted in dark purple on his front door. The consonant nearly filled the doorway.

With the exception of poisonings, the Regals were never much for subtlety. Their graphics were displayed prominently throughout Vulture. Though Finch had never seen Richard in person, he knew him to be a man of immense stature and equal terror judging from the purple embossed portraits. He could be seen slaying thirty Veins with his bare hands on a dilapidated factory wall in the city's eastern section. In a more metaphorical portrait, he held a massive, dead vulture up to the sky, clenching its glistening black talons in his giant fists, a heroic and unsmiling visage plastered to his face.

The circled purple R's might as well have been the official decoration of Vulture these days. As the preeminent gang, the tags marked their territory and warned rival gangs to step carefully, if at all. Slinking silently among the shadows, his heart throbbing in his ears, Finch looped around to the abandoned barbershop that neighbored the station. Using the old chair as a step, he pulled himself to the roof with practiced ease. Horatio watched him from below for several seconds before growing bored and retreating to his shady spot under the awning.

Finch's heart pounded as he slid on his belly to the lip of the roof. Grit and rust coated his front. Half obscured by the mesh sheet, he peered down through the top window of the radio station. He scanned for anything even slightly amiss—a sudden movement, more paint, books out of place, a henchman clad in purple-stained clothes, a triggered crossbow waiting for him behind the door. But he saw nothing. Everything looked exactly as he'd left it earlier that afternoon. For ten minutes he waited up on the roof, watching the small space that he called home for a figure to slip out from a shadow or the sneeze of some purple fiend.

At last satisfied that his home was empty, Finch clambered down, though his fingers still trembled at his side. Empty didn't necessarily mean safe. A member of the most fearsome gang in Vulture had seen fit to fix their mark to his door. His thoughts ran wild. Perhaps this was a recruiting ploy, or maybe they were expanding territory into the outskirts. Most worrisome of all, perhaps he had offended the Regals unknowingly. None of the questions now flitting through his mind portended optimistic answers.

Finch recalled his visitors from a few days before, the two Regals on the horizon that had triggered Horatio's barking. It couldn't have been a coincidence; the two events had to be linked. Regals never made house calls as friendly neighbors. Still, it felt strange to him that they wouldn't set his radio station ablaze, steal his food, or bash in his door somehow. It made no sense and Finch writhed in the uncertainty. Whatever their reasons, they all spelled trouble.

He would have to do something. Finch paced in front of his tagged door. His stomach clenched, bending him slightly forward in discomfort. He refused to flee his home like some snail scared out of its own shell. With a dog-wolf at his front door he was safer than ever, but Horatio was liable to trot off for whole days in pursuit of prey. As much as he wished to rely upon Horatio, to communicate some mutual need to his canine companion, Finch knew such hopes to be futile. He would have to be prepared to act on his own. *Self-reliance.*

Horatio panted and scratched himself in the shade, unbothered. Finch focused his attention on the Regals. The purple R stared at him like an unblinking eye. He had to act fast. Who knew when they might return, or how many they would bring for a return visit? Richard himself could kick in his door. It could happen tomorrow or even in the next ten minutes. And still the matter of the Veins that had witnessed Horatio presenting him with the head of one of their dead brethren tugged at his psyche. He felt walls closing in around him, a feeling of suffocation binding his lungs.

Self-reliance called for him to take the offensive. Those who waited in Vulture often wound up split between the beaks of the buzzards and the hungry fingers of the Cannies. No, he could not allow that to be his end. He must create some sort of challenge to the Regals, to Richard himself even. Self-preservation lay at the core of his survival. There was no room at the end even for Horatio, or his books, or his home. Or Viro, he thought ruefully, noticing a fresh green thumbprint just below the R on his door. The thought troubled him. He wasn't sure he'd actually be able to execute the necessary dispassion if the time ever came.

But he must try to maintain it all if possible. He had worked too hard to build this life to let it all go just for some purple graffiti on his door. If *self-reliance* was to be reduced to simply staying alive then surely thriving and living comfortably was the ultimate goal. But comfort fell secondary to survival, of course. And now he'd have to plot a course of action simply to remain independent, or at least alive. It felt crucial that he keep his death from being the determination of the Regals. He took a pull from his canteen, settling with his back against the door to think.

"By the way, you know you have a huge purple R on your door, right?" mentioned Viro, casually. He hurriedly redressed and applied a fresh coat of ivy-green paint to his hands and hair. It made him look as though he wore green gloves, not one centimeter of skin poking through the thick green coating.

"Yeah, Regals," he said coolly. He pulled on a pair of shorts but remained in the bed, hoping Viro might be inspired to rejoin him. Viro's presence felt like an additional lock on his door. If only he were always here. The faint smell of sweat and skin lingered over the small room and the mattress groaned as Finch shifted position.

"Are you in trouble?" Viro asked, pausing as he snapped the final button on his jumpsuit. Was that genuine concern in his voice, Finch wondered?

"Maybe."

"Well, if there's anything I can do…" replied Viro, turning to leave.

"You could let me join the Scorps," Finch said, a caustic tone escaping his lips. He couldn't help himself. If fighting was the only way Viro would stick around a little longer so be it.

"We've talked about this," Viro sighed, speaking as though addressing a whining child.

"I know. I might be in danger though," he said, grasping at this new straw.

"Why would you want to ruin this?" Viro asked after a time, turning back to him. "Haven't I made it painfully clear that if we went to the Scorps together now, we wouldn't be able to see each other anymore? Not like this, anyway."

"It wouldn't be ruined," Finch mumbled.

"So you'd just move underground, become a Scorp, and we'd just keep meeting up like this?" Viro's voice rose. The paint on his forehead scrunched as his brow furrowed. "You'd have to give up this place," he said, gesturing around the room. "And Horatio."

"Viro I just want to stay alive! Can't you see I'm terrified?"

"Finch! Do you know what Gajjea would do to you if she knew? The Regals would be the least of your worries."

Viro's strained voice had the pitch of finality. Finch had seen images of Gajjea only on the street art of Vulture. He recalled one depiction in particular, of Gajjea pointing upward from the painted sewer grate, her dark, ominous eyes following his every movement.

"Yeah, I know," said Finch, resigned.

Viro stood at the door, his green hand on the knob.

"So what, it's just never going to happen? We'll just keep meeting up like this until one of us dies? Until Gajjea dies?" Finch had spit this last part in anger and regretted it immediately.

Viro stared at him in a pitying way that made Finch squirm. He looked away, smoothing the faint green folds on his bed. Finally Viro spoke again.

"I've told you many times that things change. Nobody knows what will happen in Vulture. There is no schedule. If the opportunity arises, I will bring you into the Scorps. But things are still too unstable. The democratic campaign—"

"Enough about the democratic campaign! You're choosing her over me. You don't even care that I might be in danger?"

Finch refused to meet Viro's eye line, shouting down at his feet.

"Hey," said Viro, stepping back toward the bed and placing a tender hand under Finch's chin. "I'm trying to keep us both safe, can't you trust that?"

"Don't you love me?" Finch blurted, without meaning to. Though now that it's out, hanging in the musty air between them, he made no attempt to reel it back in. He had been wondering, after all. Viro looked at him with weary, pitiful eyes.

"You read too many of these damn books, you know that?" he said finally.

Finch said nothing. Viro kissed him gently on the cheek before stepping out the door. Finch watched through the window until the green hair disappeared into the earth. He'd be safe enough tonight with Horatio snoring under the awning. After a moment, Finch opened the door and walked outside into the night, settling himself gently onto the ground next to Horatio, careful not to disturb his friend's slumber.

"Looks like it's just you and me tonight, buddy," he whispered to Horatio, giving him a soft rub along the belly.

Finch set out in the late afternoon as the hot sun began to yawn and stretch, casting long blue shadows across the charred plain of Vulture. Horatio ambled at his heels, snapping at crickets and meandering only to follow dead end scents.

While Horatio vacillated in his path, Finch clung to the shadows, sometimes leading the dog-wolf and sometimes following as they picked their way through the ruinous purple and blue metal clumps that weaved an alley to the city center. An eerie stillness hung over Vulture as they walked, their light steps and soft breaths the only sounds permeating the silent shapes and structures that surged up around them. Up ahead, Horatio quickened his pace as he loped toward a shadowy heap on the ground. Heart pounding, Finch hustled after him, working his way gingerly from one boulder to the next. He made a habit of looking over his shoulder. Coming to Horatio's side, Finch was hardly surprised by what he found.

The dog-wolf's snout busily sniffed along a woman's corpse. She was a Vein judging from the splashes of blue paint in her short bleached hair and the small indigo arrows peppered across her skin. Scarlet pools of blood trickled from deep wounds in the woman's neck and temple. The metallic smell of blood mixed with Vulture's signature scent of burnt tar. The violent scene was punctuated by an unmistakable slash of dark purple spray paint across the Vein's eyes. The paint was dry but mixed darkly with the crusty pool of blood, making her sallow face look not unlike the broken vulture eggs occasionally to be found baked grotesquely in the sun. Clearly Finch wasn't the only one experiencing issues with the Regals.

The colors rushed up at Finch and he took a step back from the carnage. He was no safer than the body lying before him had once been in this very spot mere hours ago—or perhaps minutes—by the looks of it. Horatio quickly lost interest in the body. He sniffed curiously but didn't indulge his appetite. He prefered to kill his own food, Finch had observed. Finch wished he could be as desensitized as Horatio, pausing only briefly before moving on, never to think about the corpse again. The image of the fatal blow at her temple would forever etch itself into his memory, joining the dozens of other crumpled bodies he'd seen in his lifetime. Each dead face would emerge from his deep memory at random, setting the hairs on his neck stiffly upright. They tore themselves from the graphic scene and returned to their mission, resuming their path along the shadows. The dead Vein was a reminder that Finch doesn't need about Vulture's ever present dangers. The closer one came to the city's heart, the more likely the possibility of seeing blood.

After another half mile or so Horatio's paw prints no longer leave bloody red stamps denoting their trail. Finch began to have second thoughts. He wasn't even positive that Horatio would stick around if the Regals decided to ambush them. The purple R's become more and more frequent as they progress, painted at brief intervals over the layers of blue, black, orange, and red coating every available surface. He felt his steps slowing, plastering himself as tightly as possible to the shadows. This was deeper than Finch had ventured in a long time, maybe since his pre-radio station days when he'd been a mere beetle of Vulture, scurrying from rock to rock frightened and alone.

He took note of an old record shop as they hustled underneath the twisted irons of its fire escape. Loose bricks from its foundation lay scattered in front of the building at random. However, the shop was in decent shape compared to most of Vulture's structures. Suddenly, Finch stopped again, frozen beneath the fire escape. A sound unlike any he'd ever heard wafted down languidly from some height above his head. He stood transfixed as the melody wormed its way through his ears and into his brain. The sound traversed his spine and unclenched every muscle he held taut in his back. He yearned to keep listening, to climb up those wickedly torqued iron bars and find the source of that dreamlike sound and to lie down, close his eyes and never stop listening. Opening his eyes, he caught sight of the abundance of purple R's tattooing the walls of the shop and forced himself to move on.

At last they came to the cinema. Unlike any other building in Vulture, it stood sturdy and proud above the crumbled ruins of the city. An immense portrait of Richard himself revitalized the old building's frontal facade. Finch paused a moment in the shadows, taking in the vast mural. It must have been some Regal painter's masterpiece. It was by far the largest in the city, at least that Finch had seen. Richard's likeness towered above him, daring him to move. The gang's artists must have spent weeks at work. Even Richard's massive pinky fingers were replete with detailed creases and neat brushstrokes.

The Veins' artwork differed in style but not in detail, favoring intricate landscape portraits over triumphal declarations of strength. Most of their works showcased their navigational interests, painting resplendent maps of the city as a means of promoting their claim that more transparency and visibility among the gangs would improve the lives of all. So far none of the gangs had found enough trust even within their own ranks to begin taking the Veins' idealistic notions seriously. Plus the Veins' well-known penchant for violence gave the lie to the harmonious images portrayed in their artwork. The Cannies sprayed orange streaks laconically across each other's bodies, one leaning up against the wall while the other applied the paint, leaving crude, child-like outlines of themselves partaking in drugs and cannibalism. Judging from their artwork, their collective imagination was limited to the uncomplicated inebriation of their experience. Still, Finch appreciated the elegant simplicity of these orange markings, as they presented in unequivocal terms the violence that the artwork of the other gangs sought to obscure through the finery of their brushstrokes. The Scorps' art was always painted on the ground rather than on the upright walls prized by the other gangs. According to Viro, the desired effect was to give their enemies the sensation that they were always being watched from below. As much as he relied on it for news of Vulture's shifting currents, Finch couldn't help but enjoy the gangs' dire artwork. He was fascinated by how new images would spring up over old ones with each new happening, pictographically recording history in real time. If he could trace these histories back to their earliest point, he might have been able to elucidate some detail of Vulture's beginning, perhaps even of his own origin.

Regardless, no artwork could compare to the majesty of the Regals. Even in the dim light of dusk the colors popped off the wall. The majority of Vulture's painted citizenry would rouse as soon as the sky went from burnt orange to crow black. Finch had to act fast if he was to act at all. With a can of blue paint and a freshly dipped painter's brush, Finch hurriedly rushed to Richard's portrait. Quickly, his heart pounding in his throat, he slashed a sloppy blue V over the mural. He tipped the splayed limbs of the letter in pointed arrows, completing the insignia of the Veins. He made sure to catch Richard's face in the trail of his wide brushstroke, reaching up to his full height to do so. Horatio watched him, head cocked to one side. Finch gave the V one final coat so that it stood out over the dried paint of the portrait. His pulse raced as he hurled the can and the brush away into one of the numerous heaps of scrap metal that encircled the cinema like a buzzard's nest. The smell of fresh paint clung to his nostrils and adrenaline coursed through his veins.

It had been Shakespeare, finally, who had given him the idea. That morning he'd read through *Hamlet* for a distraction. The part in which Hamlet rewrites his execution letter, sentencing Rosencrantz and Guildenstern to death instead of himself, had set off bells in Finch's head. The purple R emblazoned on his door certainly had the portent of a death warrant. And the Veins had felt like a natural exchange for Rosencrantz and Guildenstern, a gang already at odds with the Regals and a further threat to his safety after Horatio's most recent hunt. And this way, too, perhaps Richard (Vulture's Claudius if there ever was one) would turn his full attention on the Veins, forgetting, temporarily at least, whatever plots he had for a pesky indie housed in the outskirts. The rare feeling of control had elated Finch nearly to the point of dancing, settling for an animated rub of Horatio's belly.

At about five hundred feet from the defaced mural he noticed that Horatio had disappeared from his side. Finch had fled so quickly he'd completely forgotten his companion. Guiltily, he looked back over his shoulder, and there he saw Horatio lowering his leg, having just urinated directly onto the wall under the wet blue V. Finch smiled and clapped a hand over his mouth to keep from laughing. Perhaps that dog-wolf brain of Horatio's intuited more than those unchanging black eyes let on. The dog-wolves were still prowling Vulture for a reason, after all. Horatio jogged unhurriedly after Finch and together they stole their way back towards the outskirts in the quickly encroaching dusk.

Finch's exhilaration was almost immediately tainted with regret but he forced his feet forward, quickening his pace as he raced with Horatio back to the safety of the radio station. His throat burned from the heat and dust but he didn't dare stop. Doubts and worries flew about his brain like flies on a corpse. He fretted that he'd been seen, that someone followed him, that someone would be waiting behind his door. He hadn't seen anyone yet but each minute he spent outside the bounds of the radio station in the increasing darkness left him vulnerable.

Faster and faster he ran over the ridged ground, the triumph that had initially swelled his chest deflating with each step. Pure darkness enveloped the sky as his feet struck the smooth earth of the outskirts. A small fire glowed in the distance and Horatio took off in its direction. His long limbs gathered to an incredible speed. Finch watched Horatio's long tail swish into nothingness in the dark. Even the appearance of the radio station in the distance does not quell the fear clenching Finch's stomach.

He decided to do another check of his room from the vantage of the roof before entering, hoping to avoid a potential ambush and cripplingly paranoid from his vandalism of the Regal mural already. Heaving himself up onto the building's rusty lip and clambering to his feet, he found himself staring down the rusty blade of an old hunting knife. Its serrated edges glinted in the bright moonlight. Though difficult to see in the dark, the tattoos on the hand gripping the knife were unmistakable. Finch's eyes followed the neat blue arrows adorning the Vein's fingers up to the figure's face. A solid stripe of bright blue paint and framed wild, darting pupils.

"Where have you been, indie? I was getting bored."

The Vein was tall and rangy. His close-cropped, bleached hair shined with streaks of powder-blue paint, giving his sneering face an eerie glow. The chemical smells of bleach and ink radiated off his body. His lean frame gathered itself up deliberately, twisting the blade menacingly in Finch's face.

"You see these tattoos?" asked the Vein, turning his bare arms in the pale moonlight, each of which was dotted with indigo arrows.

"See, in the Veins, you get an arrow for every kill," he said, unable to conceal his own pride. He never moved the dagger from where it pointed at Finch's throat.

Finch didn't need to count. The Veins' arms look as densely patterned as reptile scales, dozens of arrows spaced perfectly apart. He looked to be about thirty, and rather fit. The blade of his knife nearly pricked Finch as the Vein's hand adjusted on the hilt in preparation for attack.

"You know, I was sent out here to recruit you. A trained killer dog-wolf and his master could certainly be of use to the Veins. But I'm not interested in recruiting, and I don't give a damn about what the Vein elders think. They still haven't woken up to reality, old as they are. Once I tell them that you put up a struggle, that I had no choice but to cut you down, they'll go back to their musing and muttering about the collapse of the state and the fall of mankind. But what they don't see is that man hasn't fallen; he's simply embraced his purest state, relying on his senses to master his environment. Predator versus prey, period. That dog-wolf of yours gets it. But I'm not about to welcome you and that murderous beast into our ranks after what he did to that trooper. He was a friend of mine, see? And you, you don't have friends, do you? Not human ones anyway. You're an indie, and so

111

nobody will care when your body shows up painted blue on the roof of some building in the outskirts, if anyone even finds you before the vultures pick you clean."

He'd probably recited some version of this monologue dozens of times in the past. His tone was measured, though Finch detected a hint of glee rising in the Vein's voice at the prospect of killing without consequence. Just like Cannies and their Leak, plenty of people in Vulture had become addicted to murder. Finch stood frozen, his knees locked and his feet rooted to the spot. He could only stare, mouth agape, blood pumping in his clenched palms.

Would Viro find his body before the vultures? Or would the Cannies get to him first? How long would Horatio remain in his spot beneath the awning before trotting off on his own, never to return? Finch begged his feet to move, his arms to throw a punch or at least shield his throat from the looming knife blade. In this moment, *Self-reliance* called for him to meet the city's horror, sink to the villainy of its citizens so as to keep himself alive. Blinking slowly, he tried to channel Horatio's wild, remorseless energy. He balled his fists and took a sharp breath.

The Vein lifted the blade and struck downward in a ruthlessly fast, fluid motion. At the last second, Finch feinted to the side and the knife swiped at the air next to his ear. Then the man was on top of him, pinning his legs. Again the Vein drew back the knife for a killing strike.

But the whistling of the knife as it bypassed his ear had awakened a long dormant volcano in the pit of Finch's being. Years of unconsummated rage—at the Vein, at the Cannies, at Richard and the Regals, at Gajjea and the Scorps, at Vulture itself—burst to the surface, charging his limbs with unfamiliar strength. Finch watched as his left fist shot up hard into the Vein's wrist, sending the knife flying to the far corner of the roof. The Vein made to retaliate but a stomp to the chest landed him on his back, the wind kicked from his lungs. In the same moment, Finch bent low and grabbed his would-be assassin by both legs as tattooed fingers clawed at his back and neck. Finch paid the scratches no mind, still caught in the throes of his fury. In one clunking, powerful movement, he thrust the screaming Vein off the roof.

The Vein's scream ended abruptly in a muffled thump as his body hit the ground, punctuated by the audible crack of bone. It was at this moment that a bloodstained Horatio loped back toward the station, barking wildly and charging toward the whimpering, broken Vein on the ground. Seconds later he had snapped the man's neck between his serrated jaws. Horatio dragged the body a distance into the wasteland and set into his unexpected desert with vigor.

Finch watched the grisly scene in shock, unable to move. The wrathful strength left his body as soon as it had arrived, leaving his arms limp at his sides, ragged breaths emanating from his throat. A pain built in his stomach and he retched off the roof. He sat with his head in his hands, legs dangling off the edge. The animalistic sounds of Horatio gnashing paused only when loud, violent sobs wracked Finch's hunched body. Horatio ambled back toward the station to lick at the tears that spilled to the earth. Finch did nothing to quell the sound of his crying, yielding himself to the tears that streamed past his chin and not caring who might hear his sobs. He'd never killed anyone before.

As the tears began to dry in salty rivulets on his cheeks, Finch forced his drained body to take deep breaths. *Self-reliance.* Over and over again he repeated the words to himself, though they brought him little solace. He'd survived and the Vein was now entering Horatio's digestive tract. On a rational level, Finch knew that these were the only facts that mattered. Hesitation would have meant a grim role reversal. And yet he could not bring himself to savor the feeling of success that should have accompanied the moment, a feeling for which he'd foolishly longed.

Finch clambered back down off the roof despite his trembling hands. Horatio greeted him with a wet lick to his sneakers, his teeth stained red. Looking up, the dog-wolf fixed his charcoal brick eyes on Finch. Was Horatio simply seeing, or could he be comprehending Finch's defeated state? The eyes that never changed spoke to Finch differently this time, perhaps more tender than usual. Or maybe it was nothing more than a request for water.

Filling the large bowl to the brim, Finch set the water down at Horatio's feet. Horatio drank thirstily, his bloody, greasy maw casting strange red clouds swirling in the bowl before they dissipated into nothing more than a faint bronze tint. Finch walked into the station and collapsed onto his mattress. He lay in bed, closing his eyes and placing the covers over his head. No relief came in the form of sleep. Adrenaline and guilt wracked his body. Four times he got up to check the locks on his door. He lit an old candle and flipped *To Kill A Mockingbird* open to a random page, though even the book could not distract him from his conscience. He'd never felt farther from Maycomb and the Finch family. He put the book down at the description of Tom Robinson's death. Glancing outside into the darkness, he could see that Horatio had settled into a satisfied slumber, sleeping with his full belly pointed outward challengingly toward Vulture.

At last Finch blew out the candle and sleep washed over him. But his peace was short lived, as fitful images played out behind his eyelids. Time and again he dreamed himself awake with visions of his own body falling in a heap to the ground off of the roof. Sweat stained his sheets, joining the green patches left by Viro. He wished Viro were here next to him, wrapping his arms around his chest and telling him that everything would be ok. He wished he could sleep like Horatio, who had slaughtered not one but two men today and now slept peacefully with dreams of doing the same tomorrow.

CHAPTER 10

The less we say about it the better
Make it up as we go along
Feet on the ground
Head in the sky
It's ok I know nothing's wrong... nothing

— Talking Heads, *This Must Be the Place (Naive Melody)*

Rigby's eyes followed the trajectory of the Vein's body as the man with the short braid hurled him off the roof. It was the same roof she'd stood upon herself only the day before. Even in the evening's fading light she could tell that the Vein was tall and lean, a full-grown adult. She winced as she heard, even from her distant post behind the rubble heap at the edge of the city, the muffled click of the Vein's legs breaking on impact.

On a routine recon mission that had yielded little more than a few startled Cannies, Rigby had thought the night's excitement might be over. However, just when she'd set the needle down on Nina Simone's *I Put a Spell on You*, she had heard a heavy panting coming from somewhere near the foot of the record shop. Seconds later, peering through her window, she saw an enormous dog-wolf bounding heavily across the asphalt less than a hundred feet away. The indie with the tell-tale braid jogged shortly behind him. In the fading twilight, she'd shimmied silently down from her perch in the attic and followed the duo, clinging to the shadows. They too were slinking in the shadows, worming their way deep into Vulture in the direction of the cinema.

Though she could not make out the indie's face, she could see clearly now how his lanky limbs swayed as he ran, how the end of his braid fell to his shoulders. He stayed close to the dog-wolf's side, neither appearing afraid of the other. Working hard to sti-fle her own breath for fear of being discovered by the man—or worse, the dog-wolf—she watched in horror as the indie painted the Veins' emblem across Richard's portrait. Only the dog-wolf's worrisome allegiance to the man, perhaps as well as her own simple curiosity, kept her from rushing out to stop him, her hand fluttering on the electrical cord with anticipation.

But she had decided to wait. It was obvious that he had seen the Regal R on his door that she had left earlier. Now he appeared to be plotting some sort of diversion. It would have been a clever plan had she not witnessed it herself. She could only imagine Richard's fury in discovering that his mural—and thus, his very being—had been challenged. The man's brazenness shocked her, and an indie no less. Rigby almost laughed when the dog peed on the portrait. She'd never seen—or even considered —deception like this before, and she was struck just then by the fragility of the graffiti system, exploitable as it was by a creature so seemingly powerless as an indie.

She'd followed the indie back to the outskirts. He would be an enemy of the Regals as soon as the vandalism was discovered. Better to tip off Richard's fury with action and answers to the wrathful questions that were sure to come. Regal or not, surviv-ing Richard was essential to surviving Vulture.

The outskirts loomed endless and gray in front of her, dotted with the small orange glows where Cannies slaked their thirst with their awful concoctions, yowling away at the starless sky around roaring bonfires. Her feet scraped against the rough asphalt, the only sound but for the intermittent hoots of the Cannie's and the indie's bursting sobs that clenched her insides in discomfort. The man finally went to bed and his faithful hound returned to a spot under an awning adjoining the radio station only after devouring the Vein that had been tenderized by gravity.

By the time she got back to the cinema Richard was already outside, torch in one hand, a loaded crossbow in the other. She noticed Pip crouching dejectedly among the other junkers. Even in the darkness she could see the stains of grease and rust that covered him from head to toe. The rest of the junkers looked much the same, all rubbing sleep from their eyes, hunched in exhaustion. They must have been roused from the stringy junkyard hammocks by Richard's screams. Rage wracked his body, every muscle contorted. He couldn't stand still. His enormous frame twisted like an oak tree in a storm. The torch cast a villainous red light over his grimacing face. She heard him spewing curses into the night even before she came into view of the cinema.

"Every single one of you better return to this very spot with a bleach-blonde scalp in your hand by dawn or I will see fit to use yours as collateral!"

The audience of gathered Regals flinched upon every syllable, only noticing Rigby when Richard turned his ire in her direction. Every purple head stared intently at the ground. Miriam all but jumped at every word of Richard's diatribe.

"And where have you been, crafty, suspicious, Rigby? Out for a stroll? Speaking with your friends the Veins, perhaps? Answers!" His voice thundered off the wicked spires of Vulture.

His eyes were wild and a thick, dark vein threatened to burst his bald scalp open right then and there. His jaw was so clenched it looked as though his gritted teeth might shatter at any moment. Rigby forced her voice to sound calm and confident, as though speaking to a capricious child rather than a sociopathic adult.

"I've been tailing that indie, like you instructed me to. It was him. He painted the V on your mural. He must be trying to get you—us—to focus on them rather than himself. He must have seen Miriam and I out there yesterday. And if it's dead Veins you want, you'll find one back on Factory Row with purple eyes."

The audience dared not breathe as they awaited Richard's response. Rigby forced her eyes to remain level, channeling Hendrix's power chords as she stared unflinchingly back at Richard. He closed his eyes and did not open them. Rigby could see a whole range of thoughts coursing and changing gears behind his eyelids. Gradually the throbbing vein in his scalp began to subside. His white lips formed a tight smile that chilled Rigby to the core. It felt like an eon before he finally spoke.

"Clever," was all he said. His tone sounded neither angry nor incredulous, but rather amused. The crowd remained paralyzed for fear that they might break the temporary pause in his ravings. Their chins were glued to their chests, all eyes focused on their feet. Rigby alone met Richard's gaze.

"Clever, clever, clever," he repeated. Rigby began to fear that Richard was turning the word on her, an accusation that she was inventing some clever story to avoid implicating herself. She straightened her spine and squared her shoulders. "And what else have you learned of this independent man from the outskirts?" His tone was curious, his massive, stomping feet slowing to a stroll as he stepped in her direction.

"He lives in an abandoned radio station just outside Vulture where the outskirts begin. He's skinny but he's no weakling. To-night, I watched him throw a full-grown Vein from his roof like a pile of laundry. He appears to have tamed one of those dog-wolves from the outskirts. It eats Cannies but seems to like him. It sleeps outside his door. And I believe he can read. There were books all over his desk."

Richard's eyes closed again. The audience watched with rapt attention as he processed this information. Only someone as powerful as Richard could voluntarily blind himself at night, ex-posing himself to Vulture during its most treacherous hours. He stood less than a foot from Rigby and she choked on the thick scent of his ever-present cologne. Her chin was level with his or-nate purple belt buckle. His feet stretched nearly five times the size of her own. One of his hands could comfortably palm two of her heads. She fought the urge to slouch or step backward. Glancing into the eyes of her fellow Regals, Rigby could tell that disbelief in her wild report was the common sentiment. At last Richard's serpentine eyelids flicked open.

"He's a plotter, a planner, a schemer. A man of books and knowledge. Potentially a fighter. And perhaps some kind of abil-ity with wild carnivores. And he's made enemies of the Veins... This man sounds like a Regal, no?"

Dozens of Regal heads nodded in agreement, casting a rip-ple in the torch-lit darkness. Milo inched closer to Richard's el-bow as he spoke, arms crossed, nodding sagely but vigorously as though he and Richard had convened privately and come to the decision together.

"And he has not responded to our invitations, correct?"

"I've marked his door but it appears he likes his solitude, Richard."

Richard paused again, nodding as his brain digested this

information. The massive shadow billowing out from his skull bobbed in the torch light, shading the entire audience with each downward strike of his gargantuan head.

"So we shall test him. Let's we test the mettle of this incorrigible indie. Only then will we know if he is worth more to us alive than dead."

The audience murmured in agreement. When he spoke again, Richard's velvety baritone voice stifled their frantic whispers.

"Now Rigby. Would you say he cares a great deal for this canine?"

"I would, yes Richard. He gives it water and they seem fairly inseparable."

"Very well. Kill the dog-wolf. Mark it in the paint of the Veins. We will see how he responds to some violent trickery of our own. Yes. Yes Rigby, you will kill the dog-wolf, and you will make it bloody." The torchlight danced in Richard's crazed eyes. As he spoke in his strange, theatrical way, a wicked smile stitched across his face.

Rigby's immediate reaction to the thought of killing the dog-wolf was repulsion. The command felt like a punishment. She lamented her decision to absolve the Veins of blame. Having issued his decree, Richard made his way back to his chamber. The Regal artists were already at work retouching the mural. Their gentle brush strokes sent flickering shadows against the torch-lit wall. The crowd of Regals slipped into the darkness to private dealings of their own or to execute separate missions on Richard's behalf. His word was final. She'd have to kill the dog-wolf.

Nina Simone crooned smooth and soft through the record player's blocky speakers. It was one of Rigby's favorite albums. Simone really knew how to express. She sounded self-confident, but also a little scared, and by that confluence, honest. Rigby never sang along to the music. She hated the sound of her own voice but nodded her head along to the beat. She closed her eyes, her purple locks swaying to the rhythm. Simone's voice was hypnotic and relaxing, the melodies seeping through her skin and into her heart, transporting her to some golden other time.

But she quickly cut herself off from the music, wary of its distracting quality. She set the full focus of her mind on the depraved task before her. The beast was nearly three times her size and infinitely more equipped for close combat. Her electrical cord would barely damage the massive hound. And how much poison would it take to bring down such an animal? Would she even be able to get close enough to spike its water bowl? Not likely. She'd need something larger and meaner. Surely a job this vile required a weapon fittingly sinister. She'd have to purloin a crossbow from the armory, never an easy task. Each arrow was priceless in Vulture, easily lost and generally saved only for battles. Milo would need to be asked for permission to borrow a crossbow, and she shuddered at the thought. He'd make it difficult, exploiting whatever small leverage he could squeeze out of his position as Head of Inventory. And who knew how many arrows it would take to kill the dog-wolf? And would she even have time to trigger another shot once the first had been fired? She recalled the dog-wolf's long, powerful strides as it had loped past her window.

The grisly task gnawed at her psyche. She reminded herself that she'd killed a person just a day ago, and she'd hardly thought about it since. Of course, that person had worn gang colors, and they'd attacked first. Her body had taken over, killing on instinct. But something about the dog-wolf felt different. It wore no colors other than the dark fur it had been born with. Man's best friend or not, she'd have to find a way to eliminate it. After all, the dog-wolf would do the same to her in an instant. With a sense of finality, she reminded herself that a conscience was a liability in Vulture, and she was not willing to risk getting shot down from the top of some fruitless moral high ground. Miriam had a conscience, and she had a deep bruise on her chin to prove it. Rigby pushed the unsettling image of Miriam's crumpled body to the very back corners of her mind.

She placed Bob Dylan's *Highway 61 Revisited* into position on the record player. Again, she closed her eyes and swayed gently to the soft, croaky vocals. But less than halfway through "Like a Rolling Stone" the disk started skipping, harsh, intermittent chops of silence interrupting the song. Groaning, she removed the needle from the record, careful not to scratch it. She popped the dead batteries out of the clunky base of the player and tossed them into a pile of laundry in the corner of the room. Again, she groaned, sending a rueful glare in the record player's direction.

Rigby worked her way back toward the cinema, clambering through the wall of buses and skirting along the high edges formed by amalgamate metals. The soft light of dawn poked up from the horizon. Rigby had every intention of avoiding Richard until she had news for him, but there was always a decent chance of finding old batteries in the junkyard. Old cars ripped to pieces lay strewn and rotting across the expansive junkyard. The behemoth frame of a dump truck, its engine and its massive container long absent but with large rubber tires still remaining on its rusty axle, occupied the corner nearest the cinema. Rigby always thought it looked like a skeleton, all but the most fundamental pieces of the truck having melted away with time. Throughout the rest of the junkyard, all manner of defunct appliances, engines, and busted mechanical wares formed hillocks and caverns for miles before petering out into the outskirts. Smashed mirrors leaned on exploded washing machines and rusted toasters sat on great coils of copper spring. The smell of rust and dry oil emanated from every corner. The Cannies and gangs had scrupulously picked through this place, looking especially for weaponry, years ago. Still, the junkers sifted through the piles day in and day out on Richard's behalf, searching for any item that might hold some value.

Batteries were her new priority, refusing to consider the dog-wolf until she could once again play music. For the most part, the junkers overlooked batteries on the rare occasions that they were found. Nobody bothered with any electrical items at all, usually. There was no use. Every outlet was fried and any attempt to fix them had resulted in horrific electrical scarring and even death. Even if Rigby had had competition for the batteries, she knew of nobody else with a device functional enough to accept them. She hated to think about the day when all the batteries would be gone.

Crouching low, she began searching through a pile of refuse in a far corner of the junkyard. It was a section she'd never perused before, and she hoped it might yield her precious batteries. She hummed "Like a Rolling Stone" to herself as she searched, trying to stay patient. The arduous, methodical process was never brief. Over two hours elapsed and still she found nothing, moving from pile to pile. Black stains of ash and oil joined the purple crusts on her fingers.

"Hey."

Pip's voice startled her. She hadn't even heard him walk up behind her. She kicked herself for her lack of awareness, knowing that surprise could just as often mean death in Vulture. She cursed her own stupidity but felt lucky all the same. She blamed Bob Dylan for distracting her, reminding her of the liability her music—and all forms of pleasure—posed to her survival. But Pip couldn't look less threatening if he'd tried. He wore only a baggy jumpsuit that hung loose on his skinny frame. Grime and dust clung to every surface of his body. But this wasn't what made him look so harmless. It was something in his eyes, maybe. A hollowness that echoed even in his voice.

"Pip, hey, why are you…"

"Talking to you?" Pip cut her off, his voice a monotone that she couldn't read.

"No, just, out here I mean." Rigby tried to recover herself. She had never had a conversation with one of Richard's junkers before, she now realized. It was not an experience she relished. He blended into the junkyard around him, his roving eyes the only thing distinguishing him from the decaying piles of forgotten scrap.

"I live out here, remember? My hammock is just over there." He gestured in the direction of a filthy fishing net draped haphazardly between two rusting car frames.

"Right." Rigby looked away.

"Yeah, exactly." Pip's eyes refused to meet hers. She struggled to find something to say.

"So, you alright then?"

Now Pip's black-rimmed eyes shot up to her own. No longer unreadable, she saw fury boiling in his dark irises. His skinny chest swelled beneath the ill-fitting jumpsuit.

"Why did you bring me here?"

His accusatory tone caught Rigby off guard. The question leapt from his mouth like a coiled snake that's long been waiting to strike. Consumed by the investigation of the indie in the outskirts, she'd nearly forgotten that she had led Pip directly to his current, depraved fate. The junkers weren't privileged even nearly with the same level of comfort enjoyed by the Regals. Their food and water rations were smaller, they didn't benefit from the protection of the gang's limited supply of purple paint, and, worst of all, they were forced to both live and work in the junkyard. Their proximity to the cinema was their only form of safety.

"Pip, I'm sorry. I didn't know Richard was going to…I thought he'd make you a soldier."

Again she stared at her feet. She couldn't bear the contempt and sadness in Pip's eyes. At last he spoke again.

"You know I ate better as an indie?"

She nodded, still not meeting his eyes. The quivering figure before her put her unsavory task in perspective. He looked skinnier than when she'd found him, and older, dark circles sagging below his eyes. In Vulture, life could always be worse. Sometimes she forgot what an evil place it was. Murder, starvation, fatal thirst, violence, and hate were all so commonplace that they had come to feel repulsively normal to her. She wondered what other places, other collections of abandoned buildings and bumpy asphalt and humans who had survived the Water Wars were like, if such places even existed.

"Pip, I don't know what to say. You're in the bad part of a bad place. I'm sorry."

"I was okay in that mall where you found me. I could have been okay on my own. I could have died." His voice cracked and she thought he might cry.

He seemed to mention this last part as a preferable option to his current circumstances, and Rigby didn't press him for clarification. She pitied him, but she had a dog-wolf to kill. Pip's red eyes foretold many sleepless nights as they bored holes through her face.

"Are you really gonna do it?"

Maybe it was an attempt at a change of topic, though these words, too, carried a caustic undertone.

"Do what?"

She feigned ignorance. Milo was nowhere to be seen, and for once she wished he'd appear. He'd have slapped Pip and told him to get back to junking, yelled at him for speaking out of turn to a ranking Regal. She weighed the possibility of doing so herself. Anything to excuse herself from this tense, painful interaction.

"You know. Kill that guy's dog-wolf."

She paused before replying. Pip could easily run back to Richard with whatever answer she supplied. Maybe he'd been sent out here to question her in the first place. Or maybe he hoped to use her response as a bargaining chip for more food, more water. Everyone had something to gain.

"Yeah, of course."

His eyes seemed to grow sadder, were that possible. Wordlessly, he shuffled past her back to the hammock. Despite the frayed netting's apparent weakness, it barely strained as Pip collapsed into its folds.

Rigby returned her attention to the hunt for batteries. She squeezed thoughts of Pip into a dimly lit back corner of her mind, alongside the image of Miriam's stricken form on the marble floor of Richard's apartment. She left a generous amount of space for the dog-wolf back there, too. "Items to be Dealt With at a Later Date or Not at All" she labeled the space.

After another hour of searching, she gave up. There were other duties that needed her attention; she'd have to resume her search another time. With a final, sad glance in Pip's direction, she banished him from her mind and set course for the outskirts.

She needed a fresh—or perhaps rancid, more accurately—bottle of Leak. It would be easy to find. She knew from her reconnaissance missions that the Cannies had taken to roosting on the ramshackle bridge in east Vulture, at the foot of the outskirts.

Walking at a brisk pace, she was there in less than twenty minutes. Cannies could always be smelled before they were seen, and today was no different. The toxic scent was so powerful it seemed to radiate off the splintered bridge. The Cannies were lanky and naked, the men bearing scruffy beards and long, unkempt hair and the women nearly equal in grime. Their oily skin glistened in the morning sunlight. Orange paint splattered their bodies in random, distorted stripes, functioning as the sole reminder in their drunken state not to eat each other. Though this warning failed at times, even the Cannies knew that in Vulture, there was power in numbers.

"Well, well, wha' have we—"

The words were barely out of his mouth before Rigby's cord snapped viciously across his jaw. The sound of teeth shattering and falling to the gulch below caught the attention of the other Cannies, who reclined atop the beams of the bridge. The Canny yowled and clutched a clammy hand to his mouth. Even those Cannies who were in deep conference with the vile brown liquid that sloshed in the bottles gripped between their sweating palms turned in her direction.

Rigby climbed the rest of the way up to the yowling Canny's rafter and secured the bottle of Leak in her backpack. Though she screwed the cap down as tightly as possible, the stench still made her gag. The viscous liquid numbed her fingertips where she accidentally touched it. To this day nobody but the Cannies knew what went into that witch's brew that made it so horribly addictive. Some said it was a combination of rye and narcotics that the Cannies had stockpiled instead of food after the Water Wars. Others claimed it was grain alcohol mixed with human blood and the wild tobacco seed that grew in snatches along the gulch. Rigby wasn't interested in its ingredients. All she cared about was that Milo had a not-so-secret addiction to the stuff.

"I need more," she said aloud, addressing no one in particular.

Nobody appeared ready to part with his or her respective bottle. Some clutched them maternally to their chest, and others clambered like primates down the scaffolding of the bridge and ran off to the relative safety in the scrubby outskirts. Their skinny, gawky legs jerked and jolted at awkward angles as they ran. Still others remained seated on the bridge, chugging the thick liquid so as to eliminate the threat of losing it for naught.

Rigby advanced slowly toward the nearest Canny. He was a large, aggressive-looking older male who clutched a cracked yet brimming blender to his broad chest. He might've looked statuesque there on the bridge had it not been for the utter depravity of his visage. Dribbles of sticky liquid stained his chin and coursed in rivulets down his bare stomach. Just then a sharp sting erupted on Rigby's right ear. She felt blood where the rock had whizzed by, missing her head by centimeters. Turning, she saw the source of the small stone. A wily adolescent girl, streaked in orange paint, hunched forward, reloading her slingshot.

Rigby managed to sidestep the next stone bullet by ducking for cover beneath the bridge, clinging to the rafters and hauling herself from one beam to the next using her arms. She heard the drunken laughter of the Cannies over her head. The horrible noise gurgled from their Leak-slickened throats. None seemed interested in following her, instead returning to their drink. The sun had barely reached its highest point and already they were too stupefied to feel concern. More likely, they hadn't paused their carousing from last night, simply letting the bender carry them along until they passed out or ran out of Leak. One Canny slumped against a beam at the bridge's edge, his head lolling onto his chest, a long string of saliva dribbling from his lower lip.

Rigby risked a peak onto the bridge from a small opening in the old wooden slats. The Canny with the blender was still rooted in place, though he'd chugged nearly half the contents of the jug. Hanging from her hands on the rafters over the gulch, she felt her grip beginning to slip. If she could get her hands on that blender it might be enough. Finally he set it down at his side to wipe the back of his hand across his mouth. In a quick, gymnastic motion, Rigby heaved herself back up onto the bridge. Before any of them could think to announce her presence, the electrical cord struck with a sharp crack across the man's temple, sending him tumbling off the bridge and into the muddy quarry below.

She snagged the blender that had so recently been cradled in the Canny's arms and with another aerobic twist she was out of sight below the bridge, shimmying spider-like down the creaky beams. She poured the smaller jar of Leak into the blender, making a noxious, brimming mixture, which she secured tightly in her backpack before setting off to find Milo. The shrieks of the furious Cannies followed her nearly all the way down, though they remained on the bridge, caressing the jars and canisters they'd managed to retain.

Reaching the gulch, she turned on her heel and made for the cinema. Surely Milo would be lurking about, frantically calculating inventory totals or waiting for an audience with Richard. Hoping to avoid another uncomfortable exchange with Pip, Rigby avoided the junkyard on her way toward the theater. A few weary painters were putting the final touches on the restored mural. After several minutes of searching, she located the blue paint canister where she'd seen the indie toss it the night before. A quick shake told her that about half the can remained full, more than enough for her own project. Adding this burden to the increasing weight of her backpack, she gave the password to the tall guard and made her way through the revolving doors and into the cinema.

Just as she reached the locked door of the theater that had been repurposed as a stock room, it crashed open and Milo stormed out into the hallway.

"Milo," called Rigby, delighting in his surprised jump at the sound of her voice.

Regaining his composure, he turned and said, "Look who it is, shouldn't you be out on recon?"

"I'll worry about that," she said, coolly.

"Yes, as will I. And I'm sure Richard would be interested to know you've been shirking your duties as well," he replied, licking his thin lips and smirking.

Rigby knew how much he relished his high rank in the gang, but she decided against goading him further. She needed a crossbow, after all, and Milo was the only way to get one without appealing to Richard. The weapons sat polished and mounted on the wall of the stock room, locked away alongside the food, paint, and water. At least she knew how to handle Milo. Richard was far less predictable.

"Actually, I'm working on Richard's orders. About the indie." She did her best to make her tone sound casual, knowing that Milo would bite at the invocation of Richard's name. He paused, looking her up and down through narrowed eyes.

"I see," he said. "And I suppose you want a crossbow, is that it?"

He licked his lips again, luxuriating in Rigby's need.

"Yes, actually." Again, Rigby attempted to detach emotion from every syllable.

"What, you don't think you can handle the indie on your own? I thought you were the great Rigby! Untouchable Rigby! Brought up from nothing! Apple of Richard's eye! Surely you can manage to bring him in without an arrow in his leg?"

"It's not for him. It's for the dog-wolf."

"Ah yes, the boy who tames dog-wolves. No. We can't waste arrows on an animal. You'll have to find another way." He turned his back on her as though to leave, feigning indifference.

"Milo, you know as well as I do that it's the only way. You've seen the dog-wolves, nothing else will do."

"Not my concern. Be creative. I'm sure we're all interested in seeing what you come up with." He chortled with a sound not unlike the Cannies'.

Saying nothing, Rigby grabbed the cracked blender of Leak out of her backpack and shook it enticingly. Milo's ears pricked at the sound though he did not turn around.

"Aren't you thirsty, Milo?"

Finally, he looked back, staring wide-eyed at the full blender, dark liquid sloshing against its tainted glass sides. It held enough to last even the most addicted Canny for a few days.

"Where'd you get that?" he asked, unable to disguise his interest, licking his lips frantically.

"Like you said, not your concern."

"What makes you think I'd be interested in that disgusting stuff, anyway?" he said, though his eyes never left the jug. He couldn't help but take a small step in her direction.

"Fine. I guess I'll just dump it then," said Rigby.

Tilting the blender, she began to pour the acrid Leak onto the cracked linoleum floor.

"No!" whispered Milo, lunging for the jar, unable to deny himself any longer. Still, Rigby had to admire his self-control. He'd lasted longer than she'd thought he would. Clearly, he had some kind of iron self-discipline if he somehow managed to juggle his Regal duties alongside his addiction.

Just before his fingers closed around the jug, Rigby yanked it back to her chest, brandishing her cord threateningly up to his face. He stumbled backward and fell to the ground, covering his face with his outstretched arm.

"Crossbow," said Rigby, flatly. Before Milo could speak she again began pouring the Leak with dramatic slowness onto the ground.

"Fine. Fine!" he shouted, struggling to his feet. He gave her a dirty look before licking his lips angrily and trotting back into the storeroom. He left the door ajar and through the opening Rigby saw the massive pyramid of purple paint cans, the even larger pile of food, and even a sliver of the colossal water tankard housed in a corner at the rear of the room. After a few minutes, Milo returned with a crossbow, thrusting it into Rigby's arms aggressively and snatching the jar of Leak, scanning the hallway to be sure the exchange went unobserved.

Nodding curtly, Rigby turned on her heel. As she departed, she heard the gurgling sound of Milo taking a long swig.

Thus, equipped for her morbid task, she walked in the direction of the record shop. Between Pip, the Cannies, and Milo it had been a taxing morning, and bloodier than usual. Her ear still felt numb where the stone had caught her and her sweaty clothes clung to her back. She took a long pull from her canteen.

As she approached the record shop, she noticed a figure standing on her doorstep. Instinctively, she crouched low and inched closer, careful to stay out of sight. From her limited vantage under the crooked fire escape she could see that it was a young woman—a Regal judging by the purple hair, but she faced away from Rigby. Stupid, thought Rigby. Whoever this Regal was, she was blinded to a surprise attack with her back to Vulture like that. The girl's arms hung at her sides and as she got closer, Rigby saw a set of clean, purple fingernails trembling and rapping against the young woman's thigh.

"Miriam?"

Miriam jumped with a start and held a hand to her chest as she whipped her head around.

"Rigby! There you are. You scared me!"

"Well yeah, you shouldn't stand like that. What are you doing here?"

Miriam shifted on her feet and wrung her hands behind her back. Rigby cocked an eyebrow at her but said nothing.

"I... Well, I wanted to bring you something."

From within her pocket Miriam procured two small batteries, holding them out to Rigby in her clean, quivering hand. Stunned, Rigby stared at the batteries.

"I just had a really nice time, you know, listening to music the other day, and I figured you'd be looking for these sooner or later, so—"

"Where did you find these?" Rigby cut her off.

"My brother found them. There was a busted TV remote in this old shack behind the place where we stay."

Rigby took the batteries from Miriam's hand and brought them up to her face. They felt smooth and weighed pleasantly in her hand. She could smell that metallic chemical scent she'd learned to love.

"Miriam. Thank you. You have no idea... this is just... really great. Thank you."

For a moment she and Miriam just stared at each other on the doorstep, neither sure what to do next.

"Do you want to listen to some more music?"

Miriam's eyes grew wide and she nodded her head vigorously, raising herself up on her tiptoes.

"Yes! I would absolutely love that Rigby."

Rigby unlocked her door. Together they entered and sat down on the floor next to the record player. Replacing the batteries, Rigby set the needle back onto the Dylan record and switched the machine to life, holding her breath. As the lyrics began to emanate from the speakers, she released a long breath of relief. She looked over at Miriam and saw her swaying to the music with her eyes closed. A smile tested unfamiliar muscles in Rigby's face and she rubbed a hand over the odd soreness in her cheeks.

After a while, Miriam's eyes opened and her face turned solemn.

"Rigby, I actually wanted to talk to you about something."

Rigby removed the needle from the record, but Miriam didn't say a word until the silent black disc rotated to a stop. Finally, taking a deep breath, she spoke.

"I'm thinking of joining the Veins."

Rigby stared back at her, hand still on the needle.

"I've been thinking about it for a while, actually. I met a Vein during a recruiting mission a few months ago and I've started talking to him about joining. He's introduced me to a few other members and—"

"What if Richard finds out? Do you realize how dangerous

this is for you, Miriam?" Rigby couldn't stop the questions from blurting out of her mouth.

"I know!" Miriam shouted, before lowering her voice. "I know. But the Veins… They're so different. They don't kill each other, Rigby! They're not scared of each other. It'll be safer for my brother, too. Their leader isn't some psychopath. I'm sorry, Rigby but it's true!"

Rigby stared at her a moment longer before looking away and nodding.

"I understand, Miriam, I do. I just hope you're careful."

Miriam surprised her by taking her hand and looking at her with round, watery eyes.

"Rigby, you can join too. We can both go! They'd take us both, I'm sure. Everyone in Vulture knows how capable you are."

Rigby pulled her hand away.

"I'm a Regal, Miriam."

Without waiting for Miriam's reply, she set the needle back down on the record. Miriam gave her a sad look before standing up to leave. Rigby heard the door lurch closed and gentle footsteps retreating down the stairs.

CHAPTER 11

I learned this, at least, by my experiment: that if one advances confidently in the direction of his dreams, and endeavors to live the life which he has imagined, he will meet with a success unexpected in common hours.

— Henry David Thoreau, *Walden*

Horatio pawed at Finch's door, an empty water bowl pinched in his jaws. Finch had been avoiding going outside, but he'd have to collect water before the sun evaporated all the sodden patches from the sheet. This morning it produced only enough moisture to fill half his canteen, a portion of which he poured into Horatio's bowl. It was wretchedly hot today, perhaps more so than usual. The sun baked down onto the radio station, filling the poorly ventilated room with an arid heat.

Horatio gave a yip of joy when he realized they'd be going out. Viro hadn't apologized or even mentioned the tiff they'd had when he'd visited briefly in the predawn hours. But he had told Finch about a library he'd discovered on a recent recruiting mission deep in east Vulture, crumbling and abandoned but still standing. Part of an old university, it had gone largely overlooked by the gangs. Though he'd hidden his elation at the time, Finch had privately taken this information as some small act of contrition on Viro's part. Finch couldn't contain his excitement as he set out in the direction of the supposed library, all but jogging with Horatio trotting amiably by his side.

Deeper and deeper they worked their way into Vulture, setting an easterly course. The bent shapes of buildings and boulders grew less familiar as they proceeded. They strayed further and further from their usual foraging grounds. Only Finch's burning desire for books kept his feet moving forward in the oppressive heat.

He paused only to collect scrubby patches of Fiddlehead Ferns or to seek out mushrooms under promising rocks and stumps. Horatio shot off intermittently to chase down scampering lizards but always made his way dutifully back to Finch's side. He took a small sip from his canteen. The felled towers, twisted skyscrapers and flattened houses in this section of Vulture were unrecognizable to him. After a moment, he realized why it looked so odd: nearly all of the surfaces were unadorned by the gang artwork that smothered the rest of the city.

Nearly three hours passed before he noticed anything promising. Dust mixed with the sweat coating his body in a thin film. On a crooked black gate, its iron bars bent at violent angles toward the sky and finishing in sharp Gothic spikes, were the words 'Gonzaga University'. A massive spire lay collapsed on its side in the lot beyond. Picking his way past the twisted gate, Finch saw a building sitting squarely on its foundation. Three of the four walls remained intact, while the fourth had collapsed and tumbled into a pile of bricks and dirt. The mechanical drone he often heard hummed somewhere far behind him, and Finch didn't take another step until the mysterious sound had dissipated into silence.

As he scrambled over the pile of loose stones that had once been a wall, Finch's breath caught in his throat. The sweet, musty smell of books filled his nostrils and he breathed it in with pleasure. Making his way into the library, his heart dropped at the sight of large piles of ash. They had smoldered into cold gray flakes long ago but still bore the distinct smell of burnt paper. Small white scraps peered like eyes out of these insidious black piles, each one forming a car-sized island on the equally torched carpet that covered the floor. Bookshelves lay on their sides or leaned against the walls in various states of dilapidation, their empty shelves stained by streaky tattoos of smoke.

Finch thrust a desperate hand into one of these piles, turning up nothing more than more silty black and gray flakes. Even the pages that remained somewhat intact were charred beyond readability, and the movement of his hand sent cascades of scorched paper down the sides of the pile. Finch winced at the sad crunching sound his hand made each time it closed around a new, futile handful of ash.

A cork board mounted on a far wall caught his eye and he rushed toward it. A small map covered one half of the board. Scrawled in bold letters across the top of the poster is the word 'WASHINGTON' in all capitals. He scanned the map with hungry eyes. Strange words he didn't recognize were peppered across the green landmass—Tacoma, Olympia, Seattle—but one word in particular jumped out at him. 'Spokane' it said, and someone had circled the word in the choppy strokes of a dying pen. It was the same word mounted over the door of the radio station, the 'Spokane Independent Voice', and which he had seen occasionally throughout Vulture.

Finch's eyes scanned the map, trying to swallow its entirety in one bite. With a slow, gentle movement, careful not to damage the wilted map, he used his finger to trace a line up from the spot marked Spokane to a thick, wavy blue line. Under the blue line were the words 'Columbia River' in small black typeface. For several long minutes he stared at the river, following its wiggling northwest path out to the broad blue expanse marked 'Pacific Ocean'.

For years he'd wondered how Vulture began, how it fit into the world set forth in his books. A warm sensation traversed his limbs, starting in his chest and ending in his fingertips. For a long moment he forgot his hunger, his thirst, and the danger of Vulture.

The river could easily be dried up like the gulch downtown, which he now realized must once have been the Spokane River, according to the map. But something about the thick blue line denoting the Columbia River looked promising and filled him with an unfamiliar sensation of hope. He wondered how long it would take him to reach the river, what dangers might lay so far into the outskirts, how much water and food he'd need to pack for himself and Horatio. Nudging aside these details, he knew he would make the excursion as soon as he could.

With difficulty, he tore himself from the map and set his attention on the few newspaper scraps clinging to the other side of the corkboard. While smoke has obscured most of the small, inky type of these articles, he could still make out a few of the boldface headlines. The first read, "Global Illiteracy On The Rise; Experts Blame Technology." The second was cut short by smoke damage but he managed to make out the words, "Looting Rampant As President's Suicide Note Released To Publ-." On the final news scrap, in large print, were the words, "Water Wars Expected To Turn Nuclear." Finch folded the crisped papers and placed them gently in his backpack, to be added to his collection back at the station. He carefully unpinned the map from the cork board, the rusty thumbtacks crumbling in his fingers, and folding it in

140

neat creases, placed it in his backpack as well.

Horatio's sharp bark jolted him from his thoughts. His eyes flashed to Horatio, whose back bristled in a terrifying arch, his lips curled back to reveal the knife set of teeth. Finch followed the dog-wolf's narrowed dark eyes out past the tumbled pile of bricks. There, in the courtyard, stood an equally menacing dog-wolf, this one female but nearly as large. Her fur was light brown and contrasted against Horatio's jet black coat. Finch stood frozen, his back pinned to the corkboard. A low rumble emanated from the female's snarled mouth, her ears pointed low over her skull. Finch had never seen Horatio encounter another wild dog-wolf.

The two predators snarled and edged around an invisible circle, never breaking the tenuous barrier that separated them. No doubt Horatio, and Finch himself, had stumbled into territory that they had foolishly deemed unclaimed.

Finch carefully edged further away from the scene and crouched behind one of the felled bookcases. The female seemed uninterested in him, for now at least. First, she had Horatio to deal with, and she looked to be up to the task. She charged and Horatio burst through one of the ash piles to meet her attack, a plume of black flakes erupting around his flanks. The female landed a vicious bite upon Horatio's ear that he parried with a strong claw to her face. She followed with a snap at his throat that might have sealed his fate had it not been for the sharp whistle that now screeched through the air. The sound seemed to have come from the sky and even took Finch by surprise. Glancing all around, he saw nothing, but the female dog-wolf took off at a sprint into the outskirts.

Horatio too was momentarily dumbfounded by the noise, but after a few seconds he took off after the whistle. Panicking, Finch sprinted after Horatio. With his canteen, the foraged herbs, and the items nicked from the corkboard, his backpack had never been more valuable—or heavier. He was barely fast enough to keep Horatio in his sight and his feet pounded against the hot pavement. Anything—or anyone—with the ability to halt an enraged dog-wolf mid-attack with nothing more than a mere whistle almost certainly spelled trouble for Horatio.

In the rush, Finch lost track of his pace and had no idea how far he'd ventured past the library. By now it must have been close to four or five miles away. His spent lungs heaved in the hot, dry air. While the sun still sat high in the sky, he'd have a long way home at a much slower pace. And Finch had no desire to tramp through the outskirts after dark.

Finally, he caught up to a Horatio, who now stood halted on the gravely tarmac. Finch's chest heaved and he collapsed over his knees. The female dog-wolf was nowhere to be seen. When finally he managed to lift his sweating head off his chest, Finch's jaw dropped. Horatio had ambled forward into the shallow bed of a river. Finch had never seen so much water collected in one place. Certainly not in the dried-up gulch in Vulture, its dusty stones slickened only occasionally, and then only by human blood or noxious deposits seeping from the earth.

Finch had never seen coursing, blue water like this, and thus had always scoffed at the depictions of the ocean in his books describing inky seas of sublime beauty. He held Melville especially at fault in this regard. Forgetting his begging lungs, Finch stumbled forward, placing a hand in the cool water. He felt the gentle ebb of the river coursing through his splayed fingers.

The river stretched indefinitely in both directions. Small patches of green vegetation tilted in the sun along the muddy riverbank and scores of mushrooms popped their heads out of the moist earth. Finch breathed in the fresh smell of mud and splashed water on his arms and face. The river stood in stark contrast to the barren landscape that surrounded it on both sides. It was as though someone had painted a thick line of blue paint across an otherwise sandy brown canvas.

At first tentatively, then exuberantly, Horatio took to the water, splashing in with abandon. Finch followed close behind. He tore off his shoes and then his socks and sank his bare feet into the lapping water. The gentle eddies were so clear that he could see straight through to rippling versions of his pale feet. The chill of the river was exhilarating. Peeling off his clothes and tossing his shirt and pants to the side, he dove beneath the surface, submerging himself in the chilly river. When he resurfed, cool water eddying off his naked limbs, he felt as though an entire layer had been stripped from his body like a second skin.

He couldn't remember the last time he'd felt like this. The constant anxieties that plagued him every minute of the day sank to the depths of the river and he alone floated to the top, unburdened. How long had the river existed, and did anyone else know about it? It must have been that same blue line from the map, the Columbia River. The insularity of Vulture hit him in a moment of sublime clarity. The ruinous buildings sprawled only several square miles, and yet few had ever left its terrifying vicinity, wagering that a familiar threat was far preferable to the unknowable one that might lay in the outskirts beyond.

The only thing that troubled Finch about the idyllic river was that it gave him hope. Hope led to optimism, which, in his experience, had only ever led to disappointment. But maybe the rules were different out here. Maybe Vulture was truly the worst place, and everywhere else was better by small fractions that improved the further one got from the city. Thoughts of moving his belongings to a shack on the riverbank wormed their way into his daydream. Here, surely, he could execute a version of *self-reliance* truly in keeping with Thoreau's vision in his removal to Walden Pond. Finch quickly tamped these notions down. Moving was unrealistic, at least for now. Better to stay where he knew he was relatively safe, where he knew how to find food, and where he knew how to identify his enemies. And where Viro knew how to find him, he admitted to himself.

But if his home in Vulture was safe, that didn't say much for safety. Finch couldn't confirm whether his plot against the Regals had actually worked. For all he knew, there could be a purple ambush waiting for him on his doorstep back home. And the Veins had more than enough reason by now to stake him out at the station. Closing his eyes, he pushed these thoughts away, enjoying the lull of the river, lifting him up and sinking him down with gentle rhythm.

A splash next to him snapped his eyes open and he watched as Horatio lunged off toward the bank. The female dog-wolf was back, her teeth and claws bared. The dog-wolves began to circle once again, and it occurred to Finch that the river might be the water source for the many dog-wolves that roved the outskirts. Perhaps Horatio had come to this river in the days before making Finch's acquaintance, or late at night on his secret canine jaunts. Maybe Horatio no longer needed to find water on his own, as Finch refilled a bowl of the stuff for him on a regular basis. The water sheet he'd affixed to the roof of the station had never felt so inadequate to Finch as now, standing waist deep in clear water.

This time Horatio gave chase, the female taking off at high speed up the riverbank. Rushing out of the water, Finch pulled on his shoes and shirt, yanked his backpack over his shoulders, and sprinted after Horatio. Again the high pitched whistle cut through the air.

Finch slowed as Horatio came into view. He rested back on his haunches, his tail wagging beside the female. Both of them sat in rapt attention at the feet of the dirtiest man Finch had ever seen. His hair looked like a spool of tree roots that had been ripped unceremoniously from the earth. It was hard to tell if his skin had been darkened by the sun or simply coated in years of dark grime. He wore a faded pair of gray jeans that might once have been blue and an equally tired shirt made from black corduroy, which he wore unbuttoned to reveal the scrubby hair of his chest and the bubble of his gut. He must have been nearly seventy years old but it was hard to tell his age with any certainty through all the soil and dust that caked his visage. His eyes were young though, and stared out like turquoise gems from his bearded face.

"Hey there, partner. I take it this brute is your friend?"

His voice carried a deep resonance and he spoke slowly, with a sort of crooning accent that Finch had never encountered in Vulture. It took a moment for Finch to find his own voice, still stunned by the river that ebbed near his feet.

"Yes. I'm sorry about that."

The man doled out small pieces of meat to the contented dog-wolves, which had apparently lost interest in maiming each other.

"Hell, they're just animals like us," the man mused. He held up a piece of the meat for Finch to see.

"Lizard jerky. They love it. And so do I, as a matter of fact. Indulge, friend."

The man tossed a piece of the jerky to Finch. Catching it in the air, he put the small, flat, dry, lizard-shaped morsel to his mouth only after seeing the man do the same. The cured, salty flavor coated his mouth and his teeth gnashed at the unfamiliar protein.

"Thanks," Finch said, still mystified. He wondered if the heat and exhaustion were getting to his head, if he was seeing some kind of mirage. The man ran a withered hand through the tangle of gray hair sprouting from his head.

"Don't mention it. Sorry if Sheila here gave you a start. We don't get too many visitors out here."

"You live out here?"

"Here, up the river, down the river. Anywhere I fall asleep is where I live, I suppose."

"How long have you been out here?"

"Oh, I took cover here after the Water Wars and never really left. However long that is."

It was then that Finch noticed the tattooed black bands around each of the man's spindly finger digits. At first glance Finch thought he might be wearing a couple dozen rings, but closer inspection revealed the neatly spaced, jet-black ink. The man was a Bleak, realized Finch, surely the last of his kind. According to the historical graffiti records maintained by the Veins on the upright facade of the museum, all the Bleaks had been exterminated during Richard's first crusade as head of the Regals. Clearly they'd missed one. Or else the Regals had doctored the records or exaggerated the victory, as they were wont to do. The man gave his wild beard an absent tug.

"You're pretty good with these guys," said Finch, hoping not to be caught staring too pointedly at the man's fingers. He gestured towards the enormous canines chewing happily side by side in the shady bank of the river.

"Oh, I've been hanging out with these dogs for years, man. They give me just as much as I give them, if not more. Sheila's just one of my friends. I'm sure the rest of the pack will turn up soon enough. They usually don't take to strangers, but it seems your pal here vouched for you."

"You think so?" Finch beamed at Horatio, his chest swelling.

"Hell I know it! You're a strange one for someone coming from Vulture."

"How'd you know where I'm from?"

"I can smell it on you, same as the dogs. Plus there aren't too many other places to come from these days. But I won't hold it against you. Like I said, you don't seem like the others that have come through here from those parts."

"Other people have been here?"

"Over the years, yes, but mostly just those drunk fools so lost in their own heads that they wind up out here. Of course, they generally end up in the belly of one of our friends." When he gestured again towards the dog-wolves his ratty sleeve rolled up, revealing several more black bands traversing the length of his arm.

"Is this the Columbia River?" Finch had so many questions for the man but forced himself to compose one at a time.

"So you've been to the library, I take it?" The man chortled. "You're close, but this is the Spokane River—the part that hasn't dried up yet, at least. It used to flow all through Spokane—Vulture, that is."

"So where does this river go?" The questions jumped from Finch's throat before he could stop them, one somersaulting into the next in his brain as they rushed toward his mouth.

"That's hard for me to say, to be sure. I haven't ventured that way in a long, long time. The outskirts can be unpredictable and at some point I became an old man. This river stretches into a few more miles of river to the east before petering out into a swamp that you'll smell before you see."

"What about to the west?" asked Finch, transfixed.

"To the west it'll link up with the Columbia, I'd wager. And the way the sea has risen, I wouldn't be too surprised if it went from there right on into the ocean." He pointed in the direction of a rickety dock that Finch hadn't noticed before. It jut out from the bank and stood on knobby wooden legs over the water.

Finch had no idea that the ocean might be this close to Vulture, thinking the man had surely misspoken. On the map it had looked so far away. Everything in Vulture was so enclosed and melted together that it was hard to imagine anything so expansive as the ocean. Only the outskirts loomed with such largeness in his imagination.

"How sure are you?"

"As sure as any old man's memory can be, friend. And you've seen the map. Back before the Water Wars changed everything— and I mean everything—this here river just about licked the walls of those city buildings. But if you want to check it out for yourself, I have a canoe you can take upriver if you like. It never gets much use from me, anyway."

The thought appealed to Finch. A vision of him and Horatio paddling up the river flooded his mind with romantic images torn from his novels. But his eyes flashed to the sun, which had already begun its ominous, earthward descent. With a pang of sadness, Finch realized they would soon have to head back to the station. Vulture had never felt so wonderfully far away.

"Thank you. Another time. We ought to get going. But thank you for the snack. It was really, really nice talking to you."

And Finch meant it. Never before had he conversed with someone so similar to himself. Besides their age difference, the man lived on his own and relied on dog-wolves for help. It was a compatibility he didn't even feel with Viro. And every other conversation he'd ever had with Vulture's various beings had hinged on his interlocutor preparing to do him harm.

"Don't mention it. Here, take a few for the road. We'll be here if you ever feel like venturing back to these parts. Just give a whistle and I'll be where the dogs are."

Already several other dog-wolves had joined the party, eagerly snapping lizard jerky from the man's palm. Most were brown like the female dog-wolf Sheila, but others had white or reddish-brown fur. None had the same dark black coat worn by Horatio, which Finch noted with no small pride. With some difficulty, Finch was able to lure Horatio away from the horde with the jerky the man had given him.

"Sorry, what was your name again, son?"

Nobody had ever called him son. Briefly he wondered if his own father, whoever he might have been, had ever referred to him like that. Finch filled his canteen in the river, and Horatio took several long slurps as well.

"Finch."

"Finch what?"

"Finch nothing, just Finch."

"Well it sure was nice to meet you Finch Nothing. You can just call me Guy. Guy Nothing for long, I suppose." The man chuckled at this last bit. Again the easy, joking cadence of Guy's tone struck Finch, utterly different from every other human interaction he could remember.

"So long, Guy."

Guy waved a shaky hand as they took off. It took them over three hours to get back to the station, racing the sun's descent as quickly as their tired steps would carry them. And yet Finch barely noticed the distance, buoyed by thoughts of escape, discovery, and hope. In the fading light of the outskirts they were still able to make out their dusty footprints. Bonfires in the distance marked the locations of the hooting Cannies welcoming the night.

They staggered up to the station door exhausted, having run and swam and soaked in the sun in a rare day of leisure. Their stomachs were narrow with hunger and dehydration. Horatio went to sniff around the ruinous strip mall but Finch lured him back with the last piece of lizard jerky. Horatio couldn't resist. He too took laborious steps before collapsing to the ground under the awning. Finch refilled his water bowl and sat by his friend, stroking him tenderly behind the ears. For the first time, Finch took a long, uninhibited sip of water from his canteen, and even refilled Horatio's bowl. Together they rested in Vulture's arid night.

Horatio drifted off into the deep ,untroubled sleep of animals and Finch wondered at the dog-wolf's shaggy head. There was no telling how many years Horatio had ventured these lands. The hairs by his nose were turning a light shade of gray that crept up his snout. Finch laid a hand on Horatio's stomach, his fur still matted in places where the river water had dried.

Back inside, after chasing the lizard jerky with a small handful of mushrooms, Finch locked his door and lit a candle. The absence of a fresh green thumbprint on his door did little to damage his mood. Unfolding the map from his backpack, Finch followed the blue line denoting the river to the west. Sure enough, the blue Spokane River line connected to the wider blue strip of the Columbia. Finch felt his heart rising to meet his hopes, trying unsuccessfully to tamp down his excitement.

But doubt tapped at his shoulder as he read the map, tracing the snakelike river lines with his finger. The landscape depicted on the map was unrecognizable; images of verdant mountains and gleaming cityscapes populated a sidebar panel on the map. Washington apparently used to be known as the Evergreen State, and yet Finch had never seen greenery or natural peaks like those depicted in the pictures before him. The Water Wars had flattened and scorched Washington and melted Spokane into Vulture.

Still, Finch refused to give up on the river, the maps stirring a wonder and enchantment in him that he could not control. Perhaps this was one of the pitfalls of his infatuation with novels; an overwhelming passion for the unreal. The river was the answer. Surely anywhere it led would be better than Vulture, even if it led only to a more remote locale abundant in edible vegetation and fresh water. He pictured a bucolic forest miles away from the paint gangs. He and Horatio would make their escape, he decided, take a chance on the river. He yielded himself to the joyous thought that Viro, too, would join them, as soon as Finch could tell him about all that he had discovered.

As his eyelids grew heavy, he carefully refolded the map and laid it on the desk. After checking the locks once more, he blew out the candle, sending the room into total darkness. He collapsed onto the mattress and thought only for a moment about the purple R still emblazoned on his door before he was overtaken by slumber.

CHAPTER 12

Choking on the ashes of her enemy

— Nirvana, *All Apologies*

Rigby slipped on an empty Pop Tart wrapper as she lunged out of bed, but quickly recovered her footing. A nest of candy wrappers and prepackaged food wrappings encircled her mattress. Her floor was barely visible through the accumulated trash and piles of paint-stained clothing. Already the sun cooked through her window and she felt sweat forming on her back. She took a sip from her canteen, letting the lukewarm water course down her dry throat.

A fresh purple handprint caught her eye. So that's what had startled her awake, some messenger slapping their freshly painted palm against the dirty wooden plank beside her window, which served as her personal message board. Everyone with a semi-permanent abode in the Regals had one, visible only to the knowing eye that could discern these functional items—sometimes mirrors, planks, or even objects as unlikely as boots or tires—from the purple markings that covered the rest of the buildings and refuse in Regal territory. The nomadic Regals relied on word of mouth for news of meetings outside of the recurrent weekly assemblies. Old, flaking handprints floated further up on the board above the most recent addition. Once this message board became full she'd have to paint over it with a new coat of white paint. The process wasn't perfect but it worked.

An older Regal had once told Rigby that years ago people sent each other messages electronically from small square tablets. But these were outlawed and destroyed along with all the other electrical sources and weapons in Vulture by the Bleaks after the Water Wars. The idea had been to begin society anew, without any of the accoutrements that had led to the earth's immolation by the dual threat of endless Water Wars and global warming. It was the most Rigby had ever heard about the Water Wars.

A purple hand meant a meeting at the next sunrise. She'd have to bring good news. Richard would not accept stasis on the project he had assigned to her. The dog-wolf had to die today, or tonight at the latest. She placed the blue paint in her backpack and draped the crossbow over her shoulders.

As she approached Factory Row, she sensed movement. Taking cover behind one of the many rusting iron walls that lined the path, she peered out. Twenty feet ahead, two Veins dragged a third off the path. It was the Vein Rigby had killed two nights ago, purple paint dashed across her eyes and a vicious maroon scar at her temple where the electrical cord had caught her. One of the draggers was a young boy. He stood only a few feet off the ground and he moved with the shuffling clumsiness of a child. He cried silently as his older companion clamped a hand over his mouth, though she cried, too. The crooked tracks of her tears coursed skinny paths through the blue paint on her face.

Family ties were rare in Vulture, though not unheard of. Most people chose to remain single. Rigby had always equated relationships with vulnerability. Vulnerable to moments like the one now playing out before her eyes. It was difficult enough to care about oneself here. Rigby couldn't look away. The two young Veins dragged the body off the road and then lifted it together, trudging in the opposite direction. The boy strained under the weight of the corpse—was it his mother? A sister, perhaps?—but he dared not stop.

Rigby's instinct was to follow them, find out where they resided in order to lay siege at a later date. She pushed the thought away, both disgusted and proud of her utter lack of empathy. It was certainly what Milo would do. She'd grant the Veins their peace today but she made no promises for the future. The Vein's words wormed their way past Rigby's mental barriers: *Vulture doesn't have to be like this.* She moved on.

Upon reaching the edge of the outskirts, she hunkered down behind one of the painted metal heaps jutting out of the asphalt. From this vantage, she had a direct view of the radio station. Too late she realized she'd forgotten her binoculars, distracted by the purple handprint. But it didn't matter. Soon enough she would give the indie reason to present his face, up close.

A large vulture circled high overhead, the eerie sound of its intermittent wing flaps echoing earthward. It wasn't long before the station's front door opened and the indie stepped outside. The massive dog-wolf greeted him eagerly. It had been clutching a bowl in its mouth and scraping at the reinforced door with its massive paw. The man filled the water bowl from his own canteen and the dog drained the whole bowl greedily with heavy slurps. Rigby made periodic turns of her head to be sure that nobody on the Vulture side of her could sneak up and surprise her from behind. The thick purple paint smattered across her body offered plenty of protection on its own, but its power was somewhat neutralized this far from Regal territory. Of course, it was daytime so any Canny out and about was likely drunk, lost or both. It was probably why the Veins she'd seen had chosen to deal with the body now rather than last night, too. She pushed the thought away again. With effort, Rigby filed the two crying Vein children in that same back corner of her mind, which was growing somewhat crowded. Turning her attention back to the station, she saw the man and the dog take off together, running toward Vulture.

She wondered if they were going on a hunt of some kind, maybe searching for whatever strange plants and mushrooms she'd seen at the bottom of the jars in his room. The indie carried no visible weapons, though maybe with a dog-wolf at his side, he didn't need any. The outskirts were aggressively lacking in shade and the sun beat down on Rigby's neck. Once the duo was out of sight, she worked quickly. Descending the small ridge that led down from the city limits, she dashed the short distance to the radio station. She wasn't sure how long the indie would be gone, and she had to be ready by the time he returned.

Accumulated tufts of loose, coarse, dark hair littered a gravel patch under the awning of the barber shop. So this was where the dog-wolf spent its nights. Again using the busted barber's chair as a step, Rigby clambered onto the roof. Once more she marveled at the ingenious sheet strung tightly across the roof, running her dry fingers over the cool, damp mesh. She positioned herself directly above the dog-wolf's resting spot. She notched an arrow and aimed downward toward the gravel patch beneath the awning, imagining the fatal shot. Luckily the awning itself was little more than a tattered scrap of tarp hanging from a few bent metal bars, leaving very little material to impede her shot. Satisfied, she tried to make her body as small as possible, flattening herself against the roof.

She hoped they wouldn't be back until after dark. Already the shadows that loomed off the bending, twisting skyline of Vulture began to stretch ominously. The city's inky black night would descend in a few hours.

Her plan involved two gambles that she would have normally avoided had it not been for the haste of Richard's timeline. First, she was betting that the dog wouldn't smell her and raise a barking alarm. Second, she risked the possibility that the roof-check she'd seen the man complete the other night when he'd pushed the Vein from his roof wasn't a regular part of his routine. Relying on chance felt foreign and troubled her. She wished she'd had more time to design a more foolproof plan. Her finger tapped against the trigger of the crossbow. For now she kept an eye on the cityscape that the indie and the dog-wolf had disappeared into as she shifted position on the shabby roof in the smothering heat of the late afternoon.

Nearly five hours passed before they returned. Her stomach felt queasy from the several Twix bars she wished she hadn't eaten, though they were melting to goop in her pocket and she didn't dare waste them. Her back ached from lying stiff on the concrete roof all afternoon. Pins and needles pierced her feet and numbed her legs. She shook them awake feverishly as the two figures approached. Dust and grime from the outskirts had crept its way into her hair and into the folds of her clothes. She touched her cheeks with her dirt-blackened fingers. They felt tender; probably sunburned. It was the only patch of skin left exposed to the elements, the rest covered by her jumpsuit or shielded by a curtain of purple stained dreadlocks.

The two shapes trotted toward her in the dim light of dusk. Already the faint glows of Canny bonfires were starting up along the shallow boundaries of Vulture. Rigby wondered what the man had been up to all day, though she quickly tamped down her imagination. She focused on her task, shifting her body into position, tensing her forearms and gripping the crossbow in her sweating hands.

She kept her head low beneath the lip at the edge of the roof. From this crouched position, she could hear the indie's ragged breathing as he and the dog-wolf stumbled up to the door of the radio station. Peering carefully down onto the ground, Rigby saw that they were soaked in sweat and filth and looked exhausted. She wondered if they'd been running from something, or someone. She quieted her own breathing to little more than a measured whisper and allowed the sweat to run into her eyes, refusing to risk making a sound by moving to wipe it away. Rigby could tell the dog-wolf was enormous just from the thunderous rumbles of its great bearlike breaths.

Her heart skipped a beat when the dog-wolf ambled around toward the other side of the building. She held her breath, fearing that the beast had picked up her scent, but after a moment the man's voice called the dog-wolf back to the doorway. He sounded tired and Rigby exhaled a silent breath of relief. The indie referred to the dog as 'Horatio', a word Rigby had never heard before. There were some strange names in Vulture, to be sure, but nothing like that, so far as she'd heard. It seemed strange to her that a dog-wolf would even have a name. It was just an animal, after all. She repeated this last bit to herself twice more, as if trying to convince herself that it was true.

The more she thought about it, she concluded that dog-wolves and people were really after the same things: food, water, a safe place to sleep. The image of the two Veins dragging away their downed comrade flashed across her mind's eye before she could suppress the vision. She blinked hard and refocused. The dog-wolf's belly pointed up at her like a big, dark target.

The man sat beside the dog-wolf, stroking its large head. Rigby worried he would fall asleep there, jeopardizing her plan.

Show up to the meeting empty handed and she'd likely end up with a fate worse than that of this Horatio. The clack and click of three separate locks jolted her out of her overheated, exhausted thoughts. Three locks meant the indie would have to spend time unlocking all three again, buying Rigby precious seconds to make her escape. But she worried about the man's capabilities. Evidently he'd kept pace with a full-grown dog-wolf running through Vulture all day. And she'd seen him heave an adult Vein trooper off of a roof with apparent ease. This roof, actually, she noted with chagrin.

Richard's logic made sense to her, cruel as it was. By killing the dog-wolf and blaming its death on the Veins, the indie might be more receptive to receiving help from the Regals, if not to avenge his loss by killing the alleged perpetrators of the deed than for protection from a second attack. Plus, by converting the indie into a vengeful trooper sporting Regal colors, Richard could hope to get rid of a few more Veins in the process; an added bonus. Maybe the indie could even hold a position of some prestige if he showed enough promise in eradicating the Veins. With guilt-laden thoughts of Pip lingering on her psyche, she tried to convince herself that her actions would somehow, ultimately, benefit the indie.

She waited a short while longer after the sound of the locks. It was late now, the sky starless and pure black as record vinyl. Surely the indie would be asleep by now. He had looked exhausted even from the distance at which she'd first seen him approaching, and he had probably risen with the sun. The dog-wolf, too, appeared to be sleeping. Long, low breaths emanated at steady intervals up from the ground where he snoozed. The sweat dried on Rigby's lips and she tasted the salty flavor. The dog-wolf's heavy breathing beat a rhythm in the silence of the desert night.

Even the periodic yowls of the Cannies had begun to fade.

Working silently and methodically, Rigby leveled the crossbow against the lip of the roof. The nocked arrow strained against the crossbow's taut cord. She trained the arrow on a point behind the dog-wolf's ears. Exhaling slowly, she pulled the trigger. The arrow leapt from the bow with ferocious quickness. A low thrum permeated the air, the crossbow's wire vibrating with the released tension.

Peering over the edge, she looked down at the dog-wolf. The heavy arrow stuck out of its neck at a savage angle. The rhythmic breathing eddied briefly before succumbing to silence. The dog-wolf was motionless, could even still be believed to be sleeping were it not for the arrow jutting out of its neck.

Rigby had no time to waste. Her legs were stiff from sitting in a crouched position all day and she winced as she dropped to the barber's chair below. The paint canister clattered against the canteen in her backpack. She had no idea how much time she had, her heart pounding in her ears. The man could wake at any moment. Rounding the corner of the defunct strip mall's far side, she hazarded a quick glance back toward Vulture. She grabbed the blue paint out of her bag as she measured the distance to the city's ominous threshold.

The odor of animal musk and the metallic smell of blood filled her nostrils. The dog-wolf's stomach had ceased its measured heaving and now the beast lay heavy as a car on its side. As soon as she opened the canister the heady, chemical smell of paint mixed in with the olfactory cocktail burning in her nose. Hopefully the smell wouldn't wake the indie, or attract Cannies, or worse, more dog-wolves. She covered her mouth with the purple bandana around her neck and affixed the goggles, which had previously been resting atop her head, over her eyes.

Steadying her hand, she painted the Veins' insignia over the purple R she'd left last time, an arrow-tipped blue V. The soft swishes of the paint brush echoed in the silence of the outskirts and Rigby quickened her pace. The electric blue paint shined bright and unmistakable even in the darkness. She'd never painted over the Regals' colors before, and even on orders it felt blasphemous. The dog-wolf joined the others in the back corner of her mind. Her hands shook with adrenaline as she applied a thick stripe of blue paint over the dog-wolf's eyes.

A brutal yank ripped the arrow from the animal's neck and warm blood spilled out of the gaping wound, pooling at her feet. As her heart quieted, the worst of her task finished, a sudden sound caught her attention. It was a heavy, rasping sound. She held her breath, following the noise. It was the dog-wolf, breathing painful, heavy breaths in the final throes of its life. These dog-wolves were notoriously resilient, but she'd never thought it would survive a shot from such a close range. Heart thumping in her chest again, she nocked another arrow on the crossbow, leveling it against the creature's wide skull.

Just as she was about to pull the trigger, Horatio's eyes flew open. Teeth bared, he landed a vicious bite on Rigby's arm. Had she not pulled the trigger at that exact moment, she might have lost the arm entirely. She screamed and dropped the crossbow to the ground, clapping a hand over her mouth as she wailed silently. The second arrow was lodged firmly between the dog-wolf's unblinking black eyes.

Collecting the crossbow and refusing to look at her arm, she prepared to flee. Worried that her scream had awakened the man, and too weak to yank out the arrow with one hand, she snapped it off at the base, leaving the wicked arrowhead planted in the dog-wolf's thick forehead. Ignoring her pain, she moved quickly, blending into the shadows. She sprinted across the musty asphalt, and just as she reached Vulture's grisly city limits, she swore that she heard the slide of a lock. But she never looked back. She sprinted through the dark city, feeling the blood coursing down her arm and streaming off her fingertips. Her usual precautionary slyness she abandoned in favor of speed. Adrenaline carried her along like a wave beneath her feet.

The record shop came into view and she slowed to listen for footsteps. Hearing nothing, she slipped up to the safety of the record shop attic. Once the adrenaline began to dissipate, she became aware of the throbbing pain in her right forearm. Looking down, she saw blood seeping through her sleeve.

Rigby hurriedly lit several candles—a difficult task with one functional hand—to inspect the source of the blood. Gingerly, she rolled up the soaked sleeve. She must have thrown her arm up in defense when the dog-wolf had harnessed its remaining life into one final bite. Piercing her forearm was the largest bite mark she'd ever seen, a perfect dagger that had gone almost straight through her arm. It must have been at least three inches long. It had pinned like a dart in the bump of a muscle on her forearm, leaving an unmistakable, tooth-shaped cavity. An inch to the right and it would have gone through the bone, leaving her permanently one-handed. Trails of dark red blood spout from the wound, mixing with splotches of blue paint in jagged bands around her arm.

She wriggled her fingers to make sure they still worked. With excruciating pain, the digits obeyed her command. The dog-wolf had refused to die without a fight after all. Over a defunct sink in her would-be bathroom, she set about stitching the gash. Taking deep breaths, she sutured herself with messy but effective stitches. It was not the first time she'd had to dress her own wounds, after all.

For a moment, tiny dots like dust particles swirled in front of her eyes, but then she recovered herself with a few steady breaths. Blood pooled in the bottom of her sink. She took a long sip of water from her canteen and poured out just enough over her arm to clean the wound. Gradually, her pulse returned to a normal rhythm.

The tooth had broken skin and some tissue but not much more. The other issue was the blue paint. She used up a few more precious splashes of water in an effort to scrub her arm clean. The blood melted away but the blue paint remained, tattooing blue splotches on her skin. She hoped the stains wouldn't be permanent but ultimately didn't care. She didn't want to waste any more water on something as superficial as paint stains. Personal appearance had never been high on her list of priorities.

But her health was. Maybe even at the top of the list. Carefully, she dressed the incision, cleaning it thoroughly with a baking soda concoction that stung her tender flesh before carefully wrapping a clean bandage around the wound. She grit her teeth as the baking soda seared her forearm but the pain ebbed to a dull throb once the bandage was secured.

Her aching back and heaving lungs begged for the bed that she now collapsed onto. She only moved to put on a Nirvana record. Once, on a day when he'd been in a good mood, Richard had told her that the band had been part of a movement in this part of the world known as 'grunge rock', several decades before the Water Wars. Rigby's knowledge of this former world was limited to what others had told her in bits and pieces, supplemented by the visions produced by the lyrics on her records. But the name 'grunge rock' certainly resounded with the look and feel of Vulture. Kurt Cobain usually got her to sleep with good dreams, she'd found. He'd made some kind of sense of the demons in his own world; perhaps he could help to decipher her world, too.

...

Rigby forced her feet forward into the theater hall the next morning. The sun pierced through her heavy eyelids, which hung defeated over her red eyes. The guard raised her eyebrows as Rigby muttered the password on her way through the revolving door.

"Beak."

"Rough night?" asked the guard, more curious than concerned. The Regals, Rigby knew, were always keen to latch on to gossip, secreting away any rumor that might be used to elevate themselves or to tear down another.

Rigby shrugged and walked on.

"So?" Milo's eyes were jumpy as ever, his tense jaw working back and forth. He couldn't have made it sound casual if he'd tried. Rigby knew what he was really after. He wanted to bring the update to Richard himself, ingratiating himself to the regime by such small degrees.

"Fuck off," said Rigby, without hesitating or meeting his twitching eyes. She shoved him with her shoulder as she walked by, still dazed from her nocturnal escapade and a severe lack of sleep. She ignored the throbbing pain in her stitched-up arm.

Richard barely looked up when she entered. Even before everyone had filtered into the creaky auditorium seats, he spoke. His low voice silenced the audience and resonated in the cool darkness of the theater.

"Tell me."

Those two words were all he said, all he needed to say. Rigby knew the comment was directed at her. She felt hundreds of eyes turn in her direction.

"It's done."

She chose to match his concise speech. The less she said the less likely it could be used against her. To Richard, words were ammunition. Her first thoughts this morning had been of the dog-wolf's eyes flashing open last night, just before sinking its tooth into her arm. She'd woken up early after a fitful sleep and had toyed with the idea of going back to the radio station to see what more had transpired. She'd even considered checking the museum to see if the Veins had weathered any kind of retaliation. But she'd decided against it, in the end. Had she been seen, the indie could be lying in wait for her return. Rigby scanned the theater for Miriam, hoping to find her so as to apologize, though she was not yet sure what she was apologizing for. But she didn't see Miriam anywhere. An odd feeling of melancholy overtook Rigby at the thought of Miriam disappearing from her life, though she knew Miriam would be safe enough with the far less brutal Veins.

Richard's cold, measured voice snapped her attention back to the meeting.

"Good," was all he said.

CHAPTER 13

We can't behave like people in novels, though, can we?

— Edith Wharton, *The Age of Innocence*

Finch's eyelids reacted faster than his brain, flitting open while grogginess still clouded his thoughts. He sprung from the bed. But he froze, standing tensed beside his mattress, unsure what had startled him out of sleep. Stars danced in front of his eyes and blood rushed to his head. It had been some kind of scream that had woken him up. At least, that's what he thought he'd heard. Perhaps he'd dreamt it in his heavy, fatigued sleep. But he couldn't take the chance. No shred of sun had yet broken through the jet-black night that loomed impenetrably beyond the station window.

His first thought was of the purple R still adorned on his front door. Perhaps the Regals had returned to further torment him, or maybe they'd seen his vandalism of the cinema mural. He felt like one of the cornered mice he sometimes saw in the outskirts, a snake slithering closer to make the final, inescapable kill. Finch paced about the room, unable to see much of anything through his window and paralyzed at the thought of opening his door.

Surely Horatio would be barking if anything were amiss. Maybe he had imagined the scream after all. Finch tiptoed to the door. With each step the hairs rose on the back of his neck and sweat slickened his palms. Carefully, he unhitched the first lock.

Putting his ear to the door, he heard nothing but the eerie silence of the outskirts. Something smelled odd, though. It was the scent of blood, and a chemical smell he couldn't quite place. He slid the second lock. The smell intensified as the door unclamped from the frame. Heaving away the final crossbar, he whipped open the door with a powerful tug on the knob.

Immediately something felt strange to Finch, his viscera contorting in response to some primal fear. At first he saw nothing but the dark expanse of the outskirts. The smell of blood and paint cloyed his throat and brought tears to his eyes. Then he saw Horatio. Finch dropped to his knees, running a trembling hand over Horatio's dark fur. It was matted in places by blood and paint. Finch felt as though someone had just lopped off his arm, and was still too stunned to feel the certain pain. But then thick tears began to roll down his cheeks. He couldn't tell if he was crying from the reek that hung thick in the air or the agony of losing the creature that had stood resolutely by his side in this vile, forgotten corner of the earth for so long.

Bending closer and wiping the moisture from his eyes, he could just make out the blue tint of the paint splashed across Horatio's eyes, barely visible in the pale moonlight. He followed the rivulets of paint back up to the wall.

There he saw the Veins' unmistakable color, painted in the very same insignia he'd applied to the Regal mural. So they'd taken their vengeance after all. They'd known Horatio had killed one of their members, and Finch pushing the Vein off his roof had probably stoked their wrath further. Or maybe they were punishing him for leaving their mark on Richard's portrait. This possibility gutted Finch, as it would mean Horatio's death was his own fault. He slumped against the wall and stared at the immense heap of dark fur resting in a pool of blood and paint under the awning. The tears left dry, sticky trails on his cheeks.

First the Regals had left their mark, and now the Veins had added their own. While the former's designs for him remained nebulous, the latter had already made one attempt on his life and they were sure to come again. The life he'd worked so hard to build here in Vulture began to slip through his fingers. The station door remained thrown open to the elements and Finch made no effort to close it. He wished Viro were by his side as he stroked Horatio's cold, stiff ears.

Slowly, rage built from the pit of his stomach and grew to fill his chest, subsuming his despair. His fists clenched and he looked out to the wasteland and back to the ruinous skyline of Vulture, now illuminated in the dull gray light of dawn. He had wasted hours fuming and crying. He refused to think of Horatio, about how his life would be now without his loyal friend of so many years. The light bled lugubriously out of the horizon, morphing from hazy gray rays to the scalding red of the sun's first touches on Vulture. It bathed the quiet city in a pool of scarlet before passing finally over Finch, casting his hands in a reddish glow.

Finch bent over Horatio, running his hand a final time over the slope of his friend's broad head. But he stopped when his finger caught on a sharp ridge right where the fur ought to have been most smooth, right between the dog-wolf's eyes. The morning light revealed the site of the wound. Blood spouted from two distinct spots, one just behind Horatio's ear on his neck and the other directly between his eyes. Leaning closer, Finch inspected the wounds. They could only have come from one weapon. The only weapon in Vulture powerful enough to kill a full-grown dog-wolf was a crossbow. And only one gang in Vulture had access to crossbows. Finch's fists fell to his sides as these facts descended upon him in a flash of renewed clarity. It had been misdirection—just as he had tried to misdirect them—perhaps even a trap. They could be preparing to ambush him right at this moment.

Leaving the door open, Finch didn't give his books a second thought as he set off toward the museum. He paused only to lay his hand against Emerson's essay. As long as he'd had it pinned to his door, he realized he'd never taken its message to heart. He'd read the words without embodying them to the extent necessary to his survival. *Self-reliance* was his mantra, and yet he'd failed to execute it in practice. Instead, he'd become a pawn in a fatal game played by two gangs at his expense. But no longer. Finch resolved to act, embittered and guilt-ridden by his failure to do so for so long. Without Horatio by his side, he must become truly self-reliant, in demonstrative action rather than weakly taking comfort in the concept's theoretical promise. The same fire that had burned in his chest the night he threw the Vein from his roof now smoldered furiously in his limbs. For too long he had played defense where self-reliance called for offense. Fear had undermined his resolve, made him vulnerable to exploitation. First he would deal with the Veins, then the Regals. Every gang was a threat, and thus he must become a threat himself.

As he walked purposefully toward the museum, Finch formulated the crude beginnings of a plan. After taking action against the Veins and the Regals, he'd find Viro and give him an ultimatum: flee with him to the river or allow him, finally, to join the Scorps. Finch could use whatever force he applied to the rival gangs—be it destruction of their headquarters or their numbers—as proof of his allegiance to the Scorps. The thought of murder, so repulsive to him as recently as last night, felt more tangible than ever in his clenched and throbbing fists. He felt as though for the first time his eyes had been opened to the simple reality of Vulture: kill or be killed. While he'd understood this on a conceptual level from the time he was a child, he now felt its truth boiling in the marrow of his bones. His precious books had given him only a romantic sense of humanity's susceptibility to evil—Milton's Satan, Melville's Ahab, Conrad's Kurtz. But Horatio's death had illuminated that distinctly human evil in a way that the authors' words could only imitate. As he walked, all he knew was a rage that had taken the place of the dog-wolf by his side. He had never felt sharper, like a dog-wolf—like Horatio himself—loping through Vulture content in the knowledge that he would be feared.

Two Cannies jumped out in front of him, blocking his path as he passed one of the larger piles of compacted cars along the city's outer edge. The Cannies were young, drunk but lithe, and bounced from foot to foot as they leered at Finch.

"Hey there rushy, where ya rushin' off to?"

"Join us for a bite, indie?"

Finch barely broke step. Just as the Cannies opened their mouths to cackle horribly at their booze-clouded jokes they crumbled to the ground, Finch grabbing them both by their scrawny throats and thrashing their skulls together in one severe movement. Finch heard them moaning on the ground behind him as he walked on. He didn't look back. His feet resumed their resolute pace in the direction of the museum.

By the time he got there the sun was high in the sky. Intricately painted and maintained timelines were sprawled across the museum walls. Neat, pictographic histories of each gang were inscribed alongside detailed maps of Vulture with dates beginning at 1, the year after the end of the Water Wars. Over twenty years of history, amended in places by purple, blue, and green paint were represented along the sides of the dilapidated edifice. Finch wasn't tempted to pause to decipher these graphics as his curiosity would naturally compel him to do, too inflamed by bloodlust.

He imagined ravaging the museum, killing all the occupants in Horatio's name and tearing the building apart stone by stone. Every muscle clenched, he circled to the front of the building. There he halted. An indie, perhaps a little younger than himself, scurried past. Finch watched the young boy dash from shadow to shadow, could see the frantic whip of his head as he scampered fearfully through Vein territory.

Gradually, moving in frantic spurts, the indie made it past the museum and began curling back toward the outskirts. He turned to watch the young indie disappear into the shimmering horizon. Finch's arms fell to his sides as fatigue and doubt filled his limbs. The fire in his chest was blown out as though by a sharp wind, leaving him feeling empty and cold. No amount of violence would bring Horatio back, he realized, fresh tears burning in his eyes. As he turned to walk back to the radio station, he nearly bumped into Richard's tankard-sized chest.

He would have recognized the hulking man anywhere. Finch was tall, and yet Richard stood nearly two heads above him. His massive frame eclipsed the sun, and his long shadow swallowed Finch in its dark expanse. Finch stumbled backward, stunned.

The portraits of Richard had hardly been idealized. He really was nearly seven feet tall, standing on legs as thick as telephone poles. His skin was smooth and clean. It was the kind of thing one noticed in Vulture. His monumental bald head rested upon shoulders a meter wide and a chest as dense as a truck engine. Thick purple oil paint bordered his furtive eyes and neatly coated the dome of his skull. His simian jaw was contorted into a carnivorous smile.

If this was not the man who'd handily conquered Vulture,

surely no such man existed. Richard was simply too large a structure to be ignored. He was seemingly built of the very metal that clumped together and survived for decades here in Vulture, fusing into compacted, immovable masses. Richard's terrifying stature was as much a part of the city's cruel skyline as the twisted, crooked buildings that stretched up into the cloudless atmosphere.

Neither spoke at first. Finch's vision went blank as he stared up at Richard. It was not exactly fear that he felt. The loss of Horatio had left him stripped of emotion. His typically frenzied, analytical mind was muted, replaced with an exhaustion that wracked his body.

"Can I help you?" Finch asked. The words tripped off his dry tongue.

Richard's eyes flickered, surprised by Finch's irreverent tone and accustomed to immediate, unquestioned subservience.

"As a matter of fact, you can," came Richard's articulate reply. "And perhaps I can help you as well, Finch."

Finch wasn't surprised that Richard knew his name. If knowledge meant power then surely the reverse was true, too. Finch shrugged and scuffed the gravel with his toe.

"I doubt that," said Finch, moving to sidestep Richard's enormous frame. Richard blocked his way with a subtle step to his left. Finch stared at the thick, heavy knuckles hanging by Richard's sides.

"Do you? So this is you…thriving, then?" intoned Richard, mockingly appraising Finch's shrunken, slouched form with several flickering eye movements. Finch shuddered at the mirthful smile plastered on Richard's face, at the eerie white of his teeth.

"I don't need your help," repeated Finch, though he didn't try to walk away again.

"Don't you ever think the world might have more to offer you, perhaps?" ventured Richard. He took a step closer, drowning Finch in his shadow.

"No," replied Finch, shutting out an image of Horatio that flashed across his vision.

"But don't you want revenge over what these Veins did to your friend? What did you call him, Horatio?"

"You killed him," replied Finch through gritted teeth.

"Ooh, you are a clever boy. We could use a thinker like you. What do you say?"

"Not interested."

"Pity," said Richard. "But what if I told you that you could enjoy power, safety, food and water... all the books you could ever want?"

Finch tried to ignore the saliently included detail about the books, but he couldn't stop his imagination from picturing a vast library, shelves crammed with books, somewhere hidden in the Regal cinema. But what use would Richard have for books? Finch was wary. Clearly this encounter had been planned, the final domino to fall after the initial strike of the purple R on his door. Still, it seemed to Finch like an awful lot of trouble to go to for a simple recruitment. It wasn't the first time he'd been recruited, but it was certainly the most dastardly—a nefariousness befitting the Regals. When the Veins had first split from the Regals, they'd left Finch a map with the museum marked in a blue V, which they'd slid under the radio station door. The Scorps too had observed him from afar, no doubt hoping to gain an edge over the ever-expanding Regals with the addition of every indie they could get. He might have accepted their offer had it not been for Viro's subsequent interference. All of them he'd denied, wary of traps and confident that he was more suited to the life of an indie rather than acting on the orders of some gang. Still, all of the other offers he'd preferred to Richard's current proposition.

"Not interested."

"Ah, but what if I told you this paradise is indeed Vulture, where we now stand? This place can be…shall I say…Regal if you make the right connections."

"No thanks." Finch's head felt hazy, and he had difficulty forming thoughts. He forced himself to focus, refusing to let his face betray his terror. He planted his feet firmly on the ground to keep them from shuffling.

"You must think I'm some kind of a monster," said Richard, though he sported a serpentine smile as he spoke. Finch could feel Richard's hot breath rustling the hairs on the top of his head.

"On looks alone, yes," said Finch, evenly. He surprised himself with his own confidence, the words tripping out of his mouth of their own accord. But if Richard wanted him dead he would surely have killed him by now. He must want something.

Richard scoffed at Finch's remark and the twisting smile on his face turned somehow more sinister, his eyes narrowing. Finch thought he saw a ripple of anger pass over the massive face, though the change in expression was almost imperceptible.

"Enough chit-chat," said Richard, the false glee stripped from his tone. "You show promise. You may even remind me a bit of myself. Come. You can walk back with us as a free member of the Regal gang or else you'll be marched there as our prisoner until you change your mind. Thoughts?"

Finch said nothing and stared back into Richard's merciless eyes. He would have to time it carefully; enough time had been wasted already. Rearing back, Finch lunged at Richard with a vicious punch aimed at his gut, something to bend him down to a more vulnerable height. But before Finch's fist had reached Richard's body, what felt like a cement block rammed into the side of his skull. Finch reeled backwards and landed in a heap on the ground. His head throbbed and the raging sunlight hurt his eyes when he looked up. Two Richards stood above him before gradually merging back into one, wiping a clean purple handkerchief over his fist as though polishing a recently employed dagger.

"Let's go," said Richard. Two sets of hands appeared behind Finch. He felt himself being lifted to his feet and he lashed out again. His elbow connected with someone's nose and he heard a sharp crack followed by a shout. Before he could turn around to see who he'd struck, he felt zip ties being cinched around his wrists. They made a cruel plastic sound as they tightened.

Richard didn't even glance back at the commotion.

"Milo, torch it," he said.

Finch watched as the one called Milo, a lean younger man with jerking, energetic movements, set off in the direction of the radio station. He'd walk right through the open door, Finch realized with a sinking feeling. For the first time in his life he hoped Viro wasn't there. Richard took a heavy seat upon an ancient black motorcycle that Finch hadn't noticed before. It was painted with purple prints, mimicking a leopard's coat. Finch had never seen a working motor in Vulture. Of course Richard would have a motorcycle, and of course he would drive it the few miles from the cinema to the station; further luxury by which to inspire Finch, no doubt.

Finch struggled against the zip ties and attempted to break free from the other set of hands clenched tightly on his arm. This time he received a sharp knee to the ribs that sent him crashing to his knees. This was followed by another kick in the stomach, maybe a personal blow in return for the broken nose. Within a few minutes the man named Milo reappeared. He cast a sardonic smile towards Finch as he resumed his place in the rear of the party and, wordlessly, the trio with their captive began to make their way back toward the city. Richard puttered slowly on the motorcycle in front of them, the exhaust emanating horribly back into the faces of the walkers. The pungent smell of the burning gas choked Finch. He realized now where the mechanical drone he'd always heard around Vulture must have originated—the city's sole operant engine.

Then a new smell struck his nostrils, breaking through the scent of the exhaust and sending Finch's heart plummeting into his stomach. The smell was of paper burning, pleasant at first like a Canny bonfire, before changing to the sickly, thick smell of chemicals sizzling, like burnt rubber or melted plastic. A staccato popping sound followed and looking back to the outskirts, Finch watched as an enormous orb of flame swallowed the radio station he'd called home for so many years. Milo smacked him but Finch didn't look away. The smoke from the paint bomb eddied off the radio station and mingled with the still fizzling exhaust of the motorcycle. The water sheet tethered to the station roof twisted and floated in the air before falling in flames to the ground like an injured bird. It wasn't until another knee to his ribs struck the wind out of his lungs that Finch continued stumbling into Vulture. The sky was a villainous red, further illuminated by the phosphorescent yellow hue cast by the fire that raged at the party's rear, growing more distant with each step.

They didn't bother to blindfold him. Finch knew as well as everyone in Vulture where he was being taken. By nature of avoiding the cinema at all costs for most of his life, he knew exactly where it was. As they approached, more Regals began to appear. Purple markings, gilded portraits, and infinite purple R's covered every surface. Through paint-smeared eyes the Regal onlookers watched as Finch was led through the revolving door and down to the basement. With tense movements, the purple-clad crowd parted for Richard as he walked unhurriedly through the building, looking only straight ahead, his powerful, jutting chin pointed high and unmoving. Finch tried to match his captor's resolve but kept inadvertently meeting the eyes of the Regals. There were so many of them, men and women, all young and thin but not sickly like the Cannies, hungry like the Veins, or sun deprived like the Scorps. They looked healthy, like a pack of wild dog-wolves, eating regularly enough and made strong by survival.

Some troopers applied paint to each other's knotted hair and faces and spoke in hushed tones that fizzled into silence as Richard's ominous presence became known, his massive shadow obliterating any light that streamed through cracks in the building. Other Regals lounged in the sagging chairs of the theater before snapping to the seat's edge as the posse walked by. A small crowd watched as a young man and a woman in her thirties grappled brutally to settle a rank dispute. They were the last to notice Richard's giant presence. He paused as he walked past.

"Well don't stop on my account," he said to the wrestlers.

Finch could hardly stand the jocularity of Richard's tone. The two Regals resumed their fight. Both had black eyes and bleeding lips but showed no signs of tiring.

Finch felt almost naked without the splatters of purple paint that smeared everyone who now watched him with rapt attention. Perhaps that's how Richard wanted him to feel, a desire to blend in. Parts of the scene certainly did look appealing, Finch hated to admit. The figures gathered in the cinema had a strange look of pride. These were the people thriving in the wake of the Water Wars. Somehow they had all ended up here, taking on each day as though it were an opponent. Finch hated himself for being impressed. His hands throbbed where the zip ties cut off his circulation.

The purple hands delivered him into the basement. The room was dim to the point of darkness. It smelled of mildew and copper pipes and was roughly square in shape, with just one door and not much floorspace. Chains were mounted along the wall at various intervals, ending in rusted metal collars or shackles peppered with brown flecks of dried blood. A rat scurried across the floor at the sound of footsteps. Along another wall were rows and rows of etched marks, a count or tally of some kind. The thin lines started out hard and defined before petering out into weak scribbles further down the line. Dried stains of different hues of crimson spotted the floor in sticky puddles. An ancient leather armchair rested in one corner, the only piece of furniture in the otherwise bare room. Richard nodded and the two escorts left the room wordlessly, Milo leaving Finch with one final smirk.

"Welcome home," said Richard, brightly. "I think you'll find it to be equal in comfort to that dump you were living in before. Food and water will be delivered to you three times a day and anytime you feel like changing your mind and joining up with the strongest gang in Vulture, just say the word and your training will begin. I can't imagine the choice will be hard but some people can be quite indecisive."

He spoke in a casual manner that made Finch's skin crawl. Finch said nothing but turned to move toward the ratty armchair, suddenly exhausted by the exertion of the day and the sleepless night. Before he could take even two steps he felt Richard's heavy hand on weighing his shoulder. With a twist of his fingers, Richard snapped the zip ties that bound Finch's wrists. He smiled coyly as he pushed Finch into the chair.

"Perhaps the junkyard will be more to your liking. Think about it." Richard turnd on his heel and walked out the door. Finch heard the dull thud of the lock tumbling into place. The air was cool in the damp darkness of the basement though it did little to quell the intense thirst that now coated his throat.

Finch massaged his wrists as he reclined on the blocky chair. He tried to push away thoughts of the smoldering radio station and his burning books, but to little avail. They hadn't even ransacked the place for his water, or for the mushrooms and sprouts he'd never again enjoy—items so rare now as to be priceless. He thought of Viro showing up, freshly painted green thumb at the ready, only to find the station burnt to cinders. Finch wondered if Viro would cry. In destroying the station, the Regals were demonstrating how little they worried for such necessities as food and water, and how little they cared for Finch. It was the image of books burning that plagued Finch's fitful sleep that night. He thought of his novels and the law tomes and the news scraps bursting into flame, the words slowly blackening to ash on the page.

CHAPTER 14

Out here in the fields
I fight for my meals
I get my back into my living

— The Who, *Baba O'Riley*

Rigby was glad that she'd missed the action. She'd seen prisoners hauled in before and could never stomach Richard's performative reserve. Though he had always delighted in the triumphant march of a prisoner to their cell, there had never been an inmate of such personal interest to him before. Usually, the captives were used as bargaining pieces with other gangs or stripped of their colors and relegated to the junkyard. However, Rigby would have liked to see the indie up close, glimpse a face to pair with the distant body that had thrown the Vein from the station roof.

Her instrumental role in pushing the vigilante to the edge, flushing him out into the open where he could be nabbed, filled her with no small pride. She gently rubbed the tender part of her forearm. It was still sore and looked like a wicked eye, the tooth-shaped scar staring out from ominous spots of bright blue paint. The tooth mark was beginning to form a scaled crust of scab at the edges, but even a light press from her finger sent pain shooting up and down her arm. Working cumbersomely with one arm, she pulled on a long-sleeved gray shirt, to which she applied a few fresh splatters of purple paint, giving it a blotchy camouflage pattern. In addition to shielding her skin from the intense heat, the long sleeve effectively hid the wound. Any vulnerability was liable to be exploited, even by members of her own gang.

Music had become less of a simple pleasure and more of a kind of medicine for Rigby. Every time she closed her eyes she'd see the children pulling the murdered Vein out of the street. The music helped to drown out her thoughts, and gave her a different world to picture. Even touching her records, fingering their weathered jackets and smooth, ridged surfaces relaxed her.

Rigby trudged to headquarters, forcing one foot in front of the other. Her stiff back protested against the tight twists of the bus wall as she clambered through her shortcut. Only the knowledge that being a Regal helped her to stay alive allowed her to plaster a content, if wary, surmise on her face. It was the same face worn by almost everyone, as much a part of her costume as the purple paint in her hair. Blending in was safe; a smile would have been too much. She didn't join in the gossip about the prisoner. Again, she scanned the purple bodies for Miriam but couldn't locate her. Nobody was allowed down to the basement without Richard's express order. Ledo, a young Regal that Rigby had recruited from the outskirts a couple years ago, approached her. Not unlike most of the Regals milling about the cinema lobby, he was wiry and tense. But Ledo was more genuinely enthusiastic about the gang then most. Rigby didn't blame him. When she'd found him he'd been nearly dead from thirst in the outskirts. At least the gang rations had done him some good, sinewy muscles traversing his arms and chest.

"Rigby! You hear about the indie?" he asked, unable to suppress his jubilant tone.

"No, I live under a rock," she replied, sarcastically. The words left her mouth more rudely than she intended, though she let the tone linger.

"Well, I saw him," Ledo said, drawing himself up. "I heard he's read a bunch of books. Might even be some kind of genius. You think that's true?"

"He seems capable of it."

Rigby shrugged and moved to walk past but Ledo stepped back in front of her. His thin eyebrows were invisible beneath the thick coat of paint across his forehead.

"You think Richard will kill him?"

"Nah, he wouldn't waste meat like that."

Mentally, Rigby cautioned herself to be less flippant. That comment alone could be misconstrued as a critique of Richard by someone looking to undermine her. The thought doesn't seem to cross Ledo's mind. He'd always looked up to Rigby.

"So you think he'll join then?"

Rigby could see the hope burning in his jumpy brown eyes. Ledo was the perfect accolade. Ever on the hunt for someone else to follow, the impressionable Ledo seemed already to have been awed by the mysterious indie. He cracked his knuckles one at a time, even after they ceased to make the satisfying snapping sound.

"Yeah, I'm sure Richard will find something for him," Rigby offered diplomatically. From every corner of the large room, Rigby heard whispers. However, that fact alone was not noteworthy in and of itself. In the cinema, people rarely ever spoke in a tone louder than a whisper. But today, the whispers flitted around her ears and clouded the air like gnats. She made an excuse and walked on, leaving Ledo still snapping away at his knuckles behind her. From the corner of her eye she saw Milo making his way toward her from across the room, his bouncing steps recognizable anywhere. Hoping to escape the gossip, she pushed through a heavy side door and stepped outside into the rear lot.

When she noticed Pip standing alone there on the threshold of the junkyard, she tried to catch the door in its swing. But she wasn't fast enough, and he'd already made eye contact.

"Hey Rigby," he said, in that awful, hollow tone of his. Rigby winced and turned to face him.

"Pip, hey. What are you working on?"

Pip, shriveled as ever, squatted behind Richard's enormous black motorcycle. With careful strokes, he reapplied splotches of paint, ornamenting the sharp black metal with leopard prints of purple. The motorcycle was ostentatious and gaudy but Richard had never much cared for the understated. It wasn't enough that he had the only functioning motor in all of Vulture; it had to make a statement. Rumor had it that Richard had secreted a small stockpile of gas and used the bike seldom. Oftentimes junkers were tasked with the miserable chore of collecting whatever runoff gas they could find in the junkyard, spending hours just to collect a few droplets. Rigby had only ridden the motorcycle a few times in her life, and always with Richard guiding her young hands. She hadn't ridden it in years, though she'd never forget the powerful thrum of the engine as she twisted the throttle. Richard would typically only fire the old bike up for major gang raids, swooping into the encampment in a frenzied burst of raging speed and escaping unscathed just as quickly. Richard adored the motorcycle and loved more the way he looked when seated upon it, enthroned.

Pip held up his paintbrush and shrugged in explanation. Rigby nodded in acknowledgement. The brush rasped gently against the smooth metal with each small stroke. The paint oozed and bubbled on the baking hot steel frame. Not knowing what else to say and growing uncomfortable in the silence, Rigby turned precisely to the gossip she'd gone outside to escape.

"You heard about that prisoner?"

"Yeah. He's got Richard in a good mood."

The monotone of Pip's voice gave Rigby chills. She squeezed at the thoughts tucked in the back corner of her brain.

"Any idea what Richard's plans are with him?" ventured Rigby.

"Probably the same thing he does to us," mused Pip, absently. "Starve him and hurt him until he follows orders."

Pip spoke so matter-of-factly that he could have been discussing the weather. Rigby noticed a fresh bruise on his neck and looked away.

Wanting to do anything besides standing hunched in front of him, hands in her pockets, Rigby knelt down beside the motorcycle. She took the paintbrush from Pip in a weak, apologetic attempt to help him touch up the designs. But as soon as her hand formed a grip around the brush handle, a shooting pain jolted through the tendons in her arm and she dropped the brush on her lap, adding a new, unintentional smear of paint to her pants.

Pip looked up at her for the first time. The scorching sun formed pools of shadow in his sunken cheeks. He cocked a slim eyebrow while looking her full in the face.

"I'm fine," Rigby grimaced.

She tugged up her sleeve to inspect the welt on her arm. The veins that surrounded the wound throbbed and contorted under the smattering of blue paint stains.

Remembering Pip, she shot a severe look into his sad, tired eyes, which were observing the tooth-shaped divot in her arm through narrowed eyelids.

"Don't tell Richard."

Rigby had meant the words to sound like a warning, carrying with them an 'or else' tone. But they came out more like a plea.

"Sure," said Pip, offering another limp shrug after a pause. His bony shoulders rose and fell in a jerky motion.

Rigby tugged her sleeve back down and shuffled quickly back inside. The cumulative whispered hum of gossip had intensified. All around her she saw people gesticulating and peering over their shoulders, eyes wide and hands chopping the air. She wanted to go home to the record shop. It was all getting to be too much, the gang hanging like a cement necklace around her throat that she could not remove for fear that she would die. She had no interest in the indie, and her role in his capture, Richard's triumphal smugness, and the gang's excitement at the prospect of the indie's conversion to a violent, scared Regal trooper, was beginning to make her nauseous. She wanted to flood her mind with lyrics that were utterly different than her reality, something upbeat and transportive, like Sly and the Family Stone, Prince, Talking Heads, or Michael Jackson. Already lining up tracks in her head, slipping the records out of their slender cardboard sleeves and setting them gently on the turntable, Rigby struck out for the door—she'd made enough of an appearance for others to claim they'd seen her joining in the excitement, and as no meeting had been called, she needn't stay longer than necessary. Just before she reached the door, a figure stepped in front of her.

"What do you want, Milo?" she sneered.

"Aw, come on golden girl, where's that charm that everyone around here loves so much?"

He smiled patronizingly down at her. His face was mirthful, his tongue flicking back and forth over his thin white lips. She glared back into his jumpy, piggish eyes.

"Fuck off Milo, I'm not in the mood."

184

She tried to walk around him and again he stepped into her way.

"There's the charm! Cute, really. I'd watch that tone with me though, by the way."

"And why's that?"

Milo's obvious excitement worried her. His heels never touched the ground and he never remained on one foot for more than a second before shifting his weight to the other. His eyes looked especially frantic, separated by his crooked, purple nose. Maybe the indie had gotten a decent strike in before being captured, thought Rigby, smiling internally.

"I happen to know some information that I think would be of some interest to you."

"Let me guess, you want more Leak but you're too scared to go get it from the Cannies on your own?"

Again, he blocked her path and Rigby clenched the fist on her good arm. His beady eyes darted about her face and the awful smile still stretched across his cheeks, his small tongue licking his lips in spastic movements.

"Funny. Very clever, Rigby. But no. I'm talking about this."

With a quick, violent swipe of his arm, Milo snatched up Rigby's wrist—the one on her good arm—and pulled up her sleeve to reveal her tattooed forearm.

"So what? It's no secret," she said, yanking her hand away and pulling down her sleeve. "And if you ever grab me like that again I'll break that ugly nose of yours—for a second time, from what it looks like."

Milo ignored her threat and went on bouncing and grinning.

"Ah, but you don't get it, do you? I thought maybe it was just a coincidence… but then, well, have you seen him yet? Up close, I mean."

Milo was inching closer and closer, their voices growing more and more hushed. Rigby recoiled at the fetid smell of his breath but did not run away. Though the scene might have looked odd on any other day, they managed to blend in with the fervent whisperers that crowded the lobby.

"No."

"You see, I've been given primary responsibility for the captive. And the thing is, he looks like you. Well, a bit prettier, actually." Milo laughed at his own joke.

"What's your point?" hissed Rigby.

"I don't think it's a coincidence. Nobody in Vulture has tattoos like that. The Veins have their silly arrow marks of course, but not words. No, that's an old world tattoo you've got. And if I'm not mistaken, you've had that one forever, correct?"

Rigby was silent, no longer sure how much to reveal to Milo. How much had Richard told Milo about her origins, Rigby wondered?

"I'll take that as a yes," he continued. "The thing is, I have a hunch you two are related. You had a brother, didn't you?"

Milo was grasping at something—anything—to gain leverage over her. Thoughts leapt through her mind, and she had to consciously clamp her mouth shut. Milo could have already suggested this wild theory to Richard. She refused to believe him. Milo had always been a liar, always looking for other ways up the Regal ladder. If that meant tearing down the rungs below him, so be it. He was just surviving like everyone else, constantly poking around for vulnerabilities to be exploited. The existence of her tattoo and the brother she'd lost at a young age were known by most of the Regals—certainly by those members who formed the gang's upper echelon. Finally, Rigby spoke:

"Enough Milo. What are you getting at?"

186

For a long moment he simply leered down at Rigby, bouncing excitedly from foot to foot.

"He's got the same tattoo. The prisoner, I mean."

Milo spoke the words slowly and delightedly, as though each one were a morsel of candy to be rolled around in the mouth until dissolved into sweet liquid.

"How do you know, you can't read," snapped Rigby.

"Well, no, of course not. But it does look eerily similar to yours. Same thin line of text in black ink, faded with time. They might've been done by the same hand, don't you think?"

A flood of curiosities so large poured suddenly into Rigby's imagination that she thought she could drown. Never before had she so badly wanted to return to the record shop.

"You're nuts," she snarled. "And have you shared this idiotic theory of yours with Richard?"

She wasn't sure what to believe at the moment, but she was positive that the less people who knew, the better. Especially Richard. There was no telling how he'd react if he thought Rigby was related in some way to his prize prisoner. Maybe he wouldn't care. Or maybe he'd get suspicious. She decided it was better to play it safe.

"Not yet," cooed Milo.

It was clear this was the moment he'd been waiting for, his arrogant, gleeful tone reaching a crescendo on the two syllables. His tongue flicked about his wet mouth and though his eyes jumped wildly around her face, he never blinked.

"What do you want?" asked Rigby again, this time understanding the stakes. "More Leak?"

Milo swelled up dramatically, as if about to make some grandiose pronouncement.

"Oh, I'm a simple man you know me," said Milo, feigning

modesty. "But how about I come over to that old record shop you call home later and we try to figure something out."

As he spoke he took another step toward Rigby and raised his hand to brush the locks of purple hair away from her face. Instinctually, she slapped his hand away and shoved him backward, hiding the pain it caused her arm with a tight grimace. He was still smiling, staring back at her with his beady, unblinking eyes.

"I've always admired your spunk," he said, though he spit out this last word as though it left an acrid taste in his mouth.

Rigby shoved him aside with her shoulder and walked out the door, not looking back. Physical altercations were commonplace enough around the cinema that nobody paid them any mind. Over her shoulder she heard Milo's mock pleasant voice.

"Think about it!" he called.

She didn't have much of a choice in that regard. All she could do was think about it. All the way home thoughts of a brother and Milo and Richard swirled in her brain. Wracking her memories, she still came up with little more about her life before the Regals than what Richard had told her. She'd been so young when she'd first been taken in. They'd basically raised her. Try as she might, she could not shove these new thoughts into that back corner with all the rest. She needed music, old songs about chivalrous men and acts of passion, seductive women and love worth dying for. Surely none of that existed now; Milo was proof enough. She found the idea that such a romantically-inclined time had ever existed entirely preposterous, and yet all the records that lined her walls begged to differ. Or maybe those songs had been distractions back then, too, unreal auditory portals through which listeners could briefly escape their burdensome reality.

Finch stirred at the sound of keys unclenching the ancient pad-lock that sealed the basement door. Already he'd lost track of time, though he couldn't have been a prisoner for much longer than a day, he thought. A single window the size of a car's head-rest filtered in the room's only light through filmy green-yellow glass. He'd slept in snatches and woke when some grunting, purple-spattered figure slid him a bowl of rice or a half empty water bottle. Bleary-eyed and anxious, he looked toward the door. Though a hazy light strained through the small window and filled the room with foggy gray visibility, Finch could make out only a bright orange glow advancing toward him, perhaps a lantern of some kind. After seeing a working motorcycle, a lamp wouldn't necessarily have surprised him.

As his eyes adjusted to the dim lighting, he watched the one called Milo advancing toward him. Even in the darkness Finch recognized the jerky steps, the restless hands. One hand was wrapped in a grimy towel, which clenched tightly upon a long iron crowbar. The orange glow emanated from the tip of this crowbar. Finch couldn't tell if it was on fire or simply heated to a molten glow. Neither question put Finch much at ease. He straightened up on the chair that had become his island in the empty room.

"Good morning, inmate" said Milo, all too brightly.

He rocked up and down on the balls of his feet, nervous en-ergy coursing through his body and making him incapable of standing still. Finch said nothing, keeping his eyes on the menac-ing glow of the crowbar.

"Yes," mused Milo, following Finch's gaze. "Richard thought you might need a conversation starter."

Despite the faint light, Finch could tell that Milo was amused by his own joke. Milo's fingers drummed against the crowbar's handle through the protective rag.

"So. You're Finch. Want to join the Regals?" Milo asked with mock exuberance, as though he were a child beseeching Finch to play with him.

"No," croaked Finch.

His voice was hoarse with thirst and lack of use. He felt his hands and feet go clammy as Milo approached.

Without warning, Milo pushed the crowbar's business end into Finch's left shoulder. The hot metal scorched his skin through his shirt and he screamed and recoiled, falling out of the chair and onto the musty floor. Finch sprang back up onto his feet, preparing for another attack and holding his burnt shoulder tenderly. His mind went blank and his vision blurred as the heat pulsed through his shoulder.

"Relax," said Milo, the crowbar returning to the relaxed position at his side. "That was just so you know where you stand. Let's think more carefully before we answer, shall we? Sit."

Finch regarded Milo with a grim stare for a moment before reseating himself on the leather chair. He felt the blood throbbing in his shoulder where the metal had cooked him.

"It's not often that Richard keeps prisoners alive this long. Do you feel lucky?"

Milo gestured with the crowbar as he spoke, bringing its orange tip within a few inches of Finch's lips. Finch recoiled back into the chair, holding his hands up over his face.

"Yes," replied Finch. He attempted to imbue an obedient tone into his voice, though the pain was still ebbing excruciatingly in his shoulder.

"Fast learner. Maybe that's what Richard likes. That clever brain of yours. Not doing you too much good now, of course, but under different circumstances, you could be a real asset to the Regals. Still not interested?"

Finch stared back at Milo, choosing his words carefully before speaking again. Before he could open his mouth, however, he felt the savage heat of the crowbar again, this time held against his knee. Finch yelped and got to his feet again. Milo swung the crowbar swiftly and precisely into Finch's other knee. Finch buckled and collapsed heavily onto the floor with a groan.

"Let's speed this up, shall we?"

The false mirth was gone from Milo's tone. His small dark eyes were intent now, sizing Finch up inch by inch. He stood proudly over Finch's huddled body on the floor. Finch smelled the rubber and leather of Milo's boots and felt the heat of the crowbar's tip somewhere near his face.

"As I see it, you have three options: One, you join the Regals and rise in the ranks, like myself. Richard already likes you, there's your leg up. Lucky you. Let me suggest this option, strongly."

Finch watched Milo through half-closed eyelids. The pain between the two burns and his knee fused into one pulsating full-body ache. He struggled to concentrate on Milo's words.

"Two, you refuse to join. Fine, suit yourself. But Richard isn't going to just let a functioning fellow like yourself go free. I'd expect he'd have you work yourself to death in the junkyard. Most junkers only last a year or two, three years max."

As Milo spoke, Finch made his move. Springing up, he landed a left hook into Milo's jaw. But he'd misjudged the strength of his knee and he crumpled back to the ground, landing painfully on his only good arm. Milo, surprised by the attack, spat blood and swung the crowbar down heavily and angrily on Finch's back. Finch felt the metal rod thud the wind out of his chest and he yelled silently into the cement ground.

"Or choice number three," continued Milo, as though nothing had interrupted him. "You keep lashing out until you get yourself killed, either by Richard—or myself. Which is what I'm hoping for, by the way."

With a final kick to Finch's stomach, Milo walked to the door. But before he left, he poked his head back into the basement room.

"Oh, one more thing," Milo added, casually. "Viro was recruiting you quite heavily, wasn't he? I've never seen so many thumbprints on a door... and on the inside of your books, too! Curious, don't you think?"

Milo left Finch with one last wicked smirk and an infuriating, coy wink.

The question reached Finch's ears even through the throbbing, unrelenting pain coursing through his body. His eyes burned at the sound of Viro's name. Finch heard the heavy metal pieces click together with grim finality as the door was locked.

He lost sense of time, bouncing in and out of consciousness. After what felt like hours, Finch pulled himself onto the chair. He felt physically and emotionally spent from the exchange with that sadist Milo. After positioning himself as comfortably as he could on the old chair, Finch took inventory of his wounds. The throbbing from the burns had finally subsided to patches of tenderness. His knee felt slightly wobbly, but ultimately undamaged. His back felt severely bruised and it was this that caused him the most discomfort. He hoped his ribs weren't cracked.

In a daze, Finch replayed the exchange in his head. He couldn't see much of a way around Milo's three outlined options, either. Clearly the only acceptable choice was to join the gang, accept the recruitment offer, and make the best of it forevermore. Certain aspects of the option were appealing. The safety, of course, was desirable. Remaining alive, to be sure, was high on his priority list. If the rest of the gang was anything like Milo, Finch wanted nothing to do with them. He recalled the fearful look in the eyes of the Regals as Richard had approached and wondered how safe the troopers really were.

The idea of joining the gang physically sickened him. His whole life he had done everything in his power to avoid them. Hiding from them—hating them, even—felt ingrained in Finch's very DNA. Gangs had made attempts on his life more times than he could count. Gangs tore Vulture into patches which they subsequently clawed and fought over every single day, killing each other over inches of territory. Gangs had made Finch afraid. Gangs killed Horatio. Gangs had made it impossible for him and Viro to be together—at least according to Viro. His beloved radio station home had been reduced to ashes at the hands of Richard and Milo. They'd torched his books, each word a separate life, cremated unceremoniously. No, he refused to succumb. Already he had acted as an unwitting pawn in one of Richard's schemes.

Finch shifted position again, avoiding putting any pressure on his back. *Self-reliance* called for him to take option three, he decided. He'd keep fighting back. Horatio would never let these brutes change him so neither would Finch. He owed it to himself and to Horatio to try to escape, even if it meant death. But Milo's knowledge of Viro concerned him. Of course, the Regals had spies everywhere, and Milo had seen the thumbprints. And Viro was the rare Scorp that ventured above ground to recruit members, so perhaps Milo had simply connected the dots, having seen Viro make his recruiting rounds in the past. Clearly Milo had been making some kind of threat, using Viro as leverage. It was probably just a mind game, meant to rattle him, get him interested in answers that only joining would get him. Still, if Viro was in trouble, he (Finch) was at fault for having exposed him.

Finch wondered what he would do if it had been Viro trapped in this basement and his life threatened. Finch wanted to believe he would try to save him, as he felt he must now protect him.

CHAPTER 15

And I had done a hellish thing,
And it would work 'em woe:
For all averred, I had killed the bird
That made the breeze to blow.

— Samuel Taylor Coleridge, *The Rime of the Ancient Mariner*

Unable to sleep, Rigby continued cycling through her records. Hendrix bled into The Who and on into The Beatles. Each disc was the soundtrack to a different train of thought, ideas careening around her skull that offered no resolutions but only further questions. A knock at her door snapped her to attention. She silenced the soft music and snuck to her window. Lifting the curtain, her heart pounding, she peered outside. There on her shabby lofted stoop was Milo. He bounced on the balls of his feet, whistling to the tune she'd just stopped playing. House calls like this were unheard of. At the very most, some gang messenger would leave a coded purple symbol on her message board to announce a meeting or else some amendment to a plan.

Wary, Rigby cracked the door and looked up into Milo's yellow-toothed grin. He stuck his face into the gap in the door jam and Rigby fought the urge to slam it shut on his broken purple nose.

"Can I help you?" asked Rigby, icily.

"I was in the neighborhood. Thought I'd drop by for that chat we discussed earlier."

His tone was playful and made Rigby's skin crawl. His eyes were slits and he licked his lips as he spoke. In addition to the dual black eyes and the broken nose, the left side of his face was swollen and maroon.

"What happened to your face?" asked Rigby.

"Nothing," said Milo quickly, momentarily self-conscious as he rubbed his jaw. "Thought any more about what I said?"

"You're a liar, Milo."

"Oh? Well, I was just with the indie. Still looks like a match to me."

"So that's who punched you. Nice. Maybe we are related after all."

"Exactly the kind of confession Richard would be very interested to know. He wants to see you, by the way."

This news sent an icy chill down Rigby's spine before transforming into a nervous heat that flushed her cheeks. She gulped hard and strained to keep her face from betraying her fear. She felt the toes on her left foot quake inside her boot.

"Nervous? Let me in. Put that music back on and we can discuss it," said Milo.

His tone sickened her, playful and flirtatious.

"Fuck off," said Rigby, pressing against the door.

Milo wedged his foot into the frame to keep the door from closing. Rigby glanced across the room to her electrical cord, cursing herself for not bringing it with her to the door.

"You have some time before your meeting with Richard. Let me in."

His tone was no longer friendly, not even mockingly so. His eyes were black and fierce, his pupils nearly overtaking the whites. The fetid scent of Leak hung on his breath. Rigby pushed with all her strength against the door but Milo was stronger. He shoved his shoulder into the door and she fell back to the ground as he burst into her flat. Like her, he'd gone though the rigorous combat training of the Regals. Richard had always directed the training himself, cloning himself to the best of his abilities in each cadet. With grim curiosity, Milo glanced around the room.

"So you're a music buff?"

He took a few dancing steps toward her.

"Get out of here, Milo,"

She reached for her backpack, which lay limp by her bed. If she could just reach her electrical cord...

"I don't think so, sweetheart."

Milo's booted foot came down heavily on her wrist. She squirmed and lashed out but he wouldn't budge. Her uninjured arm was pinned to the ground, leaving her with just the wounded arm to defend herself. His swollen face came so close to hers that she could see the stains of brown liquid on his teeth, smell the horrible stench of the vile beverage. She saw the sharp black stubble flecked with grey that sprouted from his chin and the red veins throbbing in his eyes. His fingers danced on her shoulder, pulling at the collar of her jumpsuit.

Overcome with drunken lust, he'd forgotten to pin Rigby's right leg. Before he could get any further than exposing her shoulder, she drilled her knee into his groin in two rapid shots. He groaned and keeled back on his haunches. She shot off the ground and in one fluid motion she was on her feet, trusty electrical cord in hand. Still gasping to recover from the blow, Milo held up a meek, defensive hand. Rigby delivered another kick to his gut, which sent him onto all fours. He looked up at her, into her executioner's glare, and smiled. It took Rigby aback, her cord-wielding arm frozen over her head.

"Too late," he croaked, still smiling. For once he'd been concise.

With a final, vicious swing of the cord, the weighted end landed directly on his temple in a well-aimed shot. The dull thud of his skull punctured the silence as his body collapsed in a pile on the ground.

Rigby breathed heavily and looked around her room. Adrenaline coursed through her body, charging the whole room with such intensity it blurred her vision. It was over. She would have no choice but to leave the Regals. Milo had always bugged her but she'd never wanted him dead. She certainly never thought she'd kill him. Ethics aside, the Regals had been her safety net, and suddenly everything felt viscerally real. If she didn't act soon, the gang that had been her life would soon be her death.

She thought of hiding Milo's body, or blaming it on some other gang. She paced the room, picking up records and putting them back down. It would be too obvious. The three-pronged cuts now oozing blood on Milo's temple were her signature. With Richard already on high alert to trickery thanks to the indie, deception would be too risky. Doubts crossed her mind, begging her to remain ensconced in the safety of the gang however possible. But it was too late. She'd killed the only Regal other than Richard that outranked her, a crime for which the consequence could only be blood—her own.

She began to pack a bag, filling it at random with frantic, furious motions. She'd meet with Richard, see what he wanted, and then leave for good. Anything else would be too suspicious, and he'd send a patrol after her. No, she would take her chances in the outskirts, or maybe seek asylum with the Veins, though they weren't likely to grant her any assistance after all the treachery she'd committed against them over the years. But first she would have to meet with Richard. She was too keyed up to make rational decisions about which records to bring along on her exodus. She'd have to do that later, before she left. For now she left a half packed bag of clothes and her cord tucked neatly in the side pocket. Her eyes landed on Milo's body, which lay heavy in the middle of her floor. A pool of blood the size of a dinner plate encircled his head. She'd have to deal with that later, too. Maybe she'd have time to move the body, spray his eyes blue if only to buy herself some time. She couldn't keep Richard waiting. Otherwise her efforts might all be for naught.

Her hand fluttered at her side and she clenched it tight to keep it from trembling. Though she couldn't deal with the physical corpse just now, she mentally crammed Milo into the bursting corner at the back of her mind. He had said "too late." Maybe he'd already told Richard about the matching tattoos, or maybe it had all been a lie, a weak excuse to come by her house. Better not to find out. Better to go to headquarters, meet with Richard. Maybe then she could gauge the depth of her danger. Then maybe she could decide what to do next and how she ought to do it.

For now all she knew was that she must maintain the fearless attitude she'd relied upon her whole life. Head swirling, she set off on unsteady feet for the cinema, futile in all attempts to calm herself as she walked.

"Do come in Rigs, you needn't be a stranger."

Richard's voice boomed from behind the door.

Rigby hated the way he could predict who stood outside his door. It was some kind of game to him. Maybe it made him feel omniscient. She tugged her sleeve over the wound on her forearm. Doing her best to steady her heartbeat before turning the handle, she took a deep breath and entered the resplendent room.

"Hi Richard," she said, a touch breathlessly, as she passed the glowering, muscled guards on her way into the room. She would never get used to Richard's immense, almost inhuman size. He always looked like an enormous stone statue taking a break from some eternal pose.

"Rigs, how are you?"

He smiled but his eyes were piercing. Rigby stared at the floor. She took a deep breath.

"I'm fine. What can I do for you?"

She thought that sounded ok. She tried to remember how she usually spoke but she was too befuddled to remember just now.

"You've heard, of course, about the indie?"

As usual his voice was coated in layers of gravitas.

"Yes, congratulations."

Rigby squirmed under his gaze but straightened her spine. He could be testing her.

"Please, you did all the heavy lifting. Congratulations are due more to you than me. It was you that pushed him to the brink, made him vulnerable. Without you, he still might be free and that mutt of his would still be alive."

She wondered if it was Richard's intent to inflict as much guilt with each word as he could, cloaked in praise. Or perhaps it was her own guilt she was feeling. Squeezing her facial muscles, she attempted to assume a mask of inscrutability.

"Thank you, Richard," she said. "I appreciate it."

Best to appear grateful, though she hoped she hadn't over-done it.

They regarded each other for another long moment before

he broke the silence. Rigby wondered if he could hear the hammering sound of her heart in her chest. Sweat trickled down her back and legs.

"I want you to bring him his dinner. Talk to him. Try to get him to see the light."

The request nearly threw her off balance. Surely, he hadn't sent for her like this simply to play waiter to the prisoner. This must be some kind of test. Milo must have told him.

"Milo went down there earlier and roughed him up a bit," said Richard, his tone casual, lingering on the last word and watching Rigby carefully. "But he got nowhere. I figured you should take a whack at it…excuse the pun, I'm terrible," he added with a smirk, eyes never straying from Rigby's face.

"Of course," she said, stonily.

"Excellent. Take as long as you need," he added.

The order seemed purposefully vague; an opportunity to make a mistake of some kind. He thrust an old brass key into her hand.

"Oh, and Rigs. One more thing."

Rigby stuck her hands in her pockets to keep them from trembling as she turned around.

"Yes, Richard?"

"You remember that recruiter girl, Miriam? We had to get rid of her. She was seen talking to a Vein. Zero tolerance for traitors, as you know."

Rigby's eyes burned and she fought to hide her shock. Her heart dropped into her stomach. She couldn't believe it was true. Maybe he'd done it to punish Rigby by association, or maybe he'd simply resented letting Miriam live that first time he'd hit her.

"Just thought you should know. That's all."

Unable to speak, Rigby forced her head to nod. Turning, she left the room. His nonchalance terrified her. She felt as though the wind had been knocked out of her. And honestly, she wished it had been. At least then she might have had an idea about the identity of her enemy, and where the attack was coming from. As soon as the door closed behind her, she burst into tears, smothering her face in her elbow. She couldn't remember crying a single time in her life, and as she sobbed and gasped, she felt a tremendous release. After several long minutes she wiped her eyes and took a deep breath. Miriam joined the others at the back corner of her mind. In a daze, she placed one foot in front of the other and made her way down the stairs.

Apprehensively, she turned the key to the ancient lock. She felt woozy from the interaction with Richard and ill prepared to talk with the indie, especially after whatever Milo had done to him. For now she pushed any possibility of the man being her brother from her mind, trying to maintain her focus. She pulled her sleeve down as low as it could go over her forearm, hiding her vulnerability as best she could. The indie could be violent, waiting to pounce as soon as she opened the door. Although if Milo had already gotten to him, she doubted there'd be much fight left in the indie. Milo. She pushed that thought away, too.

She slipped into the austere basement room and took a moment to allow her eyes to adjust to the dim gray light. Little particles of dust danced in the light allowed in by the small window high on the wall. The indie was turned away from her, evidently asleep on the chair in the corner. His braid hung limp across his right shoulder, his face obscured between his lanky arm and the busted cushions of the chair.

She cleared her throat and when still he did not stir, she stepped forward. Moving closer, she set the bowl of rice down on the concrete floor near the chair as loudly as she could. Still no movement. On his left forearm she noticed a gruesome burn mark and a second down on his knee. It must have been Milo. She reached an apprehensive hand out, tapping lightly on the man's back. He looked broken and lumpy. Milo must have really broken him down.

But as soon as her fingers touched down on the indie's shoulder, they landed on a whirl of body parts and energy. Instantly the man was on his feet, eyes wide awake and wild as a dog-wolf. With his unburned arm he pinned her to the wall with the force of a steel beam. In the burst of energy, he had kicked over the rice bowl and now the white grains lay sprinkled across the cement floor. His teeth were bared and his black eyes were violent and restless.

Those eyes, so much like hers that even in the chaos of the moment she couldn't help but to notice them. The same brown-gold color framed by dense lines of long eyelashes that she saw in her own reflection. The tip of his fine nose came within inches of her own fine-tipped nose.

"Wait!" she finally managed through a rasped breath.

But already the indie was pulling back, as though just seeing her for the first time. His brow furrowed as he searched her face.

"Where did you get that?" he asked, almost desperately, pointing a quivering finger at the tattoo scrawled on her forearm, which had poked into view above her sleeve in the commotion. Rigby breathed a sigh of relief that he had not seen the tooth mark imprinted on her other arm.

"I've always had it," she said, breathing hard and not taking her eyes away from the man's face.

He looked to be about her age, maybe a little younger. But his eyes denoted years of maturity that betrayed his youthful face.

She couldn't look away. Milo was right; it was almost like looking into some kind of gender-bending mirror. The indie must have seen it, too.

"You have one, too, right?" she asked.

He looked down at the tattoo on his forearm as though noticing it for the first time.

"Who are you?" he finally asked, his unblinking eyes staring down at her beneath a furrowed brow. He dropped his arm from her chest and she slumped back against the wall.

"Rigby."

For a long moment he looked her up and down, his eyebrows low over his eyes. He barely breathed and his fists remained balled, frozen at his sides. Only his eyes moved, traversing every inch of her being. Rigby stared back at him, unable to look away. The slight way he moved his jaw, the gentle flexing of his fists and the bent kneed stance he'd assumed—all looked eerily familiar to her.

"I'm Finch," he said finally, his tone still wary.

For several minutes all they could do was stare at one another, each half-expecting the other to yank off a mask or lash out again. While Finch had no concrete memories of family, he felt that this woman standing before him could be none other than his flesh and blood. Something innate and primal in him told him it was so, despite his best efforts to be rational. The tattoo could not be a coincidence, could it, he wondered? Taking a step back, his eyes finally broke from her face.

Her hair, dark like his, was interrupted by thin dreadlocks of dry, purple paint. Her gray jumpsuit was spattered with blotches of violet in varying degrees of fadedness. A thick smear of paint covered the upper half of her face.

"You're a Regal," he said.

Though she couldn't deny it, and he probably hadn't meant it to sound like an accusation, she felt suddenly guilty and ashamed of the purple stains that covered her hair and clothes. She had so much to ask him and so much to discuss, years and years worth of time to account for, though she couldn't formulate the words. Long ago she had given up even the mere idea of this moment, eventually succeeding in forcing it from her mind and attributing any lingering thoughts to pointless daydream.

"You're my brother," she blurted. "I think," she added after a beat.

He nodded slowly but otherwise didn't move. His jaw remained tense, but his fists had gone limp at his sides. A sister. But hadn't he always been alone? His mind's eye plummeted into the deepest recesses of his memory. A small sailboat, crashed to pieces on the shore. He'd been crying. But had there been someone else? Yes. He saw her now. A small girl with a stony face and dark ringlets that cascaded off her head just like his and a small bandage on her forearm. He'd had a bandage, too. He remembered, vividly, the sharp pain in the soft flesh of his childish forearm. The tattoo, which he'd discovered upon peeling back the bandage several terrifying weeks later. He'd rubbed at the words with his hand and with dirt and even a dribble of Leak, but he couldn't remove the indecipherable symbols from his skin. The images flooded into his head before he could stop them or even make sense of what they signified. She hadn't cried. And then running. He'd run away from the girl, bawling, while she had stood resolute by the shipwrecked vessel.

"What are you going to do to me?" he asked.

"I don't know," she responded.

It was an honest answer. She was at a loss. She had no idea how much Richard knew and she didn't plan on staying to find out.

"I'll get you out of here."

The abruptness of her answer surprised even her, leaping from her mouth before she'd even fully formulated the thought. Finch's dark eyes regarded her dispassionately. There was no trust in his stare. She shivered. They were the eyes of an indie, reliant only on themselves for years and distrustful of strangers.

"Why?"

Rigby paused and looked away, thinking she ought to backtrack somehow. But it was too late. The thought implanted itself in her mind and began to grow in the fertility of her recent rebellion and nourished by guilt. Rescuing the indie felt like precisely the opposite of what she ought to do, which was why she wanted to do it. She relished the image of Richard busting open the basement door only to find his prisoner missing. How furious he'd be, and she wouldn't care because she'd be gone, into the outskirts or with this indie—perhaps her brother!—hiding around Vulture and surviving together. All the figures that she'd crammed into the back corner of her mind now burst free and swirled about her skull looking down at her judgmentally. The possibility of a fresh start had never felt closer. She wanted out.

Surely there were other, better places within reach, she thought to herself. Surely Vulture was not the last place of its kind on earth. Some had escaped the Regals in the past. Usually their bones were found in the remains of the Cannies' campfires. Others had never been found, all traces of their life gone as though they'd been erased. Richard left no stone unturned when a Regal went missing. Even a missing junker would send him out on the hunt. He'd expend inordinate energy and resources to bring them back, only to torture or even execute them upon their return as a warning to other would be deserters. Perhaps the ones that were never found had died, but a small part of Rigby indulged in the belief that they had possibly made it to some new, hopeful place. It had been so long since she'd felt the possibility offered by this moment, standing before the indie in the basement of Regal headquarters—the possibility of actual choice.

"I want to help," she said, after a long pause.

It had sounded more confident in her head. The words came out weak and unconvincing. She barely believed the statement herself.

"How?" he returned, articulating the word in a curt, skeptical monosyllable.

Finch didn't want to trust her but he could hardly help it. It wasn't as though he had many other options. Even if he killed her right now, a task he knew he could not accomplish, steal her key and leave the basement, there was an entire gang filling the floors above his head and blocking his only way out. He needed her help.

"I don't know yet. But I'll think of something."

"How can I trust you?"

"Can you afford not to? You will be dead or slaving away in the junkyard by tomorrow if you don't agree to Richard's terms. Be my guest, but I have a feeling you would have done that by now if that's what you wanted."

"You sound like that Milo guy," he challenged.

Rigby faltered at the sound of Milo's name but recovered herself quickly.

"Maybe. But I'm sure he wasn't offering you freedom."

Finch stared back at her and finally nodded in agreement. Life among the Regals had made her ruthlessly decisive.

"Where would we even go? Richard runs this place like a king, doesn't he?"

"The outskirts," she said plainly, as though it were nothing more than a jaunt across the street. Her confidence and blasé both impressed and worried Finch. She was either onto something or at her wits' end.

"I know a place..." he began, though he stopped himself suddenly. The possibility of using her to escape the cinema and then deserting her still felt like a viable option.

"Yeah?" she prodded.

Finch fought indecision. It had already been made clear that his new and best hope would be to trust this Rigby person, who was more likely than not his sister, despite the fact that she wore Regal colors. He decided to lean into the plan rather than rush it and get himself killed. Reliance on Rigby would have to substitute *self-reliance* for now.

"A river. It leads to the ocean, I think."

Rigby paused to consider this image. Her first thought was of the immense driftwood chair that Richard kept in the auditorium and that was said to have come from the ocean far away. Maybe it wasn't so far away after all. Suddenly anything felt possible. If her brother could still be alive, why shouldn't a river that led to the ocean exist? If Finch had suggested that they fly there she might have entertained the possibility.

"Works for me," she said.

She felt lighter, as though already free, untethered from Vulture and the Regals. This man who might be her brother anchored her to a past in which she wasn't a Regal, wasn't always a ruthless machine. She thought of Miriam and her siblings. All at once the figures swirling about the guilt-laden regions of her mind come bursting forth like a dust storm erupting out of the outskirts. The dog-wolf, the brother she'd imprisoned, the Vein mother and the crying children that dragged her, Miriam, and

Pip. All the lives she had ruined or destroyed in the name of the Regals.

The indie standing before her represented an opportunity, a fresh start, and she grasped at it like it was the last canteen of water in Vulture.

"But we can't go now. Better to go tomorrow morning. Most of the Regals will be asleep and we'll have less chance of being caught. Plus I'll have to grab a few things from home. Can you make it another night down here?"

"So long as Milo doesn't come around again, yeah."

"I wouldn't worry about that," she said.

"Wait. There's something else," said Finch, before Rigby could leave. He tried but couldn't help himself. He had to ask despite the voice in his skull commanding him to shut his mouth.

"What's that?" She heard the desperation in Finch's voice.

"There's a Scorp named Viro. Can you find him? And keep him safe? I think he might be in danger." Finch couldn't stop the words from tumbling forth. He wanted to give Viro the chance to join him, escape Gajjea and the Scorps and Vulture forever. His daydreams pushed their way to the front of his mind.

"I'll try," promised Rigby, noting the urgency in his voice.

"Do that and I'll know I can trust you," said Finch, thinking quickly. He knew the danger she'd be putting herself in to make contact with the Scorps.

Rigby nodded but didn't ask any further questions, time already slipping away too fast. The idea of saving a member of a rival gang rather than destroying them felt paradoxically accommodating of her new vision of herself. Before the absurdity of seeing her brother again, the thought of finding and convincing a Scorp to trust her would have sounded preposterous.

She pressed gently on his shoulder in a gesture meant to impart comfort before turning and walking out the door. The touch of her hand lingered on his shoulder long after she'd gone and the lock had re-clicked into place. He ran his finger over the tattoo. The words were all that remained of his library. Of course, Rigby's tattoo doubled his stock of words. And perhaps together they'd be able to escape to another world, one without violence and filled with books where they could lounge about in peace and reminisce about the whimsical childhood that neither of them had experienced.

CHAPTER 16

And so castles made of sand
Fall in the sea
Eventually

— Jimi Hendrix, *"Castles Made of Sand"*

Rigby felt an odd sense of peace as she left the theater, though she was careful not to show it. She assumed her usual hunched forward, eyes down posture that had served her well all her life. Her sticky purple locks swayed like curtains, partially obscuring her face. All the same, she felt as though a weight had been lifted from her shoulders. A curious lightness filled her steps. The sensation stirred her, and she wondered how long she'd subconsciously been waiting for this moment. Being a Regal had never been a choice for her, but rather an embedded part of her identity. The thought of shedding that portion of her identity felt gratifying, forcing her to question the quality of that identity in the first place. For the first time since choosing her name, she felt as though she could decide who she wanted to be.

Looking around, she delighted in her hope that this could be one of the last times that she ever saw these purple clad figures. The whispers had subsided and people had resumed their usual lurking poses and furtive glances. There were scores of people that Rigby didn't even recognize. Although she'd only just met

Finch, she couldn't deny the likelihood of the familial connection. At last, another person that shared some fragment of her pre-Regal experience had been dropped into her life. For so long she had shunned relationships, even with those that had been kind to her. Miriam's senseless death had been proof enough that she should abandon hope in any relationships outside of gang colleagues. Friendships led to vulnerability, and others couldn't be trusted to act consistently without suspicion—moments of failure which would inevitably taint all those known to be their friends as well. Thus friends were far too great a risk. But what about brothers? Direct kin? Something about Finch felt different to Rigby on an instinctual level that she couldn't explain but felt she could trust. Rigby wondered if this was what family felt like. If Miriam were still alive, she would have asked her.

Consumed in thought, her feet carried her out of the cinema and into the powerful orange wash of the afternoon sun. The heat reawakened her focus. Richard could extinguish Finch from her life just as quickly as he had been reintroduced. He had the power of a puppeteer and Finch was tied to the ends of Richard's manipulative strings now—just like her. The image of snipping these strings, once and for all, added further bounce to her step. She quickened her pace. Milo's blood would be sinking into her floorboards by now. The thought was sobering. As she thought about Richard, the weight dropped back onto her shoulders, hunching her forward. She still had no idea how much he knew. He'd certainly been acting suspicious back at the theater. It was possible that he was onto her already, testing the extent of her loyalty to the Regal regime when it was her own flesh and blood that was to be made the victim. He had made a career of being three steps ahead of everyone around him, and his cruelty knew no bounds. She rolled the thought around her brain as she traversed the swollen lumps of corroded and stained metal outside the theater.

Now to the task at hand. She had too little time to find this Viro character, and in her reconnaissance experience, the Scorps were always the hardest to track down. Their burrows and tunnel networks were known only to them, and they'd made a livelihood of becoming invisible. And she would need a peace offering of some kind, some token to keep them from killing her on sight. Rigby began to doubt that she could accomplish the errand in time. But she couldn't break the first promise she'd ever made to her brother, either. She needed him to trust her. After all, if the river he'd mentioned actually existed, only he knew how to get there.

Just then she had an idea, though as soon as she began to consider it she worried it would fail. Recalling again the urgency in Finch's voice, she raced to the record shop. With difficulty, she ignored Milo's body on her floor, stepping over it as though it was just another pile of laundry. She stripped off her purple-spattered jumpsuit and put on an old, faded gray one that hardly fit her anymore. This one didn't have even a touch of purple on it. She'd worn it during her training, before she'd earned the right to smear herself in Regal purple. Rummaging in her small personal paint bin, she was thrilled to find a single canister of ivy green spray paint with a little liquid left at the bottom. She used it sparingly. Luckily the Scorp adornment didn't require much paint. It was lucky that she didn't need to disguise herself as a Vein; the little blue arrows alone would take hours. Carefully but quickly, she gave her hands a thorough coating, making them appear as though covered by thin green gloves. The real issue would be her hair. She couldn't remember the last time she'd actually washed the paint out of it. Using rubbing alcohol, she rubbed out the brightest portions and decided to just paint over the rest despite how haphazard it would look. She did her best to cover her purple dreadlocks in green, resulting in an ugly brown color that would have to do. She used the remaining paint to coat her brow in a solid dash of green to finish the disguise.

Still dripping, she dashed out the door. Adrenaline carried her along as reason and doubt tried to halt her feet. Now she just needed to find a Scorp; never an easy task. She kept to the shadows, all too conscious of the veritable target she'd painted onto her body. She had never before feared being sighted by the Regals, and the feeling was surreal.

Rigby stopped on a dime as she saw a purple figure walking in the opposite direction, back toward the cinema. Thankfully his back was to her but Rigby recognized Ledo's bouncy, jovial gate. She wondered where he could be coming from, moving about in daylight like this.

Despite her suspicions, she didn't have time to tail him. Ignoring Ledo for now, she took off in a dead sprint in the direction of the mall. Dusk was only a few hours away and Vulture's most dangerous elements would soon become active. Scorp recruiters were the only green members that Rigby had ever seen make an appearance above ground. For recruiters of all gangs, the crumbling mall was usually a good bet for finding indies. On this occasion, however, Rigby would be recruiting a recruiter, the irony lingering only briefly on her mind. As the mall came into view, sweat from the steamy afternoon heat drove fresh paint stinging into her eyes. Heart still pounding, she paid her discomfort no mind.

She felt naked without the purple paint that she'd worn for so many years. It was a vulnerable feeling, to be sure, but also liberating, she realized. She'd left Rigby the Regal back at the cinema. In this moment, lurking in the shadows of the mall's ruinous parking structure, she was someone else, someone with options. At first nobody appeared, and she felt the silent, precious seconds slip by, never to return. Each second was another moment that Milo's absence could be discovered, or her absence. Worse still, Finch could be killed at Richard's slightest whim.

After what felt like an hour, she heard someone approaching and she took cover behind one of the many corroded pillars to spy on the figure. But it was just a Canny, wandering aimlessly and chanting up to the sky. He sipped Leak from a bowl that Rigby recognized as the one Finch's dog-wolf, Horatio, had once used. Guilt flipped her stomach and she looked away. No good. She needed a Scorp.

Rigby circled around to the back of the mall. There she waited behind a mound of rubble and another lugubrious stretch of time trickled by, though it couldn't have been that long judging from the sun's resolute position high in the sky. Suddenly a figure emerged out of a nearly imperceptible hole in the asphalt and began making its purposeful way into the parking garage. Rigby recognized the gait. They were the confident movements of a recruiter, not the frantic, darting motions of an indie. And only Scorps came from underground tunnels.

Leaving her hidden post, she tailed the figure into the garage. Her heart thrummed in her chest as the man's matted green hair came into view. His green hands swung loose at his sides. Rigby was grateful for the shade of the parking structure, as it obscured the haphazard Scorp costume she'd thrown together. Not wanting to sneak up on him unexpectedly, she decided to take the offensive.

"Hey, what are you doing up here?" she called out.

He jumped at the sound of her voice. Visible relief passed

over his face when he saw green paint coating her hair and hands.

"Recruiting, on assignment," he said quickly.

He spoke to her like an underling to a superior. He must be a relatively new member, judging from his faltering tone and his cherubic face. Gang recruiters were often recent recruits themselves, beginning their career with familiar and relatively safe daytime assignments. He bumbled and drew himself up, swelling his chest and straightening his back.

"Cool, I mean, good work. Me too. Have you seen Viro?" Rigby faltered as the man walked closer, but recovered when she saw how truly young he was. His smooth, round face reminded her painfully of Pip, though this Scorp was much chubbier. Perhaps the Scorps' food stockpile was healthier than she had imagined.

"Viro? You mean Gajjea's husband?"

Gajjea's face was renowned in Vulture, her glaring visage suffused to every sewer grate in the city. Rigby felt her plan dissolving before her. Had Finch really sent her after the Scorp leader's husband? Was this some kind of trap? Instilling as much confidence as she could muster into her voice, she pressed on.

"Right, have you seen him? Gajjea wants him."

Rigby did her best to sound authoritative and high ranking. The man nodded, his round head bouncing up and down on his fleshy neck.

"Oh. Ok yeah I think he's down 46E right now, he was there earlier at least."

Rigby winced, knowing that she had no clue where that was or even what the code meant.

"Gotcha. Thanks. That's not the new one around -"

"It's the one by that old radio station where the indie lived. Used to live, I guess. You see someone blew that place up?"

The kid yammered excitedly and Rigby was glad the trust-

216

ing fool had cut her off before she'd revealed her ignorance. He seemed excited to talk about the explosion.

"Thanks. Right, I heard about that."

"No worries. Hey, I'll go with you, I'm wrapping up here anyways. Seems like all the indies are already hiding for the night."

"Yeah, you should try going during the afternoon," suggested Rigby, sincerely grateful to the kid. She wondered if all the Scorps were this friendly, though she doubted it. It was still Vulture, after all, whether above or below ground. Maybe this kid just hadn't been broken yet, still smiley and hopeful about his new gang. But after the discovery of her brother, Rigby was willing to believe that hope could exist, even in Vulture. Perhaps the Scorps had taken empathy underground with them when they'd gone into hiding.

Within five minutes they were near the now smoldered foundation of the radio station. Scraps of the water sheet lay crisped at her feet, and Rigby twinged with guilt at her role in the home's demise. The kid led the way, talking the whole time about different recruits he'd brought in. Rigby couldn't believe her luck in bumping into this talkative, trusting fellow. He finally stopped about fifty yards from the site of the exploded station and stomped heavily four times on a patch of scrubby earth. As he stepped away, the dirt and gravel fell away to reveal a wide portal. The circular metal plate looked like a manhole cover. Slow and noiseless but for the cascading dirt and gravel drifting down the sides, the circular plate was gradually moved to the side, guided by invisible hands.

Soon, however, Rigby noticed the real hands moving the heavy plate. Green hands, to be exact. They were attached to a man at least several years her senior, who now looked up at Rigby from beneath a helmet of long, straight green hair. His eyes sparkled out from the dark tunnel and Rigby could just glimpse the sharp angle of his jaw.

"Viro!" exclaimed the boy. "We were just looking for you!"

"Who's we?" said Viro coolly. "And don't say my name above ground like that."

"Right, sorry, me and… sorry, I'm still pretty new around here, what's your name?" he asked Rigby sheepishly.

"Rigby," she said automatically, kicking herself and clamping her mouth shut so hard that she bit her tongue. She wasn't sure how well known her name was in Vulture and regretted the error.

"I don't know any Rigby," said Viro, his tone growing icy.

"Oh, well…hmm… I guess," the boy mused and looked from Rigby back to Viro.

Viro's piercing eyes traversed Rigby's body. Surely Gajjea's husband knew all the members of the Scorps, and would certainly recognize an imposter. Unless their numbers were larger than she had thought. Green eyelids narrowed over the sparkling irises. Better to cut to the chase, figured Rigby. Time was running out.

"Didn't you notice she's a Regal?" Viro asked the boy.

"What? No but…," frantically, he looked Rigby up and down. Rigby's blood went cold. Viro stood three feet below her at the edge of what looked to be a very long, low tunnel. And yet still she felt as though she'd lost the upper ground. In that same moment, she realized with an overwhelming sense of defeat that not only had she forgoed a trip to Milo's now unprotected inventory for a crossbow, but she'd also left the electrical cord back at the record shop in her haste to disguise herself.

"Get inside," Viro commanded the boy.

If the young recruiter had had a tail it would have been tucked between his legs as he scuttled down the tunnel and became lost in the darkness.

"How'd you know?" managed Rigby.

"You missed a spot," Viro said, pointing down at the purple flecks on Rigby's boots.

Her carelessness worried her. It wasn't like her to overlook details. Ever since Milo had mentioned her brother, she'd felt completely lost.

"So what do you want, come to kill me? Or maybe Gajjea?"

Viro sounded unworried. Taking note of his cavalier tone, Rigby thought briefly that the Scorps could possibly be more of a threat than she'd reported to the Regals at last week's meeting—and most weeks before that.

"It's about Finch," she blurted.

Viro froze but quickly recovered his composure. He seemed determined not to betray emotion.

"Is he dead?" he asked, his tone flat.

"No, we—the Regals have him imprisoned at the cinema."

"Was that you guys, or Gajjea?" Viro asked, nodding towards the scorched remains of the radio station.

"Us," replied Rigby, unsure why Viro would think that his wife had blown up the building. Then she recalled Finch's frantic tone. Understanding crashed over her like a wave and she stared into Viro's unblinking eyes. He must have taken to hiding out in this tunnel after seeing the ruined radio station, the home of his secret boyfriend, wondering whether he'd be next.

"Yeah," said Viro, nodding as he saw Rigby look from him to the station and back to him. "So what does he want?"

"He says you're in danger. You have to come with me."

Viro scoffed and looked out to the outskirts. His fine jaw worked back and forth.

"I think I'm perfectly safe down here, Regal." He snarled the last word, looking Rigby directly in the eyes.

"Please he…" began Rigby.

"What, said he loves me? Yeah, he does that. Kid reads too much, I tell him all the time," said Viro, cutting Rigby off and shaking his head.

"No, not that. He's my brother. I'm trying to free him, actually. I promised him I'd get you to safety. I'm not sure he'll trust me if I don't."

"Understandable," spit Viro. "But no thanks. You guys actually do look alike though," he said, again looking Rigby up and down.

Pleading wouldn't work with this man and time was running out. Rigby reverted back into the purple clad, cord-wielding killer she'd thought she'd left behind for good. She allowed her instincts to take over.

"Maybe Gajjea should know about your special interest recruiting project."

"Maybe I should kill you," replied Viro, not missing a beat. His eyes remained trained on the outskirts, his arms folded over his broad chest.

"Look, come with me now or Finch will stick around and get himself killed worrying about you. Or else he might come around here asking for you himself. You ok with either of those options?"

Finally the impassive wall Viro had constructed around himself seemed to tremble. He appeared thoughtful, then frustrated. He kicked the dirt wall of the tunnel, sending another cascade of earth pouring down. After a pause he stared intently, perhaps even angrily, up into Rigby's face. With a powerful thrust of his arms he hauled himself out of the tunnel. He was taller than Rigby, lean and agile.

"Lead the way, Regal," Viro said, resealing the portal with a kick.

Rigby's heart thumped in her chest as she set course for Vulture. Her promise to her brother might be upheld after all.

As they reached the record shop, Rigby halted. Her door was open ajar. In a panic, she tried to recall whether she'd locked up or not. She usually deadbolted the door upon leaving but today she'd forgotten that along with everything else in her frenzied mind.

"Wait here," she said to Viro, who shrugged and leaned against the fire escape, setting about picking at the green paint that coated his fingernails.

Rigby crept up the stairs and put her ear to the door. She heard nothing. Slowly, she pushed the door open, placing a tentative foot inside.

"Rigby! How nice of you to join us."

It was not lost on Rigby that Richard had declined to call her 'Rigs', the pet name he had bestowed upon her so long ago. Richard leaned like a fallen pillar against her record shelf. His voice was light but peeved, and he didn't raise his eyes when she entered. In his hands he held her copy of Radiohead's *Plastic Trees*, turning it over casually. The flat square looked small and fragile in his oversized hands. Milo's body lay slumped on the floor, his skin already beginning to succumb to the green-gray shades of death.

Rigby's mind raced to calculate the timeline, wondering how Richard could have figured her out so quickly, and how long she'd been gone. Already the red-orange sunlight of the late afternoon promised darkness within a few hours. The approaching darkness was Rigby's first thought, and it registered only after several stunned seconds in which she was unable to process the scene before her. Then she remembered Ledo and his bouncing gait. Of course. With Milo gone Richard had simply chosen a new, eager lackey. Out of the corner of her eye she could see through her southern facing window. Through it she saw the gleam of Richard's sleek motorcycle, fresh purple splotches applied by Pip just the day before. It looked like some great metallic beetle set against the backdrop of the barren outskirts.

He had set her up. He'd sent her down to the basement to get her out of the way while he searched her apartment. She berated herself for not assuming that Richard would follow through on his suspicions. Distrust was as natural in Vulture as the cockroaches that patrolled the city. Her naiveté, her stupid hopefulness that she had for so long beaten into silent submission—until today—would be her final undoing. She should have fled when she'd had the chance, she realized now, all too late. But she didn't really believe that. Even now, locked in Richard's impassive stare, she did not regret meeting Finch and trying to help him.

"It appears that Milo had a nasty fall, don't you think?" asked Richard.

False, remorseless pity coated his words.

Still Rigby said nothing. Richard's stare was unrelenting. A silence hung between them until at last he snapped the record in his hands, so easily it could have been a twig. Rigby let out a gasp that she didn't intend and clamped a hand over her mouth. She felt as though he had snapped a bone in her body.

"Ah, so perhaps that's how we get a conversation going," said Richard, a wicked smile spreading across his broad face. With one hand, he tore an entire shelf of records off the wall. They crashed to the floor in a pile and let out a puff of brown dust. Rigby imagined it was the breath going out of them as they perished upon impact with the floor. The voices that had kept her company for years, extinguished forever. She could have cried if she hadn't been frozen with shock.

When still she did not speak, Richard ripped down another shelf with such force that a second sharp pile of black shards materialized as if out of the ground. He did not stop until every record lay destroyed at his feet. The ground looked like some absurd microcosm of Vulture itself, colorful and iconic album artwork poking through hundreds of jagged pieces of black vinyl arranged helter-skelter about the floor. *The White Album* peered out from behind a cleaved record and Pink Floyd's *Dark Side of the Moon* rainbow album artwork seemed oddly content nestled amongst the destroyed collection. Nirvana's swimming baby peeked up desperately from the rubble. David Bowie's thunder-bolt-painted visage might have been considered understated here in Vulture, his luminous face poking up from the debris. Rigby knew she ought to move, run away, fight, but her body refused to obey her mind's commands. Her feet were rooted to the ground as Richard stripped all of the music out of her world in handfuls.

She did not have time to mourn. Only after the horrible cacophony of shattering records ended did her mind return to her room. Richard's low, rumbling breath reminded her of the dog-wolf's rhythmic pants. Her heart hammered in her ears.

"Have a good family meeting back there, then?" asked Richard.

It was the same tone he used to call out to people at his door, the same air of omnipotence that he hoped to cultivate until he was known and feared even in the most remote corners of Vulture. His voice triggered something in Rigby. She pushed the loss of her music collection aside and replaced it with a hatred that she did not know had been so long latent.

"Love the new look, by the way," he said, gesturing at the

green paint on her hands and head. She had forgotten about the color change, so unused to wearing anything but purple.

She balled her fists and felt rage building in her chest, hot blood pumping through her veins. It was not just hatred for Vulture or the Regals that she felt. It was hatred for Richard. He *was* Vulture. He *was* the Regals. He was the architect of this horrible place and it was designed exactly to his liking. He would not have these buildings refurbished, streets repaired, people fed, or the reign of terror ended as he would sometimes describe in picturesque terms at gang meetings. He was a deranged sociopath with a fetishistic penchant for violence. It struck her like a smack to the face. He had the power to make life better in Vulture—had had such a power for a long time—and had done nothing but accumulate more power for himself. She thought of his opulent apartment above the cinema, his domineering attitude, his demand for unquestioned obedience, his luxuriance in being feared. While perhaps she'd always known this on some level, it was only since seeing her brother again, and considering the mere possibility of family, that she could imagine an escape from Vulture's violent cycle. Before that, she'd just accepted it, and Richard, as simply being the way things were. After all, he and the Regals had been the one constant in her tumultuous life.

"Planning a vacation?" he asked, spitting the words.

She knelt down, as though to plead submission, and in some ways she really was begging for her life. Playing to Richard's ego was never a bad maneuver. She felt his eyes drilling into the top of her skull, and shuddered as his shadow consumed her in its dark expanse. He could end her right now with one solid, booted stomp from his giant feet. But she knew he wouldn't. Even now, she knew her cachet was still worth something in his eyes. He could not kill her as dispassionately as he had so many others, not without toying with her first, shaming her into a fruitless apology of some kind. She was still the abandoned girl he had found in the outskirts.

She remained inert on the ground, head bowed, chest low, waiting for him to speak. He drank in the moment, basking in her evident supplication with a vigor she could almost feel from her fetal position on the ground. When he spoke again, his voice was almost tender.

"Milo had it coming, I'm sure. Get up, Rigs. It's time we had a talk."

She shuffled to her feet, keeping her eyes averted. Anything could trigger his anger again, even an errant glance.

"How much do you remember about the day I found you— saved you, that is, from the outskirts?"

She stood silent and shook her head.

"Very little, of course. You'd been so young. Your clothes were stiff with saltwater, I remember. You'd led me back to a ship-wreck."

Seeing surprise pass over Rigby's face, he continued.

"Oh yes, this had been deep in the outskirts. Near a river that indeed leads to the ocean. I don't tell anyone about it. I never mention it, and nor should you. It gives people hope. And hopeful people like to escape."

He lingered on the last word, boring holes into Rigby with his eyes. She felt her cheeks go flush but she couldn't look away. It was the most he'd ever said about that day.

"I don't know whether your parents abandoned you on that boat, sent you off in hopes of safety somewhere else during the Water Wars, or drowned somewhere along the way. You were so young, barely past toddlerhood. And yet you had that tattoo on your chubby little arm. What kind of monster would do that to a child? But you were crying, Rigs, blubbering about a brother."

She noted how he switched back to Rigs now, caught up in his own monologue.

"And I searched everywhere for him," he continue. "Two recruits for the price of one, you see, and young. A rarity in Vulture, even today, as you know. But even our best recruiters came up empty handed and after about a month I assumed he'd been killed in the wreck or eaten by a Canny or perhaps a dog-wolf."

He walked toward her now. The wooden floorboards groaned under the strain of his heft.

"But then our friend Milo here had noticed the tattoo on the captive's arm. So similar to the one printed on your forearm. Perhaps it was the last ditch effort of a desperate parent. A permanent mark to keep their children together even after all else had been lost. Yes, that indie's tattoo got me thinking, Rigs, just like it has got you thinking, I'm sure."

His long arm shot up and she felt his thick fingers close around her forearm, but she dared not move. He studied it closely before dropping it back against her side.

"By now you've seen him. And I'm sure you'll agree the resemblance is nothing short of uncanny. But think about this a moment Rigs. Dream with me a moment. The Regals need to expand. Into the outskirts. And beyond."

He stared down at her, his eyes large and sincere. She'd never seen him like this before, or heard his voice sound so earnest and genuine. It made the small hairs on her neck prick up to the ceiling.

"To do that we need leadership. As you know, most of the Regals know only how to follow. But Finch, he's got wits and cunning. And you are the only one ruthless and experienced enough to trust. I wouldn't even trust Milo with this."

He seemed to be awaiting some kind of response. But she could not coax her mouth into forming words. Silent tension filled the room.

"Say something!" he thundered.

But before his command had even ceased echoing around the small room, a knife spun through the air like an attacking bird. Richard growled in surprise and anguish as the blade slashed across the top of his head, leaving a bloody equator across his bald scalp. He clapped a wide hand over the wound, blood seeping through his enormous fingers. Viro, a second throwing knife at the ready, stood in the doorway.

Rigby was already out the door and down the steps, and Viro followed after her as the second knife hit the far wall with a thud, missing Richard's nose by centimeters. It sang through the air at lethal speed. Richard's massive hand snatched at the air where Rigby's purple-green locks had been just milliseconds before. Blood ran down his face and mixed with the sweat and dark purple paint around his eyes, giving him a grotesque, melted appearance.

Tearing around the side of the record shop, Rigby came to the motorcycle. Her heart fluxed with a beat of relief to find the keys still in the ignition. Clearly Richard's ego refused to believe that someone would have the gall to steal it in broad daylight.

"Get on!" she cried, but Viro had already taken position behind Rigby on the seat.

Turning the key, the motorcycle jumped to life like a startled dog-wolf. Richard burst through the record shop door, his wide shoulders tearing the door from its hinges so it hung canted at a sharp angle off its frame. The collision and ensuing destruction slowed him down, but only momentarily. Ignoring the stairs, he leapt from the second floor balcony, his eyes wild with animal hatred. He landed with a thud on the ground, dust and gravel bursting up around his feet.

Rigby hadn't been on the motorcycle in years, let alone driven one. But after several moments, she found a grip around the handlebars that felt familiar under her fingers. The motorcycle tore away from the record shop, adjusting its direction with subtle movements of her hands and hips. The machine felt unstoppable, the metal and gears churning beneath her and the smell of gas filling her nostrils. She'd never gone this fast before. At first she wobbled and nearly fell over before steadying herself, learning her own weaknesses and the bike's strengths on the fly. Richard sprinted after them, nearly catching them in a violent lunge before Rigby twisted hard on the throttle and they took off with a burst of speed. As the motorcycle accelerated, Richard faded into the distance, unable to keep pace with the leaping engine.

"Nice shot. Thanks for that," she yelled back to Viro over the roaring engine.

"Don't mention it. I fucking hate that guy," he called back, smiling for the first time since they'd met.

Finch paced the length of the basement. He hated this feeling of powerlessness, this lack of choice. It was dependence in lieu of self-reliance. Everything in which he had taken small joy in as an independent had been ripped from his life. They'd killed Horatio, burned his books, torched his home. Nerves wracked his body as he waited for Richard to bust through the door to kill him at any moment. Finch are a few of the rice kernels off the ground but lost his appetite when he found himself eye to eye with a rat, both going for the same grain. Images of the smoldering radio station scorched holes in his mind. The smell of combusting books seemed to permeate the stale must of the basement prison, clinging to the insides of his nostrils. His anxiety worked itself into a tense ball in his stomach that nothing but frantic pacing could subdue to a dull ache. In a way, Rigby's visit had ruined him. She'd given him hope, something he was trying his best to live without. It had been selfish to send her after Viro. He wished he could have been satisfied with the miracle of his sister alone. Instead, he'd pressed his luck. Guilt and regret redoubled the ache in the pit of his stomach. In sending her after Viro, he risked losing them both. The Scorps didn't exactly take kindly to house calls, especially for their leader's husband. Finch couldn't imagine the danger Rigby would be putting herself in to save someone that rarely spent more time with him than an hour. It would almost have been easier to resign himself to whatever fate the Regals had in store for him. At least then there would be some certainty—anything would be better than this painful, uncertain waiting. But he forced these thoughts away. He'd just discovered he had a sister, after all. Perhaps hope was still worth something, even in Vulture.

Stopping the motorcycle proved much harder than starting it, Rigby learned as they approached the theater. She cut a wide angle and circled around to the back to avoid being seen. Unable to master the kickstand, she simply tore the keys out of the ignition and jumped down, the bike falling heavily on its side. A side mirror popped off as it hit the ground, but otherwise it looked to be undamaged. She didn't take time to assess the damage.

"Nice driving. Not so much for parking though," said Viro, with a rye grin.

"Yeah, sorry about that. Hey, can I ask…"

229

Viro cut her off.

"Why I'm involved with an indie when my wife is the leader of the Scorps?"

"Sorry, I guess I shouldn't ask. It just seems risky."

"Gajjea is a great leader. Better than most of Vulture knows, actually."

Viro shot her a knowing look before continuing.

"But underground, I don't know. Everything is so suppressed and serious. All anyone can talk about is the new order, democracy, and all that stuff. And Finch, well, you've talked to him. He reads these novels. He's a good…"

"Distraction?" Rigby cut in.

"That doesn't sound great, does it?"

Rigby shrugged as they shimmied along the wall of the cinema, keeping to the shadows.

"Listen, I think you should wait back here while I go in to check things out, ok?" Rigby said, happy to change the topic.

"And what if that giant maniac comes back? Think I can take him in a wrestling match? Plus, this place is crawling with Regals. I'll be killed on sight!"

"I'll be quick, I promise. Just trust me," said Rigby, slipping in the door as Viro once again leaned against the wall, spinning a knife in his green fingers. Rigby hoped she'd be able to uphold the promise.

Inside, she kept her head down, her shoulders hunched forward as she worked her way down the steps to the basement. With trembling fingers, she unclasped the lock on the door, praying that Finch was still on the other side. Richard's massive strides would get him here soon, far too soon.

Flinging open the heavy door, she burst into the basement. Finch was on his feet, his muscles tensed, returning her wild-eyed look.

"Ready?" she asked, already turned to go back up the stairs. Finch sensed her anxiety.

"Is it morning already?"

"Change of plans," she said, beckoning him out of the basement.

"Did you get to Viro? Is he safe?" he asked, unable to hide the frantic strain from his voice.

"As safe as we are," she said as they stepped through the doors and started up the stairs.

"Ok," he said, following after her. "Is everything alright?"

She didn't respond to the question but stopped him at the top of the stairs.

"Pretend your hands are cuffed," she said hastily.

Catching her drift, Finch glued his wrists together behind his back. She took up position behind him and shoved him through the door with exaggerated roughness.

Finch found himself in the foyer of the theater. It was the first time in what felt like days that he'd seen something other than the mind numbing gray of the dank basement. Even in the severity of the moment he appreciated the change of scenery. The theater was one of the only buildings in Vulture with all four walls still intact, plus a roof with minimal holes. No wonder the top gang claimed this place. A shove from Rigby reminded him to act like a resigned prisoner rather than an admiring tourist.

People spattered in purple paint scurried about the lobby like frightened rats, on high alert ever since Milo's conspicuous absence had become known. They hung around the door of the inventory room, and every once in a while a daring hand tried the knob. A hush fell over the gossiping Regals as they noticed Rigby escorting the ward. Rigby was ill prepared for the attention. She had always done her best to avoid these people's notice, and yet here she was, ostensibly begging for their watchful eyes with the prisoner being pushed performatively ahead of her. Again she relished the idea of leaving these false comrades for good. The silence was too tense; something had to be said.

"Richard wants me to relocate the prisoner to theater twelve."

The gathered Regals stared at her dumbly. They'd never heard her speak this loud before, other than when she was called upon during meetings. They seemed to be waiting for more.

"Also… meeting in the auditorium in two, no, five minutes. I'll see you guys in there."

She turned in the direction of the hallway that led to theater twelve, but a question stopped her in her tracks.

"Why are you green?" asked a voice she couldn't place from somewhere in the rear of the lobby. She felt sweat accumulating on her palms and her face going red beneath the hastily applied green paint. All eyes remained fixed on her and Finch cast a nervous glance over his shoulder.

"Undercover… scouting the Scorps," she replied, thinking quickly. "Richard's orders."

After a painfully long moment, the groups began to shuffle towards theater one, the gang's *de facto* auditorium. Rigby breathed a sigh of relief and noticed Finch doing the same. Ledo paused a moment longer than the herd, trying to catch Rigby's eye before joining the mass of people. Whether it had been her own clout or invoking Richard's name, clearly her ruse had worked. By fear or submission or both, honed with years of subservience to Richard, the gang had made ardent followers of these once individualistic people. Even briefly donning Richard's power, commanding the purple drones into the auditorium, sickened Rigby. Just yesterday it was her walking mindlessly where she was told, blindly following orders, compromising any will of her own for the benefit of the gang—but really for the benefit of Richard. She watched as they filed into the theater. Hundreds of purple heads bobbed in one undulating purple mass. She did not wait for them all to disappear to continue on her course down the hall.

Almost past the foyer, she heard her name. Her gut screamed for her to sprint forward, through the back exit door in theater six that she knew swung onto the back courtyard, toward escape, freedom.

"Rigby! Hey, Rigby!"

Once her mind caught up with the sound, she recognized the voice. She forced a calm expression over her face, catching and breaking eye contact with Finch in a fraction of a second.

"Hey Paul, what is it?"

She knew him only through Miriam, and she saw the family resemblance in his face. Like his sister, he too wore his heart on his sleeve, and Rigby wondered how he had survived in Vulture, and how he could remain in a gang that had killed his sister, essentially pledging himself to her murderer. Probably the same way she did, Rigby realized: ignoring the painful truths in favor of self-preservation.

"Nothing. Figured you could use some help with the indie. I'm surprised Richard is having you move him alone. Milo messed him up good but rumor is he's cunning as hell, can even talk to dog-wolves!" exclaimed Paul.

Rigby felt Finch bristle beside her. She, too, took offense. Did Paul actually have the audacity to offer her help, as though she couldn't handle the task alone, she wondered? She had more experience in her pinky than he did in his entire body. But she decided to play it cool, temper her pride for a moment. Several people were still straggling into the auditorium to attend a meeting that hadn't been called.

"Sure, thanks Paul," she said, playing along.

"Don't mention it. From what I hear this guy's a real character. Read every book in Vulture, living in some old radio station. And I heard…hey…is he not wearing handc-."

He never got the word out. Finch lashed out with a sharp elbow to Paul's skull, so quick Rigby barely saw it. Within seconds Paul's eyes had rolled back in his head and he dropped to the ground. In a surreal, reflective moment, she pondered to herself how wrong it must be that she had seen so many people collapse in front of her like that in her lifetime. She reminded herself that Richard was not yet one of those people. He was still very much alive and he could be here at any moment. The thought snapped her attention back to the moment. He would be close now, those enormous strides carrying him the mile length from the record shop to the cinema in less than ten minutes at a fast walk. Faster if he ran. Finch was already taking off down the hallway, rubbing his elbow. Risking a glance back, Rigby saw a few Regals collecting around Paul and helping him to his feet as he pointed in their direction with a trembling finger and wide eyes, still too stunned by the blow to speak. Rigby caught up to Finch and led him through the back exit of theater six into the violet light of evening.

"Damnit," intoned Rigby, looking up the wide asphalt path that wound into the city center.

Finch followed her gaze. With loping strides three yards long, Richard steamed toward them. They heard his heavy footfalls as he pounded the earth. Even from a distance they could see the firm set of his jaw, the clenched ball of his fists, and the shine of his bald, bleeding scalp.

"You got a plan of some kind?" asked Finch, his pounding

heart sending a ripple through his voice.

"No, do you?" asked Viro, stepping away from the wall.

Finch whipped around at the sound of his voice.

"Viro! I'm so glad you're safe. Milo... they knew about you... I thought maybe—"

Behind them the door bursts open and Regals poured out like puss from a scab, a torrent of purple arms and legs.

Wordlessly, Rigby pointed to the downed motorcycle. Finch was already there. Rigby joined him and together, straining against the heavy machine, they managed to flip the bike back up onto its wheels. Finch fumbled the key into the ignition. He had to use two hands to steady his trembling grip.

"Viro we gotta go!" he yelled, holding out a hand to the man leaning against the wall.

"Go where?" he responded. The question was an answer in itself.

Finch stared at him with imploring eyes as Regals hurtled toward them from the theater door. Their collective feet stampeded around them, filling the air with a steady beat that built to a roar as they approached.

"Move!" Rigby said.

Finch tore himself from Viro's impassive eyes. Moving gracefully, he surrendered the front seat, and Rigby smoothly replaced him as though they'd practiced the maneuver all their lives. The purple hoard was upon them by the time the engine buzzed to life. As Rigby pushed off with her heel, a woman taller than Finch and far more fearsome was the first to reach their party. The guard looked murderously into Rigby's treacherous eyes and yanked her off the bike. Soon Finch too was engaged with two Regals, beating them off with kicks and punches, but already two more purple figures had joined the fight. Finch cried out to

Rigby, but she was pinned to the ground by the Regal guard she'd passed so many times on her way into the cinema. Purple arms and legs blotted the sun from view.

Suddenly, however, pale faces and green hands and shocks of green hair began materializing out of nowhere. Still engaged with the tall guard, both Rigby and her combatant paused to watch the subtle shifting of sand and gravel as the holes appeared. At least four tunnels opened up behind the theater, now six, now ten. Too many to count and out poured Scorps like wasps from a nest. Viro had been right. Gajjea had been building an empire under everyone's nose. Hundreds of Scorps streamed out of the tunnels, knives spinning through the air. Rigby wondered if Viro's absence had launched this attack, or if the Scorps had simply been waiting for an opportune moment to strike.

Within moments the Scorps were overtaking the Regals, slashing them bloodily to the ground with throwing knives or else pulling them screaming down into the tunnels. Rigby felt the heavy guard turn to stone and collapse on top of her. Hauling the massive corpse off of her chest, she saw a knife protruding from deep in the center of her back. Frantically, Rigby whipped her head around, scanning for danger. It was then that she realized she was still wearing the green paint, perhaps the only thing keeping her safe from the Scorps' ambush.

First she looked to the horizon. Richard had stopped to watch the battle unfold, watching his precious numbers decline before his eyes and making no move to join them in the fight. An endless stream of Scorps poured out of the tunnels. Rigby couldn't believe the numbers Gajjea had managed to amass in secrecy underground. She turned her attention back to the ensuing battle, searching for Finch. Purple arms and green hands flailed in every direction, bursts of green hair whipping to a blur amidst the swinging purple dreadlocks. She located him finally, standing next to Viro by the wall, a few meters away from the action. She'd have to get him out of here, with or without Viro. Neither gang's victory would make things any safer for him here. With difficulty, Rigby heaved the bike back onto two wheels and clambered onto the seat, desperately searching for the keys before realizing they were still in the ignition.

"Viro, let's go! We can still escape! There's a river. It leads to an ocean but we gotta go right now!" Finch implored, pulling at Viro's hand.

"I can't, Finch," he said. His voice was stony and he looked Finch dead in the eye.

"Viro! Let's go, please!" Finch begged.

"Finch, we gotta get outta here!"

He heard Rigby's shout from several yards away, but he ignored her.

"Finch, come on!" she screamed, revving the engine for emphasis. She looked out to the horizon. She could be gone now, motoring miles away, she knew. She was unable to stifle the thought. But she stopped herself, knowing that she couldn't keep operating so dispassionately.

Finch heard his sister, but again he ignored her calls, focusing every ounce of his attention on Viro. He couldn't bring himself to give up on Viro, not even for a sister he'd known all of one day. He and Viro had a history that Finch couldn't deny even if Viro could. Viro had been the only human relationship in Finch's life, and surely that was worth fighting for. The thought rooted his feet to the ground.

"Viro, they'll kill us if we stay."

His voice was pleading and Viro could only stare his sparkling eyes back at him.

"Please. Please Viro. Maybe we can hide out in the outskirts together. I know this place, they'd never find—"

Suddenly Finch was flat on his back, his arms pinned to his sides by unknown knees as Viro let out a gasp. Looking up, Finch saw the eyes he'd only ever seen before in graffiti.

"I understand Viro here was having some trouble recruiting you," hissed Gajjea, her elegantly appointed green hands tightening around Finch's throat. "Tell me, what *wasn't* he offering you?"

Before his vision began to go fuzzy, Finch watched as Gajjea stared viciously into Viro's blank eyes. Viro said nothing, and did nothing, simply watching as his wife squeezed the life out of Finch.

Finch felt himself blacking out, pressure building in his forehead. And then, as suddenly as it had arrived, the weight on his arms was gone. Looking up, he saw Rigby seated atop the motorcycle. To his left, he saw Gajjea hunched over, a single tire track traced across her midsection. She coughed blood, all the while staring into Viro's unblinking eyes, his mouth agape.

"Get on lover boy," yelled Rigby, holding out a hand to her brother.

Finch took it and swung himself onto the backseat of the bike. Rigby cut through the crowd and the mob of battling Regals and Scorps fell away behind them. Risking a glance backwards, Finch saw Viro crouching by Gajjea's contorted body. Two dozen Scorps scurried out of the theater, straining under the weight of a massive water tankard they'd tethered to their backs. Richard's monumental form stared after them as they drove past his sightline. But only briefly. Finch knew that the notorious Richard would never give up so easily.

CHAPTER 17

To leave this Paradise, but shalt possess / A paradise within thee, happier far.

— John Milton, *Paradise Lost*

The motorcycle almost made it easy to feel safe. Once Rigby adjusted her driving to accommodate the added weight of Finch, they sped along at as decent a clip as the ancient bike could muster. As the sun reached its late afternoon peak and they passed through the long shadow of the decrepit bridge, Finch imagined the whimsy of taking a drive, whiling away time and taking in the scenery as the breeze tousled his hair, like the characters in his novels.

Rigby did her best to negotiate the abrupt divots in the terrain, but they were both glad when the bumpy city streets subsided to flatness. The unending, planar outskirts loomed in front of them. Dust and gravel kicked up behind the motorcycle's spinning tires. Thinking only of the river ahead, Finch forgot his thirst. He tapped Rigby on the shoulder. He stretched out his hand, pointing.

"I used to live there. For a long time, actually."

He had to yell over the roar of the old engine and the tires crunching over the dry earth. Rigby followed his hand though she knew where he was pointing. Given the chaos of the last few days, she had almost forgotten. The guilt ravaged her in thoughts that stung as they flitted through her mind. She had killed his dog-wolf and been party to the destruction of his home. She had helped Richard eliminate the little life that Finch had strived to preserve in Vulture. The books—bits of the past—that he had painstakingly collected over years and years only to have them ripped from his life. Just as Richard had destroyed her records, she had destroyed his books. One day she would like to talk to Finch about those books, but not today. As she took in the smoldering pile of ash that he had gestured toward, she removed one hand from the throttle to pull her sleeve as far down over her forearm as it would go.

"Do you want to stop?" she asked.

She hoped that he would say no, knowing she might not be able to bear her guilt so brazenly.

"No."

His hand dropped and he readjusted his lanky frame on the bike, every part of him facing forward as they drove on. He placed tentative hands around Rigby's waist as she accelerated, and Rigby smiled.

"You liked reading, didn't you?" she asked,

"Yes. More than anything, almost. It—the books, I mean— took me... somewhere else."

Rigby nodded.

"That was music for me. I'd close my eyes, and the sound would just wash over me. I wouldn't think about another thing until the song was over."

"I heard it once," said Finch, thoughtfully, as though trying to conjure the sound that had transfixed him under the fire escape of the record shop in Vulture.

"Amazing, isn't it?" asked Rigby.

It was Finch's turn to nod.

Vulture's ramshackle skyline faded behind them in the singular rear view mirror until the buildings looked no bigger than a jagged set of teeth. Finch directed her past the Gonzaga University gate and glanced at the piles of ash, large enough inside the decrepit library to be seen even as they whizzed past on the motorcycle. The rough, molten ground of the city gradually gave way to wind-smoothed stone and coarse sand. They sped headlong into the outskirts, far deeper than Rigby had ever been.

"Am I going the right way?" Rigby finally thought to ask, shouting over the thrum of the old engine.

"The only wrong way is back there," replied Finch.

Her smile was quickly replaced with doubt. She reminded herself that they were far from free. Their plan, in all its intricate glory, consisted of one word that neither of them had any memory of seeing: ocean. Finch had mentioned only a river and the words of some hermit that he'd once met. They had no reason to think that it was a feasible option for escape, or even that it was safer than Vulture. It had been the ocean that spat the two of them here over two decades ago, and now they raced back into its arms.

And yet still she could not help feeling hopeful. She'd never felt this much control over her own actions. Sitting astride the bike, adjusting her grip on the accelerator, she felt as though the two tires were her own feet, carrying her ever faster away from a world she'd be happy to forget. She'd been clad in purple since she was a young child, and that attire alongside fear had been enough to order first her days then her years. Each rotation of the motorcycle's tires broke the cycle anew.

Briefly, Rigby considers the possibility that she was jealous of Finch. He had lived according to his own terms, freer than her in many ways. She had forgone every pleasure but her music, denying herself any identity that did not somehow benefit her survival. Perhaps that was what had made it so easy, so automatic, to sink those arrows into the dog-wolf's skull. She was more of a weapon than a person. With Finch seated directly behind her—a brother with a face, a personality, a history—she could not imagine doing him wrong. How had she lived so long without compassion? Could she recover even a shred of the humanity that she had sacrificed to Richard and the Regals? Perhaps Finch could help her. Killing at the behest of Richard and the gang had been easier than cultivating a personal resolve. All her life, what she'd perceived as outright survival, had really been cowardice.

"Are we slowing down?"

Finch's worried voice jolted her mercifully from her mental self-flagellation. The bike did seem to be slowing down. The breeze that had been rushing over their bodies was gradually being replaced with the dead heat of the outskirts. The motor's roar subsided as though it had grown tired, now emitting little more than a persistent rasp.

"We're out of gas," sighed Finch.

Rigby could see only the dry, flat land of the outskirts stretching into the horizon. The arid expanse worried her. The possibility of a river looked as unlikely as ever, and Richard could be in pursuit by now.

"Damnit."

Her voice was flat. She looked over her shoulder, half expecting Richard to be there, smiling, stepping up out of the miles of flat earth that surrounded them. Her mind recalibrated to its baseline survivalist mode, replacing the pleasant reveries offered by the rushing speed of the motorcycle.

After another two hundred meters or so, the bike fell silent. It sailed along almost noiselessly save for the flat drone of the tires on the smooth ground. They remained planted on the bike until the moment it came to a complete halt, as though it might catch a second wind and jump back to life at any second and leave them in the dust.

Without a word they let the bike crash to the ground, its other side mirror popping off and hurtling through the air before landing several feet away. They set off walking into the far stretches of the outskirts, where the sun lay like a thick blanket over everything but the undersides of rocks. Small lizards shot off at the crunch of their approaching feet and Finch thought of Horatio, snapping up the lizards as snacks when they'd walked together.

They knew they should have been running. But the silence of the outskirts was calming, soporific even. They maintained an easy gait, matching each other's strides. Occasionally a zephyr picked up and they'd shield their eyes from the dust clouds lingering in the air. They did not speak, all energy focused on the right left pattern of their feet on the flat land. Their steps crunched pleasantly against the dusty earth, and the dry air had a pleasant, smoky scent. They were deeper into the outskirts by now than even the most remote Canny bonfires.

Finch halted, which made Rigby jump. Out of the horizon, an enormous shape loped toward them at high speed. As it came into view, they saw the four powerful legs and the lolling tongue of a dog-wolf. Rigby froze upon seeing the bounding animal, careening right at them. For a moment, Finch's mind tricked him into thinking it could be Horatio, leaping forward, fully alive. Rigby too found herself hoping that perhaps somehow the dog-wolf had survived the arrows, that the blood had been caused by something else, absolving her of the cruel murder. But both know they were chasing private ghosts with these imaginings.

As the hound got closer, the siblings grew fearful. It picked up speed, taking aim right at them, its massive paws trampling the ground in a steady tattoo that grew louder as it approached. Twenty feet away. Fifteen. Ten. The ground stretched flat and unsympathetic around them on all sides, leaving them as vulnerable as corpses to a vulture. Rigby clasped her hand on Finch's arm.

Just before the dog overtook them, a long, sharp whistle echoed across the barren outskirts. In a sharp, athletic movement the dog diverted course, rushing back from whence it came, its long tail swishing as it followed the whistle. They watched, frozen until the dog-wolf again disappeared into the horizon.

Rigby exhaled, realizing that she had been holding her breath, and let go of Finch's arm. There were soft crescent moons where her nails had dug into his skin. Finch, too, was tense. In an instant they had been made painfully aware of just how quickly their efforts could be dashed. The openness of the outskirts that had just moments earlier felt so promising now seemed submerged in doubt. Still, they did not move, as though to take a step forward would break the fragile tension that held them together.

"I had a dog like that," said Finch, his eyes low.

He'd said it so softly Rigby almost missed it, but her gut felt a twinge. She knew she could never tell him. In his voice she heard the pain of loss. She wanted to scream, to explain somehow that she had simply been doing a job, that she had just wanted to stay alive, like him. She tugged at a purple-green dreadlock and looked to the horizon.

"Sorry about Viro," she said, jumping at the first topic change she could think of. She hated to replace a bad old thought with a bad new one, but at least Viro hadn't been her fault. The dry sweat on her face and arms made her skin feel too tight.

Finch nodded slowly and took a step forward. Then another.

Together they continued on, walking in silence. After a while, he spoke again.

"He'll be alright," he said with a shrug, hoping to disguise the hurt with nonchalance. His braid knocked against his back with a steady cadence as he walked.

Rigby winced. Being an indie meant coming to terms with loneliness, and Finch was no exception, no matter how many books he'd read. She was happy to change the subject again, this time more strategically.

"Who just whistled all the way out here, a Canny you think?" asked Rigby, looking for some confirmation that she had not simply imagined the sound.

"Guy."

"What guy?"

"No. A man named Guy. He's the hermit I told you about. The old Bleak with the dog-wolves."

"Oh, right."

She felt she was losing Finch to his somber inner thoughts, his brow furrowing, eyes glazing over and staring straight ahead. They resumed their solemn journey into the depths of the outskirts, consumed with thoughts of what lay ahead and behind. With so few structures blocking its path, the late afternoon sun stretched orange and red into infinity, gilding the outskirts in a blinding shade of gold.

"Let's speed up. Try to make it before sunset," mentioned Finch.

Rigby was happy to see that his tone, and even his eyes seemed to have returned to the present. Still too exhausted to run, they quickened their pace. They walked until their feet went numb, forcing one foot in front of the other with a repetitive tempo, sweat streaming down their skin and clothes. Rigby felt hungry, thirsty, and exhausted. She hadn't even considered the possibility of dying from these ever present threats until now, when they felt like large black vultures circling above her head. Being a Regal her whole life had shielded her from experiencing these rudimentary concerns. Supplies and food were rationed, but they were always available.

At last, the sweet, musty smell of riverbank mud greeted their nostrils. They exchanged weak smiles as they mutually acknowledged the development. They quickened their pace again, this time motivated by unfamiliar hope rather than fear. On the horizon they could see it, a murky, gray-blue colored gash in the otherwise brownish landscape. The sunlight glimmered and sparkled off the water's surface. Rigby paused to admire it, mesmerized by the sight of water. Taking her hand, Finch pulled her on.

"I knew I'd see you again, Mr. Nothing!"

Guy's voice broke through the sublime of the Spokane River. At first they couldn't tell where the voice came from, the words dissipating into nothingness in the barren landscape. They noticed the dog-wolves first. They swirled like furry clouds around Guy's waist, chasing each other's tails and whimpering for the lizard jerky he tossed down to their paws and into the eager maws. There must have been seven dog-wolves in total, and still more appeared out of the outskirts as they watched. Rigby found herself salivating at the sight of the contented chewing, gnawing dogs.

The old man's voice was unlike any Rigby had ever heard in Vulture. It was casual, slow and bouncy. It's undulating cadence made her think of her James Taylor record, or maybe Cat Stevens. She took an immediate liking to the man. Hope built in her chest as she looked from the old man to the river in the distance.

"You trade in your Horatio for a girlfriend then?" joked Guy.

"Horatio's dead. This is my sister," replied Finch, bluntly.

Guy let out a low whistle, setting off the dogs in a chorus of yipping. Once he got them settled down again with a few handfuls of lizard jerky he went on.

"Take the good with the bad, I suppose," offered Guy.

Despite the simplicity of the short phrase, Rigby took comfort. It was exactly the kind of thing she wished she could think to say when Finch went numb and silent, or when Miriam would look at her with those pleading eyes. Below her feet, she saw that the crusted surface of the outskirts was darker here, the hard land giving way to soft dirt that cushioned her steps.

"Think we could get some of that jerky?" asked Finch, uncomfortable being the subject of pity.

"Certainly," said Guy, holding out a handful of small, shriveled lizards.

Finch and Rigby each took a few morsels and savored the salty taste.

"I'm Rigby," she blurted. "Thanks."

She felt she should say something, anything, before accepting this man's food. It seemed strange that food would be offered without some kind of recompense or distributed as a ration. Really she wanted to ask him how he'd survived out here in the relentless desert sun for all these years. His skin was crisped to a dark brown hue and deep wrinkles traversed his face and arms.

"Don't even mention it," he crooned softly. "You folks sound more haggard than these dog's here after a hunt. Think you'll want to come in the shade, take a load off?"

Rigby clung to his every word. This man was free, she thought, maybe even blissfully unaware of the horrors that took place on an hourly basis in Vulture, less than five miles from where they stood. More likely he was fully aware of Vulture's terrible conditions and happily avoiding them here by the riverbank. Every part of her yearned to join the man in the shade, reclining and sipping the cool water from the river and gnawing on lizard jerky, listening to stories about the past from his point of view. The black tattoos ringing his fingers intrigued her.

"We can't," said Finch, with certitude that instantly snapped Rigby out of her hopeful daydream. "Sorry."

"Well, what's the rush cowboy? Last I checked all the clocks stopped working sometime during the Water Wars," joked Guy.

"We need the canoe," said Finch, adding, "please."

Guy munched slowly on the lizard jerky, nodding as he took in the severity of Finch's tone. The dog-wolves dispersed as he walked toward Finch, chasing each other about or meandering off with their noses to the ground.

"You alright then, friend?"

He didn't sound alarmed but rather concerned at Finch's urgency. Rigby looked from Finch to Guy. A bead of sweat dribbled down the side of her brother's face.

"We will be," was all Finch offered in explanation.

"It's all yours, Finch Nothing. It's just up the bank a ways. Blew there in a sandstorm last month. Thing's more trouble than it's worth to me anyways."

The nonchalance of his tone could never communicate the impact of the favor, offering them not just a canoe but a means to escape, the key to their freedom. Rigby's heart burst at the man's unthinking kindness, so starkly different from her own selfish nature.

Finch followed Guy's pointing hand up the riverbank. He couldn't see the canoe but figured it had been cast around the bend that was shielded from view by an abrupt wall of earth.

Guy's fingernails were long and yellow, extending full inches past his ruddy fingertips.

"I imagine you'll want to head for the ocean. Now I know you feel like you've run out of turf here in Vulture, but the ocean is no promise land, especially not in my dinky canoe. I feel I ought to warn you," continued Guy, a rich sincerity entering his voice. His brown teeth poked out from his beard when he spoke.

"Richard is after us," said Rigby.

"Ah, the notorious Richard," mused Guy. "I could have guessed. He never will be satisfied, will he? Used to be a good soldier. A great soldier, actually. I knew him back then, of course. He led his troops to many a victory during the Water Wars—just before your time I suppose. Of course, that's why everyone followed him after the Water Wars ended. They trusted him, you know? But he's changed right along with this city. Started disagreeing with people, forging his own path. That's when he made us Bleaks just about extinct. Hell, now who knows where he'll stop."

A pause followed Guy's short speech, as though the words had been buried for a long time before finally springing forth.

"Thank you, Guy," said Finch.

He placed a hand on Guy's shoulder and looked him in the eye.

"Yeah, thank you," added Rigby.

Like Finch she was unused to speaking politely, to receiving generosity and returning it in kind. She crossed her arms over her chest, unsure what to do with her body.

"As I said, don't even mention it. Go on then, before the sun sets."

They set off towards the steep bank, a breeze lifting the coolness off the river and into their clothes and hair. The dirt soon turned to mud, squelching under their feet.

"I've never met someone like him," said Rigby, after a time. They might have been taking a pleasant walk were it not for the sweat and grime that coated their bodies and the exhaustion that wracked their limbs and the fear that prickled at their backs.

"Do you remember anything about our parents?" Finch asked.

"No, nothing. Richard told me something about a shipwreck once, but I don't remember."

Finch nodded ruefully.

"Me neither. "

It was the most conversational tone she'd ever heard out of him. It felt strangely calming to be talking so casually, walking along a river from which she could not remove her eyes. She wondered how long ago people had simply strolled and talked like this. Again she wished they could sit in the shade with Guy and while away an afternoon, discussing music and the past. She had so many questions. She'd said so little beyond the necessary in her life.

Finch too found himself lost in the sublime of the moment. Even though the wide river was muddy and the vegetation sparse, the landscape was beautiful to him. He longed for one of his novels, a nice paperback flexible with age and short enough to read cover to cover in an afternoon on the smooth, shady bank. *The Sun Also Rises* would have been such a novel, reading in the shady riverbank along with the characters that napped in the shade after an afternoon of drinking and fishing.

They rounded the turn and spotted the canoe, its white belly flipped up to the sky. They smiled at each other tiredly. Clambering down the clay mud of the bank, they flipped the canoe upright, the smooth old wood feeling sturdy in their hands. A paddle was pinned into the side of the bow. This too felt satisfying to the touch, hewn by a carpenter who had taken care in his work many years ago.

The last time either of them had been on the water they'd been marooned in Vulture. Still they were eager to step into the small boat, embarking onto the next phase of their escape. Finch waded into the water and pushed off, Rigby seating herself behind him. The river was lazy and flat and Finch splashed the oars awkwardly in the water before discovering a smooth, rhythmic stroke. Rigby lay back as Finch rounded the hook of land that led them back to where Guy would be waiting.

"We should say bye to Guy," offered Rigby, unsure how Finch would respond to the delay. Finch cupped his hand and ladled water into his mouth. Rigby followed suit, water dribbling down her chin.

"And ask him for some more jerky," he replied.

Right, thought Rigby, chiding herself for not thinking practically like Finch. The canoe offered no guarantees. Starvation, thirst and any number of other calamities still lay on the horizon if they were to succeed in reaching the ocean. Still, as the sun's mild late-afternoon rays caressed her hair and face, Rigby felt optimistic. She dragged her hand in the cool, murky water, feeling the silky fluidity of the river as the canoe skimmed pleasantly along. Paint slipped off her fingers in the pull of the water. A nap on a canoe in a lazy river. The thought had the makings of a song. A whole record even.

Finch stared straight ahead, learning the ins and outs of the canoe as he rowed. As on the motorcycle, it felt new and wonderful to be in control, to choose his own movements rather than relying on shadows to determine his course. Rigby's presence at his back made him feel secure in a way that he hadn't since losing Horatio. He'd asked her about their parents because it was the only concrete question he could think to ask. Infinite more questions had been dancing around his mind since the moment they'd reconnected back at the cinema. He didn't even know which of them was older. But there would be plenty of time for questions once they got the canoe upriver, he figured, a notion that sounded pleasant after the chaos of the past few days. As they approached the teetering dock near Guy's shady bank, Finch decided to make room within his *self-reliance* philosophy for Rigby. The decision existed, of course, in direct conflict with the philosophy itself, just as it had for Horatio. He'd vowed not to make such an exemption ever again after Horatio's death, but he couldn't have guessed that a sister would appear. They would be reliant on each other, and in that way become self-reliant together.

Rigby tied the canoe to one of the dock's many rusty iron outcroppings, jutting off at menacing angles. The expertly fastened knot impressed Finch. On wobbling legs they stood up one at a time to disembark. Using an ancient ladder, they clambered up onto the dock, every second prepared for the worm-eaten wood to disintegrate under their weight. Impossibly, it held.

CHAPTER 18

Nothing beside remains. Round the decay
Of that colossal Wreck, boundless and bare
The lone and level sands stretch far away.

— Percy Bysshe Shelley, *Ozymandias*

Right away something felt off. The yipping of the dogs that had become reliably constant before they'd left for the canoe had gone eerily silent. Even the slow ebb of the river had hushed, and a charged stillness filled the dry air. A rank, familiar smell of iron and zinc hung thick in the heat.

"So nice to see a brother and sister getting along."

Richard's voice somehow managed to be simultaneously sinister and sing-song all in one. Rigby's heart leapt into her throat and Finch hardened to concrete where he stood on the dock. Richard's immense frame was taller and more immovable than anything for miles in every direction. He hadn't bothered with the gash that Viro had slashed in his scalp. His face was a mask of purple paint and scarlet blood, and streaked with trails of sweat etched into his mottled face.

But he was not nearly as sweaty as the people several yards behind him, bent over their knees and heaving along the bank. Dozens of people panted and sweat on the hot ground, exhausted. Looking closer, Rigby saw that they were junkers. Somehow the combined effort of their underfed bodies had pulled him here. She spied Pip's frail chest hunched over his knees, though he lifted his head up to stare her down until she looked away.

Around their emaciated waists were fixed large, thick belts attached to long black ropes. Richard had used them like cattle, nearly fifty of them straining to pull him here at a speed relentless enough to catch up to the downed motorcycle. With their eyes, Finch and Rigby followed the ropes back to their origin. Dozens of these ropes, one for each person, stretched equal length and had been secured to the grill of a large, flat hunk of rust and metal. It took them a moment to realize what they were looking at. It appeared to be the frame of some once massive dump truck. Rigby recognized it from the lot behind the cinema, where formerly it had sat disintegrating for years. After decades of sitting in disuse, its old withered tires seemed to have barely survived the journey into the outskirts. They were covered in the dust and gravel of the barren terrain. Though only a chassis with wheels, the junkers had to have truly exerted themselves to drag the hefty, rusted beast through the desert. With the Regals tied up in a battle with the Scorps, the junkers must have been Richard's only option. He stood atop the flat metal structure, his shoulders nearly as wide as the grill of the truck.

Guy's body lay limp and unmoving at the foot of the dock, his skull caved-in by what Finch could only assume had been Richard's sledgehammer-like fist. A scrap of lizard jerky remained clutched in his hand, the wrinkled lizard head poking out from between Guy's black-ringed fingers. Finch gasped at the sight of his body, and Rigby's breath caught in her throat. Still more of the scene began to filter through the blindness of their initial shock. In the distance, the pack of dog-wolves tore into a downed animal, their maws stained with blood, too preoccupied by instinct to be conscious of the loss of their human friend. Rigby felt sick. How she'd ever had so much as a conversation with such a villain now wracked her body with shame.

Finch felt the fury rising within him. Each starved, panting man and woman before him was a fate that might have been his own. Guy's death was senseless and avoidable. Guilt clawed at his psyche, knowing that he had dragged all the violence of Vulture here, disrupting Guy's peace and ending his life. Richard's light-hearted voice and satisfied grin enraged him further.

"Not happy to see me, then?" called Richard again. He stepped heavily and with slow confidence off of his hastily made chariot.

"I'll admit I didn't expect the dog-wolves," he said, not waiting for their reply. "Luckily I brought enough meat to spare one for a distraction."

Peering closer through the mass of muscled fur, Rigby and Finch could see a slender arm that finished in a small hand. Richard had sacrificed a junker to the dog-wolves. He took long, deliberate strides toward Rigby and Finch. The dock creaked with each step, testing the tensile strength of each ancient wooden board.

"They'll probably be hungry again soon though, I'd wager. And I'd hate to disappoint them. Wouldn't you? You're a friend of the beasts, aren't you, Finch?" A cunning grin spread across his face as he stared down at Finch.

Rigby and Finch remained immobile, side-by-side at the edge of the dock. But just then Finch rushed forward, his arm raised and fist aimed high at Richard's neck. Richard hardly changed pace. With a harsh swat of his arm Finch hit the deck, and rolled onto his side. Immediately, he got back to his feet, hatred in his eyes. Again he lunged at Richard's torso, but this time a shove to the chest sent Finch hurtling backwards, clutching at a rotting post just in time to keep from falling off the dock. Finch breathed hard, the wind knocked out of him, able only to stare at Richard with murderous eyes.

"Just let us go Richard," said Rigby. She'd finally found her voice but it was weak, catching in her throat.

He chortled and took several more unhurried steps in her direction. He'd never looked so large to her. With nothing to obstruct its expanse, his shadow stretched for miles into the outskirts.

"And leave some doubt? Let Vulture know that Richard has lost a step? The balance would be irreparably upset. People need to know the boundaries."

Rigby squared her shoulders as he approached, emboldened both by rage and fear.

"There is no balance. Without the Regals you'd just be another massive oaf trying to stay alive."

"Ah, but I do have the Regals, don't I? And it's you I no longer have a need for other than as a taxidermy warning to other creative minds like yourself."

From behind his back he brandished the crossbow that had been the end of so many before her. It looked weightless in his ample hands. A heavy black arrow finishing in a ruthlessly sharp tip was mounted, ready to spring forward at lethal speed, and now he lifted it to Rigby's forehead. A fitting end, she found herself thinking. Justice served for Horatio's death.

Finch attempted to get to his feet but stumbled over again, landing hard on his hands and knees. Richard dug a heel into Finch's leg that keeled him over in groaning immobility.

"Leave her alone!" yelled Finch from his compromised position on the splintery dock. "Just shoot me and let her go back to the Regals in one piece. Haven't you lost enough Regals already today?"

Rigby stared at her brother, frozen under the trained arrow

while he was squirming on the ground in pain. His breath was ragged and he winced as he spoke but he never took his eyes off Richard. She wanted nothing more than to help him up, get back into the canoe and paddle away together.

"Not a chance. But thank you for your unwarranted input, indie." said Richard. "She's been given enough chances. You, on the other hand, still show promise as a junker. We could have used your help pulling that rusty hunk out here, now that we're down a member," he joked, nodding his head in the direction of the distracted pack of dog-wolves. "But no matter. You'll have a chance to pull us back."

While he was addressing Finch, Rigby made her move. She drove a vicious kick into Richard's oversized knee. He stumbled backward but only a step. The next thing Rigby knew, she was belly down on the coarse wood of the dock. The jagged splinters of the old sun baked boards cut her cheeks. She felt Richard's heavy boot on the center of her back, pressing so hard she thought her heart might stop. Her jaw was beginning to swell where he'd punched her to the ground.

The heavy tip of the crossbow pressed against the back of her head. The sharp end cut into her scalp and a trickle of blood dripped down her neck.

Rigby felt the arrowhead repositioning on the crown of her skull. She found herself closing her eyes and holding her breath, as if bracing for the killing shot might somehow make the blow less effective. She heard Richard positioning his giant hand around the trigger.

Nearly ten seconds passed before she opened her eyes. The muddy river stretched under her face, visible through slats in the dock. She turned her head once to the left, then to the right. Her shadow in the murky water below mimicked her movements. In the reflection she watched as her shimmering hand landed tender pats on her swollen jaw.

She no longer felt the crossbow steadied on her skull. The pressure of Richard's boot was gone too. There was a rasping sound that she couldn't place coming from somewhere behind her. Testing her strength, she pushed herself to her knees and turned around, her back to the water. Finch was resting against the rickety wooden post that stuck up off the edge of the dock. His eyes were wide, his mouth agape. Following his expression, she too felt her jaw go slack.

The rasping noise was Richard, his eyes bulging and his considerable hands grasping at the belt around his throat, a vein the width of an extension cord throbbing from his neck to his scalp as though ready to burst. Behind him stood Pip, his emotionless face focused as he maintained the tension on the belt—the same belt that had been strapped around his waist moments ago and was now tightly coiled around Richard's throat. Pip's three-fingered hand strained to grip the belt and the veins in his arms popped up from his skin. His small knuckles were white as bone. And yet despite his trembling, shriveled chest and his skinny arms and missing fingers, he looked powerful, his supple forearms tensing as the taut belt at last extinguished the life out of Richard's immense, kicking body. Pip held onto the belt for several more seconds, as though to kill Richard twice. His face remained impassive even when Richard's lifeless form crashed to the side, breaking one of the old boards in half and sending ancient dust and sharp pieces of wood bursting into the air.

Agog with shock, Rigby could hardly tell if the scene that had just played out before her eyes had been real. She took a deep breath and exhaled heavily. She couldn't peel her eyes from Richard's corpse, his huge body lying strangled on the deck and his massive head a morbid shade of blue under the caked paint and blood.

"Pip!" was all she could manage to say.

"Thank you," added Finch, meeting Pip's hollow eyes. "That was -"

"Incredible," finished Rigby.

Finch worked himself to his feet and hobbled over to Rigby, helping her up as well. The rest of Richard's now former junkers watched from the edge of the riverbank, jaws succumbing to gravity at what they'd witnessed, too transfixed to move or make a sound. Finch put a tentative hand on Pip's bony shoulder.

"Incredible," he repeated. "It really was. Thank you."

He looked directly into Pip's unblinking gray eyes as he spoke, hoping to impart the reestablished faith in humanity he had just experienced. Rigby hugged his slender frame and Pip accepted the embrace, though he did not reciprocate. Alive or dead, Richard had taken a toll on his psyche.

With little experience in intimacy of any kind between the three of them, Rigby and Finch exchanged glances. It was time to go, their eyes mutually agreed. The sun was beginning to set and the promised ocean lay alluringly ahead, a fresh start that they both craved. Returning to Vulture was still out of the question. Richard's massive void would quickly and bloodily be filled, either by another gang or, more likely, by infighting amongst the Regals. The Scorps wouldn't necessarily welcome Rigby and Finch back as political refugees, either. With both Gajjea and now Richard dead, Vulture was liable to sink to whole new levels of depravity. The Scorps had the numbers; perhaps they'd return to life above ground, establish the democracy they'd been building for so long underground. Or perhaps everyone would turn to Leak and descend to the level of the Cannies. And if the Veins had been waiting for a moment to reestablish order, surely this would be it. Still, Finch and Rigby were fugitives. Escape was the only option. The canoe bobbed laconically below them, rapping against the legs of the dock with the rhythmic ebb of the river.

"Take care, Pip," said Rigby finally, hoping her tone sufficiently reflected her gratitude.

Finch gave Pip a final, unreciprocated hug, turned to the water and they began walking down the length of the dock. Pip remained where he stood, belt still held limp at his side, bloody creases in his palms, staring blankly after them.

"She killed him," he said at last, his hollow voice resounding in the dead silence of the riverbank.

Rigby and Finch turned back at the sound of his voice.

"She killed him," he repeated. "Your dog-wolf."

Finch stared at Pip for a moment, processing the words, before turning to Rigby. His eyes narrowed and his eyebrows twisted, half-cocked and low on his forehead. Rigby stared back at Pip, shocked for what felt like the hundredth time in the past hour. Her throat went dry and her knees locked. She wished she was still pinned under Richard's crossbow.

"Why?" was all she said, her voice faint and defeated.

But she knew why. Either for revenge or pure malice, Pip had learned how to operate in Vulture. The evil of the place had corrupted him, killed the person he was and made his body a vessel for its cruelty. But those same forces had allowed him to kill Richard, and they would not easily be unlearned. He would not allow Rigby to unlearn, either. These were the survival instincts of the frightened boy in the mall, realized in full.

"Check her arm," said Pip, his voice still a haunting monotone. Grime clung to the underside of his fingernails. His skinny legs remained planted behind Richard's massive corpse. Although half her size, he terrified Rigby.

Finch eyed the sleeves covering Rigby's forearms. His hand shot out and he grabbed the wrist opposite her tattooed arm and yanked up the sleeve. He took in the sight of the blue paint stains, the indisputable mark left by Horatio's tooth imprinted in the center. Rigby didn't resist, didn't even speak. Finch dropped her arm after looking at it for only a moment. He'd seen enough. It fell to her side with a dull thud.

She supposed she should have known this moment would come eventually, though she hadn't expected it so soon. She had thought that maybe, for once, bliss could last longer than a three-minute track. Once he'd figured her out for the coward she'd always been, Finch would have thrown her off the canoe just like he'd thrown that Vein from the radio station roof, she reflected now. Pip hadn't killed Richard to save her, but to save himself. He saw an opportunity and took it, just as she had never had the courage to do. Vulture had created Pip, as did she, and in turn he had destroyed her.

Finch's eyes were dark and low, not with rage but betrayal. He too was busily chiding himself internally. No sooner had he again made an exception to his credo than it had been subverted against him. Again. Friendship, family, romance. All it meant was vulnerability. Death. He had been foolish to have ever foreseen a hopeful future with Rigby. He had blindly forgotten—or simply ignored—the fact that she was a Regal simply because it felt good to talk to another human being, a sister, a connection in his lonely world. He'd been weak, he knew now. He wondered if he would have believed Richard to be his father had he turned up at the radio station with a matching tattoo, if he would run back to Vulture if Viro called his name. He felt stupid, humiliated, and furious with himself. *Self-reliance.* First Horatio, then Viro, now

Rigby. Perhaps one day he would actually live up to his mantra. For now, he would begin again, following Pip's example.

Finch cast a final withering look into Rigby's downcast eyes and turned from her, resolute. Without looking back, he clambered down the splintering ladder into the canoe. She heard the rope slap the water as he untied it and set off. The rhythm of the paddle swished through the water as he pushed away from the dock and into the slow current of the river. Rigby plopped down at the edge of the dock, looking out at the water, which was gilded in ruby as the sun smoldered at the edge of the horizon.

Finch's back and arms begged him to relent his furious pace, but he refused. He wanted to get as far away from Vulture as he could, and as fast as possible. He felt the water's depth increasing beneath his body and the canoe began to feel less and less significant as the river widened. Each pull of the oar was a blow struck to Vulture, to Rigby, to Richard. Never backwards, only forwards. Good or bad he would take on the sea. He paused his manic paddling only when a current took up under the craft and carried him into a wide, brackish estuary, the canoe suddenly feeling perilously small. The smell of salt water clung to his skin and clothes and he plunged onward. If he had looked back, he would have seen his sister's silhouette etched atop the dock against the red sunset.

Looking down the river, Rigby could barely make out the speck of the canoe. Her brother pounded, angrily it seemed to her, at each stroke of the paddle. She felt empty, drained of all emotional and physical energy. It was not despair, but the painful sensation of normalcy. Alone, plotting her next move, accounting for food and water, keeping watch over her shoulder; she thought she'd left the feeling behind for good. And yet nothing could or would ever be the same for her in Vulture. All the records that she'd once counted on for comfort lay in pieces on her floor. There was nothing for her to return to in Vulture. She'd grown up in the Regal gang, now leaderless and perhaps stripped to nothing by the Scorps. The only constant in her life had been snuffed out like a candle. Her knees wobbled and she gripped the wooden rail of the dock for balance.

She turned at the sound of the belt falling from Pip's hand with a thud to the deck. Without a word or even a glance in her direction, he set off up the dock, rejoining the still dumbfounded squadron of junkers. The dog-wolves had begun sniffing excitedly at Richard's immense corpse. With a stiff back and a set jaw, Pip passed through the junkers and walked on, back towards Vulture. Decisions suddenly their own to make, the once enslaved junkers helped to free each other from the collars and belts that had bound them for so long. Some followed after Pip, still unused to life without a leader. Others jumped in the river, their giddy laughs echoing in the still dusk of the outskirts, splashing in the cool, muddy water.

THE END

CPSIA information can be obtained
at www.ICGtesting.com
Printed in the USA
BVHW072258220222
629774BV00008B/861